ADVANC
A Place for

—

Like all novels that linger in the heart and mind long after they are read, *A Place for People Like Us* is a journey. With honesty, nuance, and empathy, Botha shares profound insights into the complexities and complications of identity, belonging, and relationships, perhaps most importantly the one we have with ourselves.
>   —**Anita Kushwaha**, author of the
>   *Secret Lives of Mothers and Daughters*

With this fascinating glimpse into Toronto's Orthodox Jewish Community, Danila Botha tells the story of Hannah, a woman caught between her boyfriend's world of tradition and security, and her girlfriend's wild nonconformity. A gripping tale about love, belonging and betrayal.
>   —**Elyse Friedman**, award winning author of
>   *The Opportunist*

As she prepares to convert to Judaism, Hannah, our protagonist, is so enthralled by Jillian that she ignores this early warning: "She's the sexiest, most charming person ever, until she decides to fuck up your life." But how could Hannah—or anyone else, really—resist this "arresting presence, like a tornado quietly building"? The link between these contrasting, complex women grows in intensity and depth as Hannah embarks on a life-changing journey that ultimately reveals the true essence of everyone around her, strips family secrets bare, and forces her to come to terms with both reality and her own self. In these more-righteous-than-thou times that we currently live in, this novel is not only important: it is necessary. John Steinbeck believed that most of our vices are nothing more than "attempted short cuts to love", and *A Place for People*

Like Us is Danila Botha's poignant, razor-sharp, and courageous exploration of the lengths that some people are willing to go to satisfy their fundamental human need for acceptance.

—**Martha Batiz**, author of
No Stars in the Sky and *A Daughter's Place*

In *A Place for People Like Us*, Danila Botha brings her characters to life with verve and compassion. Desperate to redefine herself and break from a traumatic past and troubled family, Hannah confronts life-changing decisions in which romantic, religious, moral and material desires clash and intersect. In prose that is bold, warm and fearless, Botha interleaves her insights with a twisty plot that keeps us on the edge of our seats right until the end.

—**Catherine Bush**, author of
Skin and *Blaze Island*

depth ... I'm always grateful when I stumble upon a writer who is still into raw realism. But if that is accompanied by some magical realism—especially drug induced—even better. Botha's exploration of identity and trauma ... lives in her dark humor, her storytelling, and the deep absurdity she pulls from life ... This is the kind of book you read in one sitting and then carry with you for a long time.
　　—**Michela Politti**, *Swamp Pink Magazine*

... *Things That Cause Inappropriate Happiness* touches on themes of generational trauma, substance abuse, and love ... In "Able to Pass," a young woman uses Jewish folklore to try and contact her grandmother's sister, who disappeared during Second World War ... The title story follows a disheartened woman with debilitating rheumatoid arthritis. As she wonders "how much happiness was appropriate now that I knew I had an incurable, chronic illness," she meets a man who whisks her back to when she was young and healthy ... Heartbreaking ... this collection contains elements of magical realism and eccentric, inquisitive prose. The sun rises "like tiger's eyes on a disappearing grey satin canvas," and first kisses feel like "glitter in my bloodstream." Botha flourishes in introspective moments of everyday life as her characters search for a sense of belonging.
　　—**Megan Brearley**, *Literary Review of Canada*

Botha ... captures the subtleties of human relationships, the desires, expectations, disappointments, cruelties, and, yes, moments of inappropriate happiness ... The Chekhovian humanism and pulsing empathy throughout is more than evident ... Botha captures the deep contradictory currents of the heart. She is also capable of delicate ironies and dark humour.
　　—**Michael Bryson**, *The Miramichi Reader*

Prolific and profound, Danila Botha is an author ... who always looks deeply into the hearts and minds of her characters. In her latest short fiction collection, *Things That Cause Inappropriate Happiness,* she explores cultural and religious identity, displacement, and the way that we grow to depend on interpersonal relationships of all varieties. The result is a collection of stories that shows vast range and depth.

—*Open Book*

A highly creative assortment, with its multiplicity of female protagonists ... it's not the mix of drama, humour, or quirkiness of [her] characters that makes Botha's collection hard to classify. It's the persistent contravention of ... boundaries, including those of realism ... the layer of subversiveness ... demonstrating both mastery of elliptical storytelling and Botha's own brand of satire ... One admires the writing, the tension Botha effects, and one winces at the same time ... Also, to Botha's credit is that the Holocaust is a haunting but not lachrymose presence ... Botha's artistic eye is firmly on her subjects—always perceptive ... *Things That Cause Inappropriate Happiness* is replete with lives—those that could have been, those that were, and some that might yet be. Most meaningful ... are the stories with characters who are determined to go on living despite the calamity they've endured, if only for the sake of those who didn't get the chance to.

—**Olga Stein,** *Great Lakes Review*

Danila Botha's third collection of short stories is a beautifully written, deeply rendered series of portraits of people struggling to define themselves in harsh circumstances. Dealing with often generational trauma, especially around Holocaust survival, the stories relentlessly strip away façades. From the bullied teenage girl to the woman who self-harms to get attention from her husband, the pain is deep. The stories often enter the realm of the fantastic, yet the stories never trade deeply felt experience for something easier and more escapist. The short stories of *Things That Cause Inappropriate Happiness* will remain with the reader long after the book is finished, and in each re-read, there are new discoveries and revelations.

—*Indie Reader*

Most of the characters in Danila Botha's pulsating and often moving third collection of short fiction are young and seeking direction, and/ or meaning in a world offering a dizzying array of options ... Throughout the book, a theme emerges of the past reaching into the present, and making itself felt, either through the revelation of truths previously hidden or with a swelling of emotion as characters grope towards a new or clearer understanding of one another. In Things That Cause Inappropriate Happiness, Danila writes of the tenacity of the human heart, its battle to remain true to itself. This is a book brimming with raw emotion that touches the reader deeply.

—**Ian Colford,** *The Seaboard Review*

The stories in this collection lure us in then challenge us, giving us an unfiltered look into the darkest sides of the human condition, which ultimately means the darkest sides of ourselves. The stories cover a wide range of topics, some with the horrors of the Holocaust prominent in the rearview of the characters' lives, some in the era of #MeToo and others focused on love, love lost and the act of creation. It ... conjures the rare magic of truly great, rich prose. Botha's ability to convey complex emotions in the gray areas of our lives is stunning. She's a remarkable talent destined to be recognized in the upper echelon of Canadian Fiction ... Botha's skill is plain for all to see. She is not just a writer's writer, but a reader's writer as well. Incredibly powerful.

—**JJ Dupuis,** author of the *Creature X Mystery* series

This is Botha's third collection of short stories and it really proves her to be a master of the form. As the title of the book might suggest, her characters are provocative, unruly, complex, and conflicted—and the twists their stories take make for a propulsive read. The stories explore what it means to be Jewish, what it means to be an artist, and what it means to be a woman, and they do it with a sharp wit and a big heart.

    —**Anuja Varghese,** award winning author of *Chrysalis*

How to capture the joy of reading this, this collection of more than two dozen tiny perfect literary gems? Each story distinct, but at its heart, this is a cohesive collection— tearing through layers of yearning and isolation, revealing narratives centering on the lost, the lonely and the disconnected ... These beautifully-rendered characters manage to remain detached, restrained, or simply understated in their revelations, leaving the reader all the more touched by the gaping vulnerabilities exposed, amidst the gracefulness of their telling ... Sensational.

    —**Terri Portelli,** *Bookly Matters*

This generous collection features ... a kaleidoscope of critical life moments and raw emotions. Botha's characters ... are internally fractured by intense longing, shame, and love, and yet fight to stay true to themselves. Unabashedly, they pursue "inappropriate happiness" through various means—embracing the rough outdoors, experimenting with mind-altering drugs, exploring once-suppressed sexuality, and above all, steadfastly refusing to compromise their art.

    —**Su Chang,** author of *The Immortal Woman*

Essential Prose Series 231

Guernica Editions Inc. acknowledges the support of the Canada Council for the Arts and the Ontario Arts Council. The Ontario Arts Council is an agency of the Government of Ontario.

We acknowledge the financial support of the Government of Canada.

A PLACE
FOR PEOPLE
LIKE US

—a novel—

Danila Botha

GUERNICA
EDITIONS
TORONTO • CHICAGO • BUFFALO • LANCASTER (U.K.)
2025

Guernica Founder: Antonio D'Alfonso

Michael Mirolla, general editor
Heather Wood, editor
David Moratto, Interior and cover design

Guernica Editions Inc.
1241 Marble Rock Rd., Gananoque, ON K7G 2V4
2250 Military Road, Tonawanda, N.Y. 14150-6000 U.S.A.
www.guernicaeditions.com

Distributors:
Independent Publishers Group (IPG)
600 North Pulaski Road, Chicago IL 60624
University of Toronto Press Distribution (UTP)
5201 Dufferin Street, Toronto (ON), Canada M3H 5T8

First edition.
Printed in Canada.

Legal Deposit—Third Quarter
Library of Congress Catalog Card Number: 2025931490
Library and Archives Canada Cataloguing in Publication
Title: A place for people like us : a novel / Danila Botha.
Names: Botha, Danila, 1982- author
Series: Essential prose series ; 231.
Description: Series statement: Essential prose series ; 231
Identifiers: Canadiana (print) 20250147734 | Canadiana (ebook)
20250147742 | ISBN 9781771839808 (softcover) |
ISBN 9781771839815 (EPUB)
Subjects: LCGFT: Novels.
Classification: LCC PS8603.O915 P53 2025 | DDC C813/.6—dc23

I had never known, never even
imagined for a heartbeat, that there
might be a place for people like us.
 —**Denis Johnson**, *Jesus' Son*

That girl thinks she's the queen of the
neighborhood I got news for you, she is!
 —**Bikini Kill**, *Rebel Girl*

Do not say, oh find the good in it,
do not say, there was virtue;
there was no virtue, not even in me.
Let us begin from there.
 —**Dionne Brand**, *Ossuaries*

CHAPTER ONE

THE FIRST TIME I met Jillian was the night I was about to meet my potential new roommate, and instead of texting me like a normal person, Cassidy called, frantic, and all I could hear was her breathy, high-pitched voice clarifying that she was "sitting near the bar" and "been waiting here for fifteen minutes," and even though I knew I was less than five minutes late, I could feel my heart start to race.

It was hard to hear anything over all the noise, the people behind me yelling their orders above the blaring speakers at the bar, the band who was sound checking on a small stage in front of them, White Stripe-y garage rock like it was 2006 instead of 2016. I edged closer to her and heard the metallic scrape of her Coke Zero against the graffitied wooden table. Cassidy looked exactly like she did on Instagram, sandy blonde curly hair subdued in a ballerina bun, with a few loose ringlets framing her heart shaped face, glowing skin, no makeup except for a little mascara and lip gloss, a pink hoodie and black high waisted jeans that made her look like a fit suburban housewife with two kids, instead of a twenty-one-year-old, third-year undergrad like me.

"Look, I've got to go soon," she said, tapping the dusty table with her phone like she was Judge Judy condemning a particularly unskilled criminal. "I have to get up at 5 a.m. every morning to run." She repeated the words partial athletic scholarship three times. It would have made a good drinking game if only I still drank, and she had even the tiniest sense of humour.

Her phone case was full of gold glitter that moved around when she shook it. She wanted to show me photos of the extra room in her apartment. I leaned over, and from what I could see, it looked clean and bright, with a decent sized window, but it was definitely small. She said she had an extra futon and a bedside table, so I didn't even need to bring my sidewalk-scored half-damaged Ikea crap with me, which was an extra bonus. Her parents paid her rent, she'd told me, but if she rented out the other room, she got to keep some of it, and her dad was impressed with her entrepreneurial spirit. She liked that I was a business major in one of the elite programs everyone knew was hard to get into. It was weird going to school in the most expensive building on campus. Webb Gallagher had intimidating marble floors and gold lettering, its vast open spaces filled with bright light and office building-like chairs and tables. Cassidy had no reaction to my double major in film.

We were both trying to act like we weren't desperate, even though school started again in less than a week. Jen, Cassidy's old roommate was a faster runner, and when she found out she got a full track and field scholarship to Purdue, she ditched Cassidy without a second thought. "She turned out to be the worst kind of friend,"

Cassidy said. "Cutthroat and so inconsiderate. So I decided, I'm never going to live with another friend again. This is a business arrangement, right, so we're going to get along, but it'll be easier to have boundaries."

She pulled up a contract on her phone. "I just need you to read this and initial here."

I took a deep breath. The kids I babysat loved the *Little Mermaid* movie, and I felt like Ariel, signing my voice away for the vaguest potential of happiness.

I knew I couldn't spend another second in the messy, revolving door communal artist house I'd been living in no matter how cheap it was. For one thing, it was almost an hour from campus. What started out as interesting and relaxed quickly started reminding me of childhood. Officially, there were four music majors from my university who were in a band together, along with the lead singer's and the drummer's girlfriends. They were called Shut Your Eyes and See, which was apparently a James Joyce quote, and they sounded like a cross between The National and Arcade Fire. They smoked an obscene amount of weed, did mushrooms and drank, practiced and fought at 2 a.m. It was the dirt streaked, sticky wooden floors, the endless nights of rice and lentil dinners, watching them cheat on their Drama or English major girlfriends, who always played dumb or cried and screamed but then took them back.

I skimmed and signed.

I looked at Cassidy's little diamond studs, and her chunky silver Tiffany's heart necklace. She was talking about being a kinesiology major and her plan to become a physical therapist.

For the past two years, I'd worked for a wealthy family in Leaside. They had a full-time live-in house-keeper and hired me to take care of their kids. My boss, Stephanie, taught me all the subtle signifiers of wealth.

She gave me tons of her old clothes. "Better you than the Salvation Army," she'd said, which made me feel both excited and queasy, like a pig gorging on the pile of truffles it was just supposed to dig up.

When I told my mom about my potential new roommate, when I took a selfie in Steph's clothes, with squeaky clean hair and a tiny, delicate gold crucifix around my neck that she'd given me for my birthday, she was so relieved. I knew all she wanted was for me to be able to push my past further into the rear-view mirror.

I wanted for the millionth time to just be able to buy a pint of whatever was on tap, and drink it slowly, like Cassidy was doing. I fantasized about a pitcher of Sangria, the deep purple kind with thick juicy slices of orange and canned maraschino cherries floating in it. I could tie the stem of the cherry into a knot using my tongue. It always distracted people from how much I could down quickly.

Whatever I did, I committed to all the way, which my mom always said was just like my father. I wished I was different, but for the past year, I'd been fully committed to sobriety. I went to NA and AA meetings every week.

I rubbed the knuckle of my index finger under my nose, wiping away traces of imaginary powder. I only ever drank to make the coke last longer. Just thinking about it filled my stomach with a tantalizing mix of ex-hilaration and fear.

I glanced over at the stage. Another band had started playing, louder, heavier rock, and I got up, turned my camera on and started filming. The singer, who was wearing red leather pants and a cropped black tank top, was dancing her way into the crowd. I look at her, and, in one of those surreal moments that only happens in movies, the singer walked right up to me, took my phone out of my hands and kissed me right on the lips. I pulled away and regretted it immediately.

The singer had a big red grin that was both charming and devious, like a cross between Taylor Swift and the Joker. She looked like she'd been expecting me to wait around. "I'm Jillian," she said. "I always look out into the audience and choose someone who looks like they need some shaking up."

Cassidy thought the whole thing was hilarious, and I was too embarrassed to talk much to Jillian. I wanted to ask her what her last name was so I could creep her on Instagram or at least hear more of her music. "Hopefully we'll see each other again," I said, trying to sound casual and she grinned at me. "Don't worry, we will." It sounded like a promise.

I moved in with Cassidy two days later.

CHAPTER TWO

IT WAS ANOTHER two weeks before I saw Jillian again. I managed to find her band, Dissolve into the Sky, and she was in the centre of all their Instagram photos, all glittery and magnetic, her dark eyes framed by Bette Davis style baby bangs and cobalt blue eyeshadow. She was wearing a bright read jumpsuit in my favourite photo, throwing her head back, laughing like one of her bandmates had just told her the best joke ever. They had songs on SoundCloud, and I listened to their music for hours, Jillian's voice textured and beautiful, alternating between softness and booming, like a cross between St. Vincent and Beyoncé.

I figured the musicians I'd lived with probably knew her, so I dropped in on them one day after class. Ewan, the singer, whom I'd hated the most when I lived there, said she was "sexy like crazy women always are. Like, feral," he said, grinning, "biting, hickeys everywhere, all that. She's a great performer. Crazy as fuck though. Remember when I was dating Cheryl? Jillian and I hooked up, and she wanted me to break up with Cheryl, even though Cheryl was living with me. Jillian was the one who smashed my guitar and confronted Cheryl in the middle of the night, screaming that a guy like me was too special to be with a girl like her."

He snorted. "Wait, you really don't remember this?"

I shook my head.

He looked me up and down.

"Why are you asking?"

I shrugged. "No reason. I saw her play a while ago. I just wasn't sure what I thought."

He grinned at me. "She's the sexiest, most charming person ever, until she decides to fuck up your life."

On my way out, I bumped into Carrie, who sometimes did backing vocals for the band.

"Yeah, I know her," she said. "I'll give you her finsta."

She spelled it out for me: *El verí de la mare.*

"What does that mean?"

She shrugged. "She spent a summer in Barcelona. I think it's Catalan. Mother's poison, or something like that." She rolled her eyes.

I added her, and she accepted and followed me back a few hours later. I thought about sliding into her DMs. I wrote two drafts, but they both felt weird and read like a mix of a love letter and fan fiction. I was too embarrassed to send them.

I finally saw Jillian again in an elective class that I almost didn't take. For my film major, I had to take one writing class outside of screenwriting, and I found myself in an Introduction to Creative Writing class. I submitted a short story that I wrote on the bus. It was about growing up in rural BC, in a collective called the Tribe. I wrote about all the rituals, the singing and the chanting, the ideology of living off the land. My dad compiled a book called the *Teachings* that we took turns studying. It borrowed from all religions, but he especially liked Buddhism and Taoism, though he was born Jewish. His parents were Holocaust survivors. His father's family had been wealthy and established German Jews, and his mother's family were peasants from the Slovakian countryside. "The lesson," he would tell everyone, a serious look in his usually gentler blue-grey eyes, "is not to get too comfortable." Life was about freedom, he always said, freedom from the status quo, freedom from the trappings of the material world, freedom from fixed ideas of what things should be. We called ourselves a loving, conscious community, and we shared everything, from food and water, to clothing and supplies and even a phone line where everyone took turns chipping in money.

We called each other Kin, and when people talked about my father their eyes would glaze over, and their smiles would stretch across their cheeks. I wrote about myself and my fifty something siblings, running around among the trees near Kootenay Lake.

It wasn't fiction, but I had a feeling it sounded like it. The professor emailed me to say that my story was original and that I had great imagination.

In person, she had wild, dark red streaked curls and was wearing red fishnet gloves underneath her black suit jacket. She made a joke about T.S. Eliot looking out of his window, thinking what a hole the landscape was. "Imagine what he would have thought of this campus," she said.

And then, after we'd finished reading the first three verses out loud, she said: "Now write about your idea of 'The Waste Land.'"

I stared at my laptop screen. I thought of the building they were in, a beige high rise that looked like twenty-five stories of cinder blocks. We were close to townhouses full of kiddie pools and small manicured bits of yard. Normal people found it boring, I knew, but being around people whose biggest problem was a lack of stimulation was comforting. *The suburbs were a haven, a hive of inactivity where everyone lived in subdivisions that were comfortingly all the same. I had the feeling I could walk into the wrong house easily, walk into some other family's kitchen, where they'd feed me some kind of casserole and ask me about my day, like in a nineties family sitcom. Everyone had a routine, school, soccer, after school jobs. My mom became a real nurse, she got legally married for the first time, changed our last name. "We're not hiding from your father, we're becoming our real selves," she said, and I tried hard to believe her. She loved the self-help books my dad hated. Louise L. Hay and Deepak Chopra were her new gods, they're practical, she kept saying, feeling good is useful. We decorated our new house in white, the colour of the walls was angel's kiss. For the first time ever, I went to a real school and did homework and ran track and cross country, and my stepdad gave me a hard time about coming home late and it all felt like a fever dream until I fucked it all up and then I woke up all alone.*

I felt the bile rising in my chest when I looked at the words. I put my hand down hard on my backspace key and deleted them all. When the professor asked for a volunteer, I heard the jangling of bracelets as a hand shot up. I recognized Jillian's raspy voice and turned around to look at her. She was wearing a shiny crinkly dress, her black hair piled into a messy top knot. Her cheekbones were as high as I remembered them. She looked like a living version of the *Woman in Gold* painting one of the musicians had a poster of.

"December is the cruelest month," she read, her lips flashing with what looked like big chunks of red glitter, "breeding flashing neon anger towards Christmas / the claustrophobia of strip malls/ the nasal drone of Alvin and The Chipmunks singing the Hula Hoop Song or Jingle Bells / the silver tinsel hanging in narrow doorways/reminders that we are not Christian or Canadian / Only in the summer / do I feel human."

In the bright daytime light, Jillian's skin was the colour of milky tea. Her eyeliner was smeared under her eyes. Her purse looked like it was made from the back pocket of a pair of jeans, and it was covered in band buttons. I pointed to a pink and black one with two raccoons on it that said Live Fast! East Trash!

"That's funny," I said.

"Sonic Youth," she answered. "Ever listen to them?"

I shook my head. "Your poem was so original," I found myself saying. "I loved it."

A splash of red crept across the skin on her neck like tie dye. I wondered if her skin felt hot.

She angled her head towards the door. "Thanks. Let's go get a smoke."

We walked outside and she fumbled with her bright green lighter.

"It's really good to see you again," I blurted out.

Jillian laughed. "You too. I'm glad you added me."

We stood in silence. We smoked, a chunky silver ring with a bright pink stone moving up and down on her skinny middle finger.

"You look like a Hannah."

"What?"

"You've got this regal, bohemian thing going on, like Hannah Arendt, you know, like you've got too many important thoughts on your mind to think too much about your clothes, but you still look good."

I had no idea who that was. I looked down at my rumpled blue button shirt and scruffy loose jeans and laughed.

"So, you're a writer?"

"I wish. I'm a business major at Webb, but I'm also a film major. I liked the assignment today, but I felt weird about sharing. Writing feels good but, I don't really know what I'm doing."

Jillian shrugged like a cat stretching in the sun. "Me neither. I'm a music major. I just took this because I figured it would help with lyric writing. It's good to approach art from different angles, you know?"

"Yeah." I took another drag. "Do you play instruments too?"

"Piano and guitar. I've been playing since I was a little kid. I think my favourite instrument is my voice though."

"Oh yeah?"

"I always had classical training, spent all these hours of practicing, and then one day, I was waiting for one of my teachers in her house, and her daughter was playing all this '90s music, hip hop, and R&B. I heard Jill Scott for the first time, and I don't know why, but it changed my life. I wanted to sing from the depths of my soul like that, I wanted to move people. The first summer we moved to Canada, my sister and I saw this amazing concert downtown, Janelle Monáe, Solange, SZA, this amazing singer from Toronto, Kennedy Rd, and of course,

Jill Scott. She had this huge, powerful voice, but also, it was her personality, she was so funny and real. She called herself Jilly from Philly. She walked around like she owned the stage, like she was comfortable in her body in a way I'd never seen. I was like, that's it, I'm changing my name."

"What was your name before?"

She sighed. "Miriam. Pretty common in Israel. When I found my sound, I became a new person. And then, late one night when I couldn't sleep, it occurred to me, I could live a more exciting fulfilling life, I could become someone whose nickname rhymes with thrill."

It was the kind of detail a famous person would mention in interviews.

She linked her arm through mine. "What do you say we get out of here?"

There was another hour left of class. I never skipped class. Why would I after spending so many years not being in school? I loved school.

Still, I found myself nodding. "Sure."

"Want to go get something to drink? Or eat?"

I almost laughed. I had about twenty dollars to get me through the next week and a half.

"Nah. I'm not hungry. Do you want to just come over? I try not to drink, and my diet is boring now that I don't take Adderall anymore."

Jillian smiled. "Adderall is pretty great. Where'd you get it?"

I felt my face contorting itself into a grimace.

"My stepdad owns a few pharmacies around Hamilton. I used to live with him and my mom and work for him, as a pharmacy assistant. I had to either open or close, so I had access to all the best stuff. Everything. Valium, Oxycontin, Fentanyl, which also a great way to make extra money. I wish I could do things lightly or casually, but the way I'm wired, I go all the way or not at all. You know what I mean?"

"Hell yeah. I read this great quote the other day, everything in moderation, including moderation."

I laughed.

"I don't know why, I can't just eat a scoop of ice cream, like a normal person, I have to eat a whole carton and then go to the convenience store at 3 a.m. in pajama bottoms to get two more. Until I get them, I can't even think about anything else. And that's ice cream. You should have seen me with drugs, I was ridiculous. Fentanyl preoccupied all my thoughts. My stepfather was furious, and my mom was disappointed, like she'd always suspected I was capable of dying in a gutter somewhere, experiencing the kind of poetic justice she wishes on my dad."

Jillian put her hand on my shoulder.

"But look at you now, doing so well, in one of the most prestigious business programs in the country."

I snorted. My dad and the Tribe were against all school, including what they called Con-iversity. I imagined his tissue paper pale lined face when I told him that, not only was I seriously in debt, I was also studying the capitalist ventures that destroyed individuals and communities. My dad was a child prodigy with an insanely high IQ, and everyone thought he was going to a be a surgeon or a concert flutist. He got accepted into

Harvard, but he ended up going to UBC for Cognitive Science for two years before he dropped out with barely passing grades.

I wasn't brilliant like some of my siblings either.

"The most exceptional thing about you," he told me once, "was the way you were raised."

My mom was cautiously optimistic, I could tell because she'd been calling me regularly again, but she'd never been the effusive type.

"It's hard to imagine what life will be like when we graduate, but the thought of money and stability is nice. I do love doing film stuff though. I love how three dimensional it is, how you can capture so much nuance and imagery and story. I love taking photos too. I don't know, in a perfect world, I could make a living combining the two or make enough money in in a corporate job to quit and go make movies." I laughed. "I don't know, I haven't really thought about the details."

"No, that's awesome," Jillian said. "Maybe you can show me some stuff you've filmed, and I can show you where I can record. Have you ever filmed bands playing? Maybe you could come to one of shows and get some footage."

My heart was racing. "Yeah," I said. "Let's go."

CHAPTER THREE

I T WASN'T LONG before I was spending all my nights at Jillian's. I could hear my mom's voice, telling me not to accept anything from anyone unless I could reciprocate. She turned into a sitcom mom after we settled in Ancaster. She'd say ridiculous things like organizing your room will help you organize your mind, education is the thing that matters the most, and, of course, there's no such thing as a free lunch. I'd get headaches from rolling my eyes so hard. I mentioned it to Jillian, and she laughed, not her throaty, dry laugh but her squeaky one, the one where she sounded delighted at the very thought of something.

"That's ridiculous, I have more space than I'll ever need."

Jillian's parents were property developers, and they not only owned her apartment, but the entire building she lived in. Jillian lived in the penthouse, which was less luxurious than it sounded, being six minutes from our concrete jungle campus and not at all glamorous neighbourhood, but it was large, with a huge wraparound balcony full of fancy lounging chairs.

"My parents are just happy that I'm not living alone anymore," she said. She turned me down every time I offered to chip in on rent.

"They overcharge everyone for all of these units, trust me, they don't need your money."

I felt guilty, and she knew it. She sat down heavily beside me on her bright green velvet couch. Jillian called it Esmeralda. Her other favourite thing was a plastic swivel chair that hung from a heavy metal hook in her living room ceiling. It looked like an extra from a 90's music video. I was scared to break it the first time I sat in it.

She reached over and squeezed my hand.

"It's just a chair, it's okay if it breaks, but it won't."

I swung my legs back and forth, like a little kid in a playground.

"Okay I love this," I found myself saying.

"Style has more depth than people realize. You can show people your quirks just by collecting things you love and displaying them. I read somewhere that someone said our generation's thing should be 'I consume, therefore I am' and I think it's true, but it's not necessarily bad."

Her kitchen was always empty aside from the few foods she liked, brown or red rice, a handful of pink lady or green apples, half eaten bags of peach rings and blow pops, and expensive varieties of green and mint tea.

Her living room floor was covered in a fluffy purple carpet and her desk was full of coffee table books about Aretha Franklin, Prince, Bjork, and well-read stacks of celebrity gossip magazines that she bought in bundles online. On her bedroom wall was a pink plastic framed poster of Bambi, which was her favourite movie as a kid and a framed paparazzi photo of Lindsay Lohan, blonde and passed out in the front seat of a car, with the words *Sleeping Beauty* graffitied above her head. Across from were two more framed photos, one of Britney with a shaved head, holding an umbrella, and a black and white surveillance photo of Solange and Jay Z in an elevator, Solange swinging and kicking in his direction, with the word Tension graffitied underneath.

Her bedroom floor was splatter painted in bright greens and yellows and oranges, with some reds and pinks peeking through from underneath. It looked like Jackson Pollock had done it. There were notepads full of scribbled song lyrics everywhere and pencil crayons full of teeth marks. In her bathroom there was a framed series of photos above her toilet. I leaned in and it was a bunch of dick pics, each one printed on fancy paper and covered with tiny pink and purple Swarovski crystals. She laughed when she saw me staring.

"It's a reminder to never back on any of the dating apps. It's kind of funny to turn it into art, don't you think?"

Her bathroom cabinet was wide open. It was full of bright pink and red lipsticks, stacks of cheap eye shadow in every colour of the rainbow, and the kind of tiny liquor bottles you get on planes. She laughed when I pointed it out. "Some people take those packets of Stevia with them everywhere, some people take those little salad dressings, I take tiny Ketel Ones or Absoluts."

It was like waking up inside an artist's fantasy. It was more than I'd ever dreamed of. I mentioned this to her one day, and she turned to me, taking both of my hands into hers.

"It's a haven for artists, for weirdos like you and me. That's exactly what it's supposed to be. So no matter what happens on the outside, in the world, if there's rejection, if there's people who don't get us, if things feel hard or impossible, we have this refuge where we're always just safe to be ourselves. So whether we're making music or jewellery or going to school and living our lives like some kind of performance art, there's a place for people like us."

And then, she added: "Your mom is wrong, you know. Not everything is about money."

It can sometimes feel like it when you don't have any, I thought.

"You're a great friend, you're so loyal and easy to talk to, and if you ask me, that's priceless."

I rolled my eyes. I was never any good at taking compliments.

The situation with Cassidy became untenable once she got accepted into Alpha Sigma Pi. At first she kept encouraging me to rush with her, and when she officially joined she became one of them, all glossy white toothed smiles, highlights, and natural looking bronzer. I could tell because Cassidy was naturally so pale. The girls she joined with were all size zeroes, but if you asked them about what they ate or if were runners like Cassidy, they'd shrug and look at you with a straight face and say, "I don't think I'm skinny, I think I'm just normal." At first it was funny, and Jillian loved hearing all about them. Cassidy's Instagram handle was Cassiekins12, and Jillian always called her Cassiekins and wanted to know what she was up to, like she couldn't believe people like her existed. I'd squeeze myself into Jillian's two sizes smaller than I wore clothes the next day just to be able to stay longer.

I decided to tell her I was leaving after I overheard Cassidy and her friends talking about me. I got in late one night, and the sorority girls were drunk on a bottle of pink champagne.

"She acts like she's too good to hang out with us. Do you know she used to be a nanny?"

I heard Amber, Cassidy's best friend whoop. "We should get her to serve us drinks. We could have our own personal waitress and bartender."

When I told Jillian, she insisted that I move in officially. "Bullies are always the same," she said shaking her head. "They hit you where you feel most insecure. But the thing is, they never have any imagination, which is why they never amount to anything."

"I hope I amount to something," I said.

"Of course you will," she said. "You're going to make amazing movies. And you're going to make all our music videos and film our live shows, and we'll both get famous together."

When Jillian performed, she was an arresting presence, like a tornado quietly building. The audience would sit, glued to her every movement, watching a piece of her wavy black hair come unpinned as she tossed her head back or transfixed as she read from or tore up a set list. My favourite part was her lyrics, which were always so precise and resonant. It always felt like she was narrating a story I'd lived, like she was writing just for me. I knew this was impossible, logically speaking, since most of her songs were written before we'd even met, but they felt personal somehow.

My favourite was a song called "Believe Me," which once I heard I had on repeat in my head for days. I could imagine it in the world, blasting from speakers, on the soundtracks to movies and people's lives. The heavy rock chorus, which was simple, but cut through my heart, went *If I said it / I meant it, I'm sure / when it comes to love there's nothing I won't endure / I don't want to suffer any more / So if you want me / if you need me / just tell me/ because I love you / believe me.*

I started filming Jillian going about her daily life, reading, folding laundry, even watching TV, writing and doing rehearsals with the band. I used them for the song's verses, and then when we got to the chorus, I used up close footage of her performing, her eyes on the camera with an indescribable urgency, like it was the most important person in her life that she needed to convince of something. One night, I filmed her backlit on the balcony, mouthing I love you, her brown eyes wide and vulnerable and I used it right at the end, where the lyric changed when to *when it comes to you / there's nothing I won't endure.*

Even I was surprised by how moving it was.

My other favourite was "When I'm Gone." I wrote down the first verse in my notebook when I heard it.

I see you / I see her / I don't know what to say / And it's like the radio / same shit / different day / You see me coming / you look at her / you look away / I don't know why / I'm so surprised / But it hurts me anyway.

I went downtown and filmed street art, graffiti, fabric stores with the bright colours hanging in their windows. I got two people from one of my film classes to act like a couple, both beautiful, walking arm in arm down the street, their eyes on each other or down on the ground, avoiding anyone's gaze but each other's.

When I got to the punch line, *You could always see who I was / You're going to miss me when I'm gone,* I interspersed footage of Jillian going wild on stage, full of emotion and red lips.

"Oh my God," Jillian squealed. "These are so beautiful. You really get me, Hannah. You understand what I'm all about and what my music is all about."

Her words felt like warm tea in my throat. She uploaded them right away to the band's social media, and they started getting thousands of views.

"I fucking told you," Jillian said. "I told you this was going to work, that we were going to inspire each other. This is just the beginning."

Jillian suffered from insomnia and, if she couldn't be productive at 2:30 or 3 a.m., she'd come and join me in bed. Her fingers and toes were always cold. She'd rub her feet behind the backs of my knees. Sometimes she'd talk about song idea, or tour ideas or album cover art. She found an Alexander McQueen floor length dress one day, in a vintage store on Ossington. It was an ombre rainbow made of layers of silk and lace, from its cherry red halter top to yellow, green, blue. and its sidewalk sweeping amethyst. When she put it on, along with smoky eyeshadow and messy, loose hair, including overgrown bangs that were hanging over her eyes, she looked like she belonged on the cover of *Vogue* or *Rolling Stone.*

Jillian was the kind of person that a lot of people were a little bit in love with or jealous of. The fact that she chose me to be her closest friend and confidant made me feel so special.

Sometimes she told me stories that made me sad, like the time she was twelve and was convinced a strange woman was chasing her, so she ran terrified into the thin glass table in her family's dining room, smashing glass and cutting up her thighs. It was the first time that her parents insisted on taking her to the psych ward. She couldn't remember much about it.

She told me about guys like Evan who were turned on when she told the story. "I'm not a fucking manic pixie dream girl fantasy for guys like him, you know?"

I nodded. "Of course."

"I knew you'd understand."

"I can't believe you've never used a vibrator before," she said one night, laughing at my flustered expression when she pulled out two tiny ones from her purse, one that looked like a two-inch tube of lipstick, the other that looked almost exactly like mascara. To say it felt like a slow building thunderstorm was true, but it was also true that I preferred the easy intimacy of Jillian's fingers and fists.

If I drank a little with Jillian sometimes, a little bit of red wine or one or two beers between us, or if we shared an Adderall to help us focus and get our school-work done, we weren't doing fentanyl or meth, and I was still totally in control of things.

"I mean you have to be careful, but you don't want to deprive yourself either. Everyone only gets one life, so we have to make it worth it," she said, and it dawned on me that this was the real reason why my mother had left my dad and the Tribe. She wanted to think for herself, to do things without a sense of absolute right or wrong, to do whatever felt right without the guilt of abandoning a whole belief system.

I never knew quite what we were; if were friends or lovers, or artists in a situationship, or just each other's biggest support systems, but the future felt more real and more exciting than I'd let myself even dream about before.

CHAPTER FOUR

EVERYTHING CHANGED WHEN I met Mark Gold-water. He'd been in one of my classes for a while, but I'd never thought much about him. He looked like a Snapchat filter come to life, around 6'4" if I had to guess, with wild, wavy blonde hair. The only thoughts about him I'd ever had were whether his hair colour was natural or if his brilliant white teeth were veneers. He always wore expensive streetwear, hoodies with the word Supreme or Off White written across the chest, black jeans or sweats, and an enormous collection of Nikes in every eye burning colour from bright red to highlighter yellow. When Jillian wore things like that she looked eccentric and artistic, while he looked like he was trying too hard to prove his individuality.

He was pretty quiet in class, so we never really talked until a marketing professor assigned us to the same group to create a strategic branding plan.

Mark looked at me and mumbled something about liking my hair, which was a faded lavender that Jillian had started painting on one night and stopped halfway through when she got a new song idea.

I nodded. "Thanks," I said. "My roommate did it."

"Really?" he said. "It looks like balayage."

I laughed. "Yeah, I'm sure that's what she was going for."

He smiled. "She's talented," he said, and I grinned.

"You have no idea."

The assignment was more in depth than I expected, and he seemed very serious about it. We divided up the work, but he had an opinion on every sentence I wrote. He'd change whole paragraphs on our Google doc and then send me screenshots if I didn't reply right away. I got so annoyed, I threatened to ask for a different partner. We agreed to meet in person at the Webb Library to work on it together. I got there fifteen minutes early, and there he was, looking like he'd been there for days. Under the fluorescent lights, his eyebrows looked like lightning bolts, and his face looked extra pale. He was bent across a table, his sleeves rolled up, a second table full of his books and notes.

"Hannah," he said, and when I started to answer, he kept talking. "Trust me, you want to do this the way I've said."

I was startled by his bluntness. "Why?" I asked. "Why do I want to?"

"No one could be in this program if they didn't care about their GPA. I've seen you taking notes. You care."

"Of course I care, but why do you assume I'm wrong? You took out all my important research, including the most recent consumer statistics."

"Okay, calm down," he said. "Have a seat."

I stayed standing.

"I'm good right here."

I thought about a conversation I'd had with Jillian a

few days before. She had last night's mascara and eye-shadow pooled and smeared around her eyes, which made her gaze seem more feverish. She mentioned that her parents weren't exactly supportive of her music, that they were happy that she was in school, but they wanted her to finish already so she could go to law school, like her sister. She'd recently made a deal with them: she was going to take a whole year off school, starting next semester, to pursue her music full time. If she didn't make serious progress towards something, she'd start studying for the LSATs. She begged me to take time off with her, but I told her that there was no way I could. I wasn't even sure I wanted to. As this Mark guy talked, I wondered if I was making the right decision.

"Look," he said, speaking slowly like I was an idiot, "I know because Bryce grades on a curve, people tend to take it easy. But isn't it more fun to be the people who set the curve instead?"

I shrugged. "I mean, how do you really know what Bryce is going to like or not like?"

He shifted uncomfortably on his feet. Today's sneakers were white low tops with black and white stripes.

"I know, okay? I interned with JKX over the last two summers. I was basically one of his assistants. I know he likes the copy clean, short sentences, not too many extraneous facts. It's not that what you researched is wrong, he's just not going to care. If you really want to keep it in, we have to make it shorter and move it to the end, where we summarize our main thoughts including market trends."

He looked at me like he was proud of winning but also like he somehow wanted to smooth things over.

"It's okay," I said.

He smiled at me. "You're different than other people in this program."

"What do you mean?"

"You know how competitive it is, everyone is so serious about everything, they want to fight you until you die and then stand on your carcass. You're like, yeah, okay, you're right. It was just … unexpected."

"I mean … you are right. And you're right, I do care about my GPA, and if you did all this extra work so you know what our professor wants, the least I can do is go along with it."

"I try not to get too competitive," he said, staring off into the distance. "But I hear my dad's voice in my head sometimes, 'I didn't just make the Dean's list, I was number one on the Dean's List in my day,' and it's hard to ignore it, and not just want to be the best at everything, you know?"

I leaned in close to him and touched his arm. "Can I tell you a secret? I've never cared about being the best. I'm just trying to keep up, do well enough to deserve to be here. I am different to all of you."

"What do you mean?"

"I mean, you can afford to do free internships. You probably have parents that are thrilled that you're in this program, that are encouraging you and even paying for school. I mean, how'd you get to intern for Bryce anyway?"

His cheeks flushed. "My dad set it up."

I looked him right in the eye. "Exactly. My dad was in jail for eight years, and he actively discourages programs like this. I got in because of my grades, I guess, and my old boss's husband, who works in finance and wrote me this really kind reference letter. I work as one of their nannies in the summer."

"Wow, really?"

"What?"

"That's impressive, it's a hard job. Trust me, I know. My sister and I used to torture our nannies when we were little. You must be a very patient person."

I laughed. "Nah, they're good kids, two sweet older girls and their younger brother. It's easy."

"What did your dad do, that he went to jail?"

"Trust me you don't want to know."

"Try me. My brother went to jail for three years. He was a plastic surgeon doing tummy tucks and boob jobs for all these people in our community who were obsessed with him. He was living the good life, fancy cars and constant vacations, and then all of a sudden, he was a criminal and no one wanted to talk to him."

"What did he go to jail for?"

"Insurance fraud. He'd pretend it was all medically necessary and get people's insurance to cover cosmetic stuff. Eventually he got caught. He's not allowed to practice medicine anymore."

"Wow, that's a lot, but my dad's story is much worse, trust me. You'll never want to talk to me again if I tell you."

"Because of something your dad did? Why?"

"It's not a comfortable subject. And it kind of was my fault."

"What? What do you mean?"

"My dad was the spiritual leader of a group that the media called a cult. They blurred a lot of boundaries, but they eventually got into legal trouble over my dad's love of young girls. I mean very young girls, little kids."

I watched Mark's hand fly over his mouth, and I flinched.

"Including you?" he asked quietly.

I nodded. "But it wasn't just that. My dad fathered a lot of kids, and to use his words, he had special affinities with a lot of us." I felt vomit rising in the back of my throat. "I had the chance to testify against him, and I did. I was part of the reason he got a long sentence."

Mark looked at me. "Hannah, that's really brave. And that's a good thing, if he was guilty…"

I took a deep breath. "He was. But lots of people from the group stopped talking to my mom and me, then started threatening us. My brother, like my mom's other son, just stopped talking to us altogether. It's why we moved to Ontario."

My hands were shaking. "Sorry, I just really need to talk about something else. I've never talked to anyone about this, besides my mom, and she has a lot of her own feelings tied up in it."

"Of course. If it makes you feel better, I think I would have testified against my brother if I had to. I was too young, and I didn't know anything, but I hate the way my family pretends that nothing really happened, that none of it is a big deal."

I nodded. "I like everything you've added to the project. I have to go. Thanks for telling me what you know about Bryce. I believe you. You should hand it in the way it is now. Forget my changes."

He shook his head. "No, no, we'll add them at the end like I said. Do you need a ride home?"

"No, thanks, I'm okay to walk."

He stood up like was about to hug me, then second guessed himself and patted my arm.

I almost wanted to hug him, but I held myself back.

It was dark outside, and the sidewalks were slippery from the earlier rain.

I was in the lobby of our building when my phone pinged.

"Thanks for all your hard work on our project. Was good to spend time with you. Let's do it again sometime, not for school."

I was too surprised to answer him. Three days later, he texted me again. It was Thursday, and we had our class that afternoon.

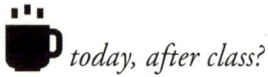 *today, after class?*

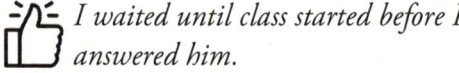 *I waited until class started before I answered him.*

CHAPTER FIVE

I'D BEEN SPENDING less time with Jillian lately. We liked working creatively at the same time. She'd sit writing and playing guitar or singing, and I'd edit videos or write ideas for treatments or concepts. She'd started skipping class, even though she wasn't supposed to take time off for another two months. She'd send me texts when I was on my way to class that read like mini grocery lists.

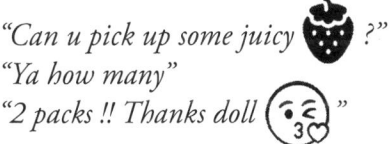

"Can u pick up some juicy *?"*
"Ya how many"
"2 packs !! Thanks doll *"*

Every time I told her I was worried or implied that it might not be in her best interest to just stop showing up, she'd either whine or snap at me about how productive she was being.

"I have all day to do nothing but work," she'd say. "I'm going to have a whole album's worth of material soon."

Her mom started showing up unannounced, usually with Tupperware full of food for her daughter, though I'd wind up eating a lot more of it than she did.

Jillian's mother's name was Esther, and she looked a lot like Jillian, except that she was taller and fuller figured. Esther was beautiful with the same olive skin, high cheekbones, and dark wavy hair, but she was more carefully put together. She wore pinstripe button-up dresses and, despite the yellow turmeric streaks or stray flour on her hands, she always had perfectly manicured light pink nails. She once wore a necklace made of aquamarine stones that looked like a row of shiny, ocean-coloured candies.

In no universe could I imagine a world where my mom was so worried about me that she'd take a day off work to come over with food she'd made for me. It was Moroccan food, Jillian said, and my favourites were *mujadera*, a rice dish made with lentils and crispy fried onions, fried eggplant slices in tomato sauce, and *ma'aroud,* these buttery dessert rolls stuffed with dates and date syrup and coated with powdered sugar. It wasn't just the flavours or the textures, I tried to tell Jillian once. The first time I tasted her mom's food, I could taste the love. I could taste the energy and the nurturing that went into every bite. I was actually jealous.

Jillian said her mother was just trying to make her fat.

"It all seems very generous until you think about what she's doing. She wants me to keep kosher, so she brings kosher food, and then it becomes easier to just go along with it. That way she can tell people I'm still keeping kosher, and she isn't lying. She wants me to gain weight, so she brings carbs, so she can tell everyone my *eating disorder not otherwise specified* is better. Forget how I'm feeling, just as long as I look fatter."

"But she wants you to get better," I said weakly. "You know that no matter what, she really cares."

My mom was at best a brief emailer. She made a fine art of talking about the weather. No matter how maddeningly vague her messages were in their inquiries about me, they always ended in the hope that I was "staying dry in this rain, xo" or "enjoying this brief respite from the below ten degrees chill, xo" or "wearing your warmest long johns in this cold snap xo." She might as well, I sometimes thought, just come out and write, "You're more of a disappointment that I'd ever imagined, hope you're enjoying this heat wave xo" and call it a day. I never let myself do more than respond to the few facts she tells me about herself, about her garden or my stepdad or whatever barbeque with neighbours down the street they went to that weekend.

I wanted Esther to like me. Lately she'd been bringing extra food and asking me to encourage Jillian to go to class.

"You're such a good influence, Hannah," Esther said. "I'm sure just being around you is good for her." I was ashamed of how good her words made me feel.

I came home one day to find Jillian writing with this girl Marla, whom she'd talked about with such a mix of reverence and desire, it made me feel sick.

"Marla's so accomplished," she'd say, and I could hear the gut twisting awe in her voice.

Marla had long dark hair and full red lips, and her right arm was covered in a blue and purple sleeve tattoo of a mermaid, swimming through waves, with the words Daughter of the Sea in the middle.

They were bent over a notepad, concentrating so hard

that I don't think they heard me when I walked in. Either that or they were ignoring me, which wasn't great either.

"Hi," I said, as loudly as I could. "What are you guys doing?"

Jillian turned around and looked up at me for a second before turning back to the page.

"We're writing lyrics. Marla's helping me, isn't that cool?"

"Yeah, I guess so."

I moved closer to them, and Marla barely looked up.

"Look, we're trying to work," she said. "We have to concentrate; the Adderall can only do so much."

Marla's lipstick was smeared a little under her bottom lip. She was wearing those drug store long eyelash strips, the kind you glue on top of your own eyelashes, and her left one was starting to peel in the corner of her eye.

I tried to smile. "No worries, I wasn't planning to stay. I just came to drop off my bag."

I threw my red backpack in front of my bedroom, and it hit my door with a thud.

I grabbed my jacket from the hanger behind the main door.

"Hannah," Jillian said, "You don't have to leave, this is your apartment too."

I shook my head. "No worries, I had other plans anyway."

I decided to take the stairs instead of the elevator, and by the time I got outside she'd sent me six texts.

> *WTF*
> *Hannah, seriously*
> *Come back!!*
> *HANNNNAHHHH*
> *Want to hear what you think of the new song . . .*
> *Wait, so now you're ignoring me?? WTF Hannah*
> *You know I haven't been feeling well lately . . .*

I didn't have anything to say so I didn't answer. It was kind of satisfying to think of her sitting there, getting angrier and angrier.

Maybe I could do something creative too. I thought about going to the film building, trying out some new equipment. Maybe I could study.

I sent Mark a text.

> *What r u up to?*
> *Not much. Want to get* 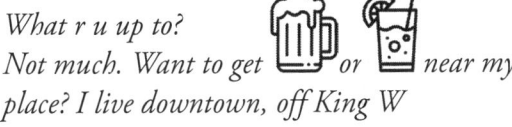 *or* *near my place? I live downtown, off King W*

I smiled thinking of putting that much distance between me and Jillian for a night.

Would she worry about me or go back to hanging out with Marla, her texting just a momentary, bratty outburst?

I wrote back.

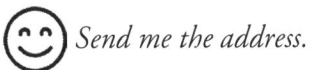 *Send me the address.*

CHAPTER SIX

TRIED TO imagine where Mark would want to meet. I couldn't decide if it would be generic but comforting, like Starbucks, or an over-the-top hipster place that sold twenty-dollar hemp seed milk cold brew coffee and micro brewed kale kombuchas. Jillian would act underwhelmed, and he'd fall all over himself trying to impress her. She was the kind of person who could name and get excited about the array of rare spices in a dish without bothering to eat it. She was always so charming that no one ever questioned her. There was the time she got us into a hip hop concert for free, when the tickets were sold out and had gone for hundreds of dollars. She walked right up to the bouncer, and told him she'd lost our tickets, then burst into tears. She had this whole story about how the tickets were a birthday present, and she couldn't forgive herself for losing them, and the big hulking bodyguard melted and ushered us in, then looked the other way. Another time she took me for dinner with two guys she called great connections. One was a publicist, and one was a producer at a major record label.

She wore a black low cut tank top, her nipples poking

through the thin fabric, and deep red lipstick and gave them each a business card.

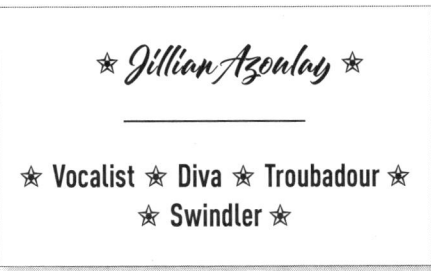

☆ *Jillian Azoulay* ☆

☆ Vocalist ☆ Diva ☆ Troubadour ☆ ☆ Swindler ☆

If I tried, I could be someone people liked, but I couldn't be fascinating and magical, no matter how much I studied her sleights of hand.

Mark surprised me by taking me to a place called Tiger and Rose. It had high ceilings, exposed brick walls and shiny purple, pink and green shutters that were covered in semi-precious stones, including pieces of amethyst and agate.

The host who seated us had the posture and tight manbun of a ballerina. He gestured us to a booth in the back, which Mark told me was his favourite spot.

"It'll be great, we'll actually be able to hear each other."

I laughed, surprised by how nervous that made me.

"So you bring a lot of girls here?"

"No, not at all," he said, the tops of his cheeks brightening as he looked down. "I live down the street from here, just over on Portland. Sometimes the library at Webb is just too intense, and it's far. This corner is quiet enough to hear your own thoughts, so I figured ..."

I laughed. "It's fine, I was kidding."

My legs stuck instantly to the brown leather seats. I stretched them out, and it felt like I was ripping off ten Band-Aids.

I grimaced.

"Yeah, that can't be comfortable." He smiled. "I've never seen you dressed like this before," he added quickly.

I pulled down my skirt a little. It was dark green and stopped mid-thigh. It belonged to Jillian. She'd gone into her closet and pulled out a few things that she insisted were way too big for her, including this skirt and a pink and brown striped tank top with pink lace straps that I was wearing on top of it. I'd tried it on for Jillian, and she gave me her sexy, wolfish smile.

"See, this is how this shirt is meant to look." She reached over and tweaked my left nipple, then squeezed my breasts together. "I never filled it in right."

I groaned. "Is this your subtle way of pointing out that I'm the fatter one?"

She looked genuinely distressed for a second. "No! It's my totally non subtle way of pointing out that you're the sexy one. You have the best shape, Hannah. I'd kill to look like you."

Yeah, okay, I thought, but I said thank you.

Mark was smiling at me.

"You look great," he said, and somehow I believed him.

"So, how'd you pick this neighbourhood? I mean, it's awesome, but it took me forever to get here."

He laughed. "Yeah, but you probably took the subway and a streetcar, I have a car. My parents own my unit, so I get to live here for free. One of their wholesale

38

offices is on the main floor. Import/export. They're in the diamond business."

He said the last part quickly, as if it was a fact that he didn't want to have to tell everyone.

"One of my part time film jobs is making promo videos for this jewellery company's social media. Diamonds are really fun to shoot, the way they reflect the light. It's actually fun to shoot different stones. I had no idea how beautiful they were."

"That's so cool. Which company?"

"Coco Bijoux, they sell handmade jewellery and antiques. They gifted me with the ring I'm wearing, I love it so much, I never take it off."

"Oh yeah, I know them. Can I see?"

I held out my hand and flexed my fingers. It was a small rose made of white gold. The petals were made of pink tourmaline and the leaves, which wrapped around my finger, were made of green tourmaline.

He ran his fingers over mine. "That's beautiful. Twentieth century for sure, like 1920s maybe?"

"Yeah."

I took it off so he could look at it more closely.

"What are the tiny black stones here? Tourmaline or onyx?"

"They're onyx."

"My grandmother was obsessed with stones and us knowing all of them so we could go into the business. She had this traditional gold and silver cluster ring that had stones that were designed to look like old mine cut diamonds. She always said when she had money one day, she'd get herself the real thing. She worked for a few years as a diamond sorter at this big company in Belgium and got out just before World War II started. After she and my grandfather met and got married here, they started Goldwater International."

"That's so interesting. How come it seemed like you didn't want to talk about the company before?"

Mark sighed. "My family and the company became infamous after my brother got arrested. There were millions of dollars that he hadn't declared legally, and then some of it disappeared, and so did he. He took one of those 1 a.m. flights and hid with an Ultra-Orthodox community in Israel. It was so weird, for years he was telling us to disconnect from Orthodox Judaism, he even become a Buddhist at one point, and then he gets in trouble and that's the first place he runs to. But that wasn't even the worst part. Before he disappeared, he used the money to buy diamonds. Then his ex-wife, Iris, had them made into rings and necklaces and wore them into Hong Kong, where you don't have to declare how much jewellery you're carrying. As far as the world is concerned, those diamonds were never recovered. His clinic was called Goldwater Health, and there were newspaper headlines like 'Goldwater Medical Fraud: What happened to the Goldwater diamonds?' which was not exactly the kind of attention the rest of us wanted. My brother, of course, wasn't around to take the blame for it, so it looked like we were colluding with him, or like we were idiots who somehow missed what he was doing. I don't know what made us look worse."

"Wow. With my dad, the articles were mostly about him. There was a more in-depth article later, that named the seven women who decided to stay with him, even after he went to jail. They mentioned that their kids had been taken by Children's Aid but didn't name any of them or any of us. They also didn't name the other members who'd left. That would have been worse."

I was startled when I felt him reach for my hand.

"I've never been on a date like this, where you can just talk about everything, even terrible things. Have you?"

I laughed. "Is this a date?"

His cheeks turned pink. "I mean, no, I haven't, but I'm probably not the best person to ask. A lot of the time, things just kind of low key happen, and then you're just with someone, you know, or you never see them again."

He smiled at me and wiggled his eyebrows a little.

"Do you go on a lot of dates?" I asked him.

"Depends on your definition of date. If you mean do I ask lots of girls out like this, then no. But my parents are Orthodox Jews, and they think I'm getting to that age where I should be considering settling down."

"Okay ..."

"So they have these two matchmakers whose job is to find girls that they think are appropriate. It's so weird, you get these printouts, which are basically dating resumes. There are one or two pictures of the girl, always dressed modestly, her elbows and knees and collarbones covered, and then another piece of paper that tells you what Jewish community she's part of, if she goes to university or college, what she's looking for in her life, and in the case of one matchmaker, the girl's height and clothing size."

I grimaced.

"Yeah, it freaked me out too. Because in the end, if you

don't actually like each other, if the chemistry isn't there, and you don't click, who cares about any of that stuff?"

I nodded. "Yeah. Do the girls ask for the guy's clothing size too? Do they want to know his shoe size or his glove size?"

He laughed. "Ha. You're funny. No, the girls have almost no power in that situation. I mean, they can tell the matchmaker if they want to keep seeing him or not, but really, the guys are the ones who decide everything."

"Is that how it's been for you?"

"No, I've never gotten past a first date with any of them. I've never wanted to. The dates have to be in a public place, like the lobby of a hotel or a crowded restaurant, somewhere so full of people that nothing inappropriate could ever happen. These girls are afraid to order or eat anything. They want to show you how nice and easy going they are, so they don't give real answers, and neither do you. It's like two bad actors reading from the world's most boring script."

"If they're so bad, why do you agree to go on these weird dates?"

"I don't do it that often. I just go every now and then to get my parents off my back. They just want to avoid any more controversy. I'm already kind of doing things differently, going to business school but not wanting to work in the family business, not living at home. Underneath it all, we all do our own thing, especially my mom. But on a superficial level, we all have to conform."

"That's interesting. Is that how your parents met through a matchmaker?"

"Yeah, but it was different. My mom was twenty-five, which was considered ancient for that world, especially back then, and she was the heir to a huge fortune, which she'd only get if she got married and had kids. She was very strategic when she picked my dad. She always talks about how he gives her space to be herself and do her own things. In a different way, I think I'd want that kind of freedom too. Do you know how your parents met?"

"Yeah, in class at UBC. My mom thought he was really well read, and he'd play his expensive flute and quote all these poets. I picture him like the Pied Piper, leading all these random, starstruck girls off the edge of a cliff, charmed by the different ways they fell, like it was performance art. He liked my mom because she was harder to impress."

He smiled at me and touched my arm just above my wrist.

"Kind of like you."

"No, I'm not that hard to impress. My mom has always been really cool, you know, restrained, composed no matter what the situation is. I've always wished I could be more like that."

"It's okay. You're a warmer person. I think that's better."

"I've never thought of it that way."

"Come on," he said, moving his head in the direction of the door. "Let's get out of here."

We walked from the café to his apartment. The downtown air was smoky and cool against my skin. We held hands, and Mark laced his fingers through mine.

His apartment was huge and airy, lightly furnished and brightly lit.

Sex with him was not what I expected.

He needed me to reassure him, to guide his hands, and he kept telling me how beautiful I was, like he was in awe of having the experience, and he was trying to find a way to say so.

He asked me to stay the night, and I wanted to refuse, but I remembered Jillian and Marla.

I'd never stayed out like this before.

He put his arm around me when we fell asleep and, when I rolled away, I felt him stretch one of his long legs over both of mine.

The next morning, he made us both mint tea and brought it to me in bed.

Part of me wanted to curl up into a ball and stay, under his incredibly soft, well ironed cotton duvet and sheets, his hand running through the back of my hair.

I forced myself to get up. "Thanks for a great night, Mark."

"Call me Naftali," he said. "It's my Hebrew name, but it's what everyone who knows me calls me."

"I like it. Does it mean anything?"

"Yeah, he was a character in the Old Testament, one of the sons of Jacob. There's this chapter where Jacob blesses all of his sons, and he describes Naftali as 'swift as a deer,' which my mom always liked." He grinned. "Mark's just the name on my driver's license."

He picked up my phone. "Here, I'll change it for you in your contacts."

He offered to drive me home, so I had time to get ready for class.

I let him kiss me goodbye.

I liked the person I was when I was with him.

CHAPTER SEVEN

WHEN I GOT inside, Jillian was sprawled out in a pair of peach cotton underwear and matching sports bra on a green couch. It wasn't her black, ratty period granny panties, but it wasn't her lacy come and get it underwear either. She looked up at me casually, and I knew how this was going to go. She'd act too cool, and it would be a competition to see which one of us cared less. Obviously, it was going to be her.

"How was your night?" I asked her.

She shrugged. "It was okay. Marla left early, about an hour after you, so I've been bored."

"Did you write anything new?"

"Not really. We weren't as productive as I hoped. Where we you last night, anyway?"

I started to answer but then I stopped myself.

"It's okay, Hannah, we're not exclusive," she said quietly. "Even though you live here."

I tried not to look too eager. "Why, would you want to be?"

"No," she said, and I felt each word scrape the inside of my teeth.

She gave me a strange half smile. "So, who's the guy?"

"Why do you assume it's a guy?"

She rolled her eyes. "Because this is obviously your first foray into being with a woman. Sometimes you just seem so straight, like you're just putting in just to feel what it's like. You don't even have any gay friends."

I interrupted her. "I don't have that many friends in general."

"Oh, stop being self-deprecating. When we go to any gay community stuff, you always stand there like you don't know if you belong."

"Maybe I don't feel like I do sometimes. So what?"

"When I met other people who were queer, it was a revelation. I grew up religious, where the rules of life are completely prescribed, and I had no idea that there was this whole world full of people like me, but better because they're confident in who they are and they're not hiding."

She turned away from me.

"I tried coming out to my mom, who you think is so great, and she thinks it's just a phase, like I'm screwing with her, and one day I'll marry a wonderful Jewish guy and all will be well. I've known since I was a kid. I tried being with guys, twice, just to see, one of them was the son of a friend of my parents and everyone was so happy, but it wasn't for me. My friends in the queer community changed my life."

I nodded. "I just, I don't know. You're right, you are the first woman I've ever been with, but I'm not just like trying it out. Ever since I've met you, it's just felt good. I don't know if I'm bi or pan, but I'm something."

I stopped to take a breath.

"You're right though, I did meet a guy. I wasn't sure I liked him at first, but it's possible I might, a little."

"Tell me about him," she said in a softer tone.

"What do you want to know?"

"Well, for one thing, where'd you meet him?"

"In class. Marketing."

"Is he our age?"

"No, he's two years older. He spent two years in Israel that he couldn't get course credit for at Webb."

"Wait, is he Jewish? What was he doing in Israel?"

"Yeah, he's Jewish. He was studying in a yeshiva in Jerusalem."

Jillian started laughing. "it's ye-shee-va" she said. "Your pronunciation is so cute. Wait, so is he like me? Another religious kid who's off the *Derech*?"

I stared at her. "I don't know. What do those words mean? He seems pretty religious. He put on that thing this morning, you know, with the black leather straps and the black box on his head when he was praying."

Jillian laughed again, her musical leading lady, everything is hilarious and delightful laugh.

"Off the *Derech* means off the path, what they say about someone who was raised religious and becomes completely the opposite as they get older. The box is called *tefillin*. And you're right, it is a religious thing, to lay *tefillin* every morning. Wait, does he think you're Jewish? Did you tell him you were because of your dad?"

I felt myself getting annoyed. "I always thought Judaism went according to the mom, that's what my dad always said, so I'm not Jewish, right? No, I mean, of course not. Why would I tell him that?"

"No, it's just, it's interesting if he's even a little religious, that he'd date someone who wasn't Jewish. Even traditional not very religious Jewish guys wouldn't do that."

I raised my eyebrows. "I mean, we only hung out once."

"Just be careful. I know lots of religious guys who are supposedly saving themselves for marriage, and all it means is that they're not sleeping with Jewish girls. They think it doesn't count if you're not Jewish. So they go around, acting religious, sleeping with girls they have no intention of ever being in a relationship with, and then they marry some Jewish girl their parents' matchmaker sets them up with, and it's like those other relationships never happened."

I was pretty sure Naftali wasn't that kind of guy.

"It's okay," I said. "I just met him. I don't even know if I want to see him again."

She sat up. "I wonder if I know him. What's his name?"

"Mark. Mark Goldwater. But he says people who know him call him Naftali."

"Oh my God, is his sister Devorah Goldwater?"

"I don't know. He mentioned a sister, but I don't know if he said her name. He mentioned his sister-in-law or ex-sister-in-law."

She looked at me quizzically and I found myself telling her more than I wanted to. Jillian always had that effect on me. "Apparently his brother was involved in some kind of white-collar crime. He was a plastic surgeon, I don't know exactly what the story was."

"Oh my God, yes, that's totally Devorah's brother. Michael Goldwater." She was fidgeting wildly with her hands, her eyes glowing.

"Yeah, it was a huge story. I know girls who went to

him. He did tummy tucks and breast lifts. All these religious young moms would go there to tighten up post baby. Oh, the sister-in-law! Right, the one from Kowloon. The one who wore all the diamonds and saved him and his family from financial disaster. Oh my God, I can't believe you're getting involved with these people. What are the chances?"

I laughed. "I hardly know him."

"But he told you about his family."

"Yeah, a little. We both talked about our families, him and me."

"And he didn't mention his sister at all?"

"Not that I remember. Why, do you know her?"

Jillian walked into her room and put on oversized black t-shirt that fit her like a dress.

She sat down and played with the hem.

"We were ... friends in high school. We went to the same religious all girls' school. It was about a year after I moved here."

"And?"

"We became more than friends, but she didn't want anyone to know."

"Because she was religious?"

"No, she wasn't back then. She acted the way she was supposed to, but she was just going through the motions. She never said it, but I think she couldn't stand the thought of being anything like her mom."

"What do you mean?"

"Her mom comes from this Ultra-Orthodox but very rich family. Apparently her marriage is super weird. At least that's always been the rumour. It's easy to hide things in that world. If you're Orthodox, you wouldn't kiss or hold hands with your spouse in public because it's not considered modest. There are so many women's only events or men's only events. Their mom's name is Malka, which really suits her."

"Why?"

"It means Queen. She'll be totally polite, but then she'll make a comment that's ruthless, but accurate. She's like Martha Stewart, elegant and savage, but also very Jewish.

"I kind of loved Devorah, but she didn't love me. She and I even talked a lot, like real conversations. She was so beautiful and self-assured. She wore the brightest colours, lime green or bright yellow, or blue tie dye and crazy make up. She's the one who got me into glitter. She did gymnastics so she had all these muscles, thighs that could crack concrete when she moved. I was in love with her, and I was sixteen, and it was my first time. It always felt like she was out of my league, and I just wanted a little piece of her, any part of herself she was willing to give me, you know?"

I really do, I thought, but I just nodded.

"We had a couple of sleepovers at her house. People expect teenage girls to have them. She was always hot and cold with me. She'd be complimenting me, have me sitting beside her at lunch. Once she even had her hand on my thigh, in front of everyone. And then a few days later, she'd just nod, like hi, and keep walking like she had somewhere better to be. I was always guessing, always too much for her, and then one day she fully ghosted me. She told the girls in our school that I was obsessed with her. I showed up at her house one day after school, so we could talk, so I could tell her to stop spreading rumours about me, and then she told everyone I was stalking her. Then she had their housekeeper escort me off their property."

"That sounds horrible."

"Yeah, it was. Is her brother into game playing too?"

"I don't know. Not so far."

Jillian laughed. "Where's the fun in that?"

I rolled my eyes at her. "I don't know. It feels … weirdly safe to hang out with him? Not in a bad way."

She snorted. "Boring."

I laughed.

"I can invite him over, and you can hang out with us and tell me what you think."

"Yeah I can do that," she said, giving me a half smile. "But I probably won't like him."

CHAPTER EIGHT

EVER SINCE I told Jillian about Naftali, we'd been spending more time together and he'd started messaging me more. It was fun getting so much attention from both of them.

I didn't tell him much about Jillian, except that she was incredibly talented, and that I got to film stuff for her. I also mentioned that she was taking time off, and that she wanted me to go on the road with her and film, and I was thinking about it. I asked him if he wanted to come with me to see one of her shows.

Jillian was wearing a Blondie halter top and jeans, and she was lining her eyes with a charcoal pencil, purposely making it thick and messy when he walked in. I was wearing a light green dress that belonged to her. Lately, without really trying, I'd lost weight, and I could fit into more of her clothes.

He kissed me quickly, and I was caught off guard and embarrassed when I saw Jillian looking at me.

"Hi," she said, and he looked at her like he was trying to place her.

"I remember you. You went to Ohr Temima with my sister, right?"

I heard myself groan, and I saw Jillian start fiddling with her bracelets.

"Yeah. She's a couple of years older than me. I haven't seen her in a long time. How is she?"

"Baruch Hashem," he answered, "She's having another kid this month, number three."

"Wow. What is that, like a kid a year since she graduated? That's wild."

He laughed. "Not quite, but yeah, it's a loud house."

"What's it like being an uncle?"

"It's fun, I guess. Easier than having my own kids. But I've been an uncle for a long time, my older brother has kids too."

"Right, of course," Jillian said quickly. "Your famous older brother."

Naftali laughed, but I could tell he was uncomfortable.

"Let's talk about something else."

"Why?" she asked. "He's fascinating. The whole story, the money, the diamonds, it's like a movie. He's not still in jail, right?"

I could see Naftali squirm. "No, he's been out for a long time. He got remarried, and he has more kids now. He became religious. He changed a lot, *Baruch Hashem.*"

I tried to change the subject. "What does *Baruch Hashem* mean?" I asked, and they both started laughing.

"It means thank God," Naftali said. And at the same time Jillian said, "We're probably the first Jews she's ever met," while looking at him.

"My dad's Jewish," I said quietly. "You know that."

"What's your mom's background again?"

"British and Scottish. She says there's some Jewish

ancestry somewhere on her dad's side, but I don't know if it's true or just a story she thought my dad would like."

Jillian got up and put on some music. It was Jill Scott's first album, *Who Is Jill Scott?*

"This is her favourite album," I told him. "It's where she got the name Jill from."

"Right, yeah. In high school you went by Miriam, right?"

She sighed. "I never really identified with Miriam. I'm thinking of getting it legally changed."

She got up suddenly. "Let's have something to drink. You drink, Naftali?"

"Yeah."

"Great. I've got vodka, gin, whiskey, whatever you want."

"I'm good with anything."

She disappeared into her room and came back with a bottle of blackcurrant flavoured Absolut and Scooby Doo shot glasses.

"I've been meaning to try this."

She poured mine first, in the cup decorated with an especially dopey looking Shaggy. It was overflowing a little. After she poured for both of them, we clinked our glasses together.

"*L'chaim*," she said loudly, and then elbowed me in the ribs. "That's like the Jewish version of cheers."

"Yeah, I got that."

She turned to both of us.

"I was watching such a good movie earlier. Have you guys heard of *But I'm a Cheerleader*? It's old, from the 90s, I think it stars a young Natasha Lyonne. She's a teenager, but she's into girls, so her parents send her to this super intense conversion boot camp. It's supposed to be satire, I think, but if places like this were real, it's totally where my parents would have sent me."

I looked over at Naftali to gauge his reaction, but his expression betrayed nothing.

"How would your mom react," Jillian asked me, "if you told her you were bi?"

I tried not to react. "I don't think she'd care."

Naftali raised his eyebrows at me, just a little.

Jillian laughed and leaned against Naftali's knee. "Oh, she didn't tell you? Hannah and I had a thing for a while. I mean, you know, she's a lot of fun."

I wanted to kill her.

Naftali shrugged. "Hey, we've all been there. I was in a yeshiva for two years. It's a very strict world. Guys aren't supposed to see or be around any girls or waste any seed, and they're eighteen or nineteen. What do people think is going to happen, you know?"

I stared at him, somehow not totally surprised.

"It was my *chavrusa*, my learning partner, Ezra." His cheeks flushed, and he grinned then looked away. "He was British, very proper and very sarcastic. It was just, something to do, to release the tension, but then it was a little more … But he's married now, and we're not in touch anymore. We both thought it would be weird to still talk."

Jillian reached over and gave Naftali a high five. "Okay, fine, I guess we can be friends."

Naftali laughed.

That night he stayed over at our apartment.

"It's nice how much Jillian cares about you," he said, and I fell asleep smiling.

CHAPTER NINE

NAFTALI'S ROOM ALWAYS smelled like the lemon and fig all-purpose spray he used on his bedside table and the tiny sachets of lavender his sister brought back from a trip to Provence. Somehow, even though he lived downtown, the air smelled fresh.

He had framed photos of St. Martin to Tulum to Casablanca to Petra and Tel Aviv, beach scenes and street scenes, outdoor markets selling spices and jewellery and vibrant graffiti in Spanish, Italian, Arabic, and Hebrew.

He caught me staring at them one day. "I've always been intimated by the thought of travel, the costs, the logistics, getting a passport, but I'd love to travel and capture everything on film. I've never been outside of Canada."

"You should definitely travel. There was this famous art school, Bezalel, right near my yeshiva, and I bought a few of these there. The students there are truly talented."

"Wow, I don't know anything about Israel, but I have heard of Bezalel. My dad's grandmother, my great-grandmother, studied there in the twenties. They moved there so her dad could study in a yeshiva in Hevron. She was a painter. One of my dad's few earthly possessions is this oil portrait she painted of her grandmother. She never got to finish her degree because they married her off to an older Jewish man in Germany. My dad talked about her and Bezalel Academy of Art a lot."

I could tell he was surprised too. "That's amazing."

"It's hard to explain but my dad has these moments where he seems like he's all there, and you can actually talk to him and feel connected to whatever he's talking about. Like family history, say. And you think, it's so cool to know something about my family, maybe I should go there. But the next minute he's pumping you full of his paranoia, telling you that they'll reject you there because your mom isn't Jewish. They'll put you on a no fly list to Israel because of his 'so called crimes,' that's how he says it, with wild gesticulating, like the whole thing is ridiculous, and he didn't do anything wrong. What's hard is that the consequences are real for everyone else, even if they aren't for him."

"Do you think he doesn't believe he did anything wrong? Because that's how my brother talks too, like he can act like he feels guilt or remorse, but he doesn't understand the effect it's had on other people, and I don't know if he'd care if he did."

I sighed. "I'm pretty sure that, in my dad's mind, he's a little kid. He always told us that his favourite age was six. I think he really doesn't think it's wrong, because he doesn't see himself as an adult."

"Wow, that is fucked up."

"I know, but there are these moments where he can make you feel like you're the only person who gets him, and I think that's how he gets people to stay loyal to him. It's one of the reasons I know I have to keep my distance. He makes me feel sorry for him."

Naftali sighed. "Yeah, I get that. I keep a certain distance from Avrumi too."

"What kind of name is Avrumi?" I asked. "Is it Hebrew?"

"Yeah. His Hebrew name is Avraham, which means Abraham. But since he changed his life and became more religious, he took on Avraham's original name, Avrum. After Avrum become religious, he changed his name to Avraham, which in Hebrew, is only one extra letter, an h for Hashem, which means God. Avrumi wanted to remind himself to stay humble because he still had so much growth and change and amends to make."

He rolled his eyes. "It's almost believable, right? Once he changed it, our grandmother started calling him Avrumi, like my little Avrum or something, and then he said he liked it and everyone started calling him that, which is weird when I think about it."

"When we were kids, he went by Mikey back then, he was always the loudest person in the room, whether it was for his grades or how talented he was at violin or basketball. He and my sister used to fight all the time, always telling on each other and spying on each other. One time I remember he had a shouting fit at one of her birthday parties, there was a magician I think, and he kept having to stop his act because Mikey was arguing really loudly with someone. Anyway, he stormed off and walked face first into a wall, and he knocked out his two front teeth. My parents had to rush him to an emergency dentist, there was blood everywhere, and her party was instantly over, but I swear he looked happy about it.

Imagine being that jealous just because it was someone else's birthday."

"That's ... wow."

"We've never been close. Apparently, when I was two, and I don't remember this, but my mom told me, he scratched me here, on my neck, because he wanted to see how I'd react. He was nine, almost ten. Apparently when I didn't cry like my sister did, he did it again, which is why I have this stupid scar. She said she eventually got him to apologize, but it was a battle. It's not like your dad, where he can convince some people that, deep down, he's actually good. It's like everyone who knows him knows he isn't good, but he can talk a good game, and if you're not too close to him, he can seem kind of normal, and it's easier to go along with it than fight it."

"Hannah, can I ask you something?"

We were sitting on the edge of his bed, the photo of the Moroccan souk so close we could almost touch it. He was staring at his socks.

"Yeah, sure."

"Do you remember the things you dad ... I mean, have you like blocked it from your mind? Or does it come up for you, like in memories or in dreams?"

"I ..."

"Because it happened to me once too, with Avrumi."

"Really?"

He looked away, and I reached for his hand.

"Only once that I can remember anyway. We were in the basement on the couch, and he was worried someone was going to see us, which made me so scared that we were both doing something wrong. I remember being able to feel my heart in my head and in my throat. He told me not to tell anyone, but I told Devo, who just told me not tell anyone else. I've kept my distance from Avrumi ever since."

"Wow, I'm sorry," I found myself saying.

"Do you ever worry that you're going to be like him or like people like him? It's one of the reasons I wanted to have that experience in yeshiva. I had all these complicated feelings, he was my brother, he was a guy, and it was scary but I kind of liked it, and I didn't know ... and I did like it, but I also like being with girls, so ..."

"Yeah, but I mean, one thing was a traumatic experience and another was just attraction ..."

"Yeah, but in my family, no one talks about anything. There's like ten elephants in the room at any given moment, and you're just supposed to ignore them. I don't want to be like that. If I'm scared of something, I want to be able to confront it, I want to know."

"Wow. I have always been afraid of being like my dad, but because everything is wrapped up in his philosophies, I've wanted to be the opposite of all of it. I've always wanted to fit in. I've always wanted more friendly but distant relationships with people. I've always wanted to go to university, to make money, to belong in a different way, in a way that I've chosen myself."

He leaned in close. "I feel so close to you right now," he said, and I nodded. I felt really close to him too.

When I tried to tell Jillian about it a few days later, when I tried to tell her about how much freer I felt with him—he knows about my past and he still wants to date me! He has his own serious problems, I'm not the most messed up person he's ever met—she said what we had was a trauma bond. "This might not be the deep connection you think it is," she told me, and I was surprised by how angry I felt.

I told her how we had sex once in the Starbucks washroom at Queen and Bathurst, my bare butt pressed up against the dingy stall wall because I told him I had to go home, and he wanted me to stay a little longer. I thought she'd be jealous, but she just shook her head at me like she felt sorry for me, which made me even angrier.

Jillian and I still hooked up sometimes.

"I knew this girl Tracy, who lived in my neighbourhood in Thornhill. Her dad was a partner in an otherwise all Jewish law firm and all her friends were Jewish. There was this one guy, who was Jewish, and they liked each other. She was beautiful and he played along with her, flirting with her, making out with her and getting her to be his *Shabbos goy*."

"What's a *Shabbos goy*?"

"Someone who's not Jewish, who can do stuff for you that you can't do for yourself on Shabbat. He'd have her come over on Shabbat with a tray of Slurpies for everyone from 7/11. He'd use her to turn on lights and turn phones or computers on and off. He was turned on by the Christian stuff. He'd ask her to cross herself, and or wear her Catholic school uniform. I guess at some point he dumped her. And a few months later he was married to a nice Jewish girl. I just don't want to see that happen to you."

I told Naftali the story late one night at his place.

"Yeah," he said quietly, "I know guys like that too. They're assholes. They're not even just lying to the girl; they're lying to themselves. These are religious people. They're supposed to treat their fellow human beings with respect. My problem is I still feel connected to Judaism. Sometimes I wish I didn't. I still pray and I think what some people get out of yoga and meditation, that's what it's like for me. It's the same with keeping Shabbat. It gives me a break, a real rest away from life and I get to recharge. It would be easier if I didn't."

He looked straight at me, his blonde eyebrows furrowed into what I knew was his most serious expression.

"Hannah, I really like you. I want you to meet the people in my life, my friends, my parents. The only problem is that you're not Jewish. I'm not saying this because it matters to them, I'm saying it because it matters to me. Judaism is matrilineal. From a young age, you get told about how bad intermarriage is, how if you marry a non-Jewish girl, the kids aren't Jewish. In the world I live in, everything moves much faster. Dating is different, you go out a bunch of times, you decide you want the same things in life, you get engaged. There's no living together before you get married. What we have right now is amazing, but this can't go any further unless ..."

"Unless what?"

"Unless you convert to Judaism."

For a brief period of time, after the Tribe disbanded, but before the charges and arrests, my dad had floated a similar possibility by my mother. We could move to Toronto, where his sisters and their families lived. We could officially join a religion, have relatives and be a legitimate part of a real community. My parents could get married. My mom suspected that he only wanted to do it to try to seem normal and avoid what was coming.

Later we found out that he'd made a similar offer to convert to Catholicism for a couple of his other spiritual wives.

"Wow," I said. "I'd really have to think about it."

"My sister-in law, Iris, is a convert. She and Avrumi are divorced, but she's like my sister, in some ways more than Devorah is. She's still part of our family. Do you want to talk to her? She's awesome and very direct and she'd be honest with you about everything."

That night, I mentioned it to Jillian.

"What do you think? Is it crazy that I'm actually thinking about it?"

"Meeting Iris, or becoming Jewish?"

"Meeting Iris. No, both. I don't know."

"You should definitely meet Iris," she said. "If nothing else, she's probably fascinating."

The next time I saw Naftali, I told him he could introduce us.

"Just come by the house," he said, "even if I'm not there."

"Whose house?"

"My parents. It's a huge place, and Iris and her daughter live there too."

CHAPTER TEN

IRIS WAS MORE interested in speaking to me than I expected. She called me the next day.

"This is a big deal," she said almost immediately. "You're the first girlfriend that he's ever even mentioned. I'm excited to meet you." And then added: "Trust me, I know what it's like to be an outsider. If everything works out, I'll be here for you."

I laughed. "Thanks," I said. Then she gave me their address.

"A trip to Chateau Goldwater," Jillian said.

"What's it like?"

"Let's put it this way, my parents are in real estate, so I've been some pretty impressive houses. Their house is incredible. I remember being especially wowed by their elevator, because I'd never seen one in a house. Devorah had said her dad had it built for her grandmother, who was very old, but still, an elevator in a house with five storeys. There were other things too: an indoor pool, a massive yard with a tennis court, a section where the housekeeper and maids lived. Each kid had their own wing of the house. Their basement was amazing. They had this mini arcade with a pool table and air hockey and a little movie theatre. I'd just never seen anything like it, you know, all the marble and the paintings and G monogrammed stuff."

I laughed. "Are you messing with me? G monogrammed stuff?"

She held her hands up and grinned. "I'm really not. G for Goldwater, in cursive gold lettering. It's on their towels and their napkins. You'll see for yourself."

Naftali had a casual way of explaining things that always downplayed their wealth. It didn't seem like he was embarrassed, just that he was matter of fact about the one or two details that were important to him, and happy to ignore everything else.

I stood outside the house for twenty minutes before Iris came to get me. The house looked like a movie set.

Iris had told me to walk around to the side of the house, to a grey stone side entrance where the mail and packages were delivered.

"If you go to the front door," she said, "Clara, the housekeeper will let you in, and you'll have to explain who you are, and what you're doing here. It's less complicated this way."

Iris was wearing a long-sleeved red velvet dress that fit her long, lean figure like a second skin. She had on a light red lip stain and charcoal winged eyeliner that wouldn't have been out of place on a beauty influencer. She was incredibly beautiful.

"I love your make up," I said, but Iris shrugged me off.

"Oh, Frida, the family's make-up artist did it. I have no idea how to do stuff like this, and I normally don't even try but we had a work meeting earlier that I had to look nice for. I'm sure you'll meet Frida sometime. She does Shabbat make up for us on Friday afternoons."

"What's Shabbat make up?"

"Make up that lasts from before sundown on Fridays to sunset on Saturdays. But she uses amazing stuff, so it doesn't come off or bleed, so we feel beautiful on Shabbat."

I had so many questions, I didn't know where to start.

I followed her inside. I took off my shoes, and a maid in pink scrubs appeared out of nowhere to put them in a closet. Then she disappeared. I blinked and took in some of the details: grey and green marble floors, cream carpeting in the hallway that led into Iris's room.

"My daughter Victoria's room is next door. She's still at school."

"I like the name Victoria, it's very classic."

"We named her after a rooftop restaurant in Victoria Harbour, in Hong Kong where Avrumi and I first met. The view was so beautiful, and the sky was so open. There was a feeling that day that anything was possible, and when I named her, that's what I wanted her to feel.

"I didn't become Jewish until after we had her, but when Avrumi's life changed, Victoria and I converted, and we both chose Hebrew names. Everyone in this family has Hebrew or Yiddish first names, but she's such a Victoria, you'll see when you meet her. She's elegant, and I love that you said classic."

"What did you give her as a Hebrew name?"

"Esther, as in Queen Esther. I chose Na'ama which means pleasant for mine. I meant it to be tongue in cheek, like a joke about becoming a well-behaved Jewish woman. I was still angry with Avrumi, because he wanted me to change my name to Iris. My Chinese name is Aihe, which means waterlily. I always thought I'd go by Lily in North America, but he preferred Iris. He thought it sounded more Jewish. So that was our deal. I'd change my name, but Victoria wouldn't have to change hers. Although in the end it's easier for her, at her religious all girls' school, to go by Estee with her friends." She rolled her eyes. "I guess you can't win them all."

"Does she have a Chinese name?"

"Of course. It's Zhen, which means precious."

I looked down at the royal blue and gold rug at my feet.

It was like being inside a castle, full of décor and furniture as delicate as the ceramics in the Gardiner Museum, except that real people actually lived there.

Iris took my arm and squeezed just above the elbow. It felt surprisingly good.

"You like that? It's an acupressure point. Not that I know tons about it, but sometimes little massages help."

"It feels great."

"Don't worry so much. We're all odd birds in this family, and there's something special about having our own particular flock. I mean"—and she leaned in conspiratorially and said very quietly—"except Devorah, she and her husband and kids are pretty much the Jewish community gold standards. And in some ways, so is Avrumi and his new wife and kids. But as long as you know what to expect, it's okay."

"What do you mean?" I asked, trying to keep my voice as low as hers.

"I mean, they don't like to think. They come out and strongly share whatever opinion is popular in their community, whether that's where to donate charity, or why your kid should leave the Jewish school they're in because it'll affect their future marriage prospects, or why they shouldn't eat at a certain kosher restaurant in the neighbourhood because, after Shabbat, boys and girls hang out there, unsupervised."

"Wait, what?"

"Oh, yeah. It's all insane. Try to ignore them when they talk. They love to get into discussions where they shout people into submission. I'll tell you a secret: Devorah doesn't actually believe anything she says, no matter how much conviction she speaks with. I've seen her go from one end of the spectrum to the other without even blinking. Tomorrow, she could decide she wants her daughters to live more open lives and be citizens of the world, and she'll talk with the same confidence about how that's who she's always been. Try not to take anything she says seriously."

"Okay."

"Naftali is not like that at all. He thinks deeply about everything, and he's one of a kind. It takes the right kind of person to fit in with all of us, and he thinks a lot of you."

"Oh, I don't know ..."

"It was more complicated with me. I was with Avrumi, for years without converting, which bothered them but for years he wasn't religious at all, so they had to pick their battles. Naftali is the good son and family member, the one who's always managed to have decent relationships with everyone. In a way, there's more pressure for him, to meet everyone's expectations. Which means, if you decide to keep seeing him, you're going to have to convert to Judaism."

"I don't know. I mean, it's early days. I was looking online at all the different kinds of conversions, Orthodox, Conservative, Reform ..."

"Orthodox," Iris interrupted me. "It can only be Orthodox with this family. That's the only kind of conversion they think counts."

"But Orthodox conversions take forever. I was reading online; it can take people three or four years."

"It won't take you that long. For one thing, your dad is Jewish, so it won't be totally foreign to you. For another thing, one of the sponsoring Beit Din rabbis, that's the Orthodox Jewish court that presides over this stuff, is very close to Jack and Malka. His name is Rabbi Brown. I can give you his contact information. Aside from all the drama with Avrumi, the Goldwaters are incredible community members. They're huge charity donors, and Malka comes from a rabbinic dynasty. Her dad was a big deal rabbi in New York, and her grandfather sat on the Beit Din in Israel. They'll help you. You just need to be serious about it and committed to it. I'm not going to lie to you, Hannah. If you decide to do this, it's hard."

"Yeah, I'm sure. That's why I haven't decided anything yet. Was it worth it for you, to go through all that?"

"I think so. You learn a lot and you think deeply about things and make yourself vulnerable in a way that's not necessarily normal. Was it worth it? Yes. Do I wish I could have skipped some of the waiting around or uncomfortable questions? Of course. But it gives you a culture and a community. If you've ever felt like you're looking for something but don't quite know where you fit in, it may be that you have a Jewish soul. According to the Kabbalah, Abraham and Sarah, the original patriarch and matriarch of Judaism, created many Jewish souls, and some of them try to return to their origins. I know when I did it, it felt indescribably right, like things falling perfectly into place in ways I didn't know I wanted."

I felt her words deeply, but I hoped she couldn't tell.

She leaned in and tapped my knee with her perfectly manicured candy apple red nails.

"I didn't grow up wealthy either. Naftali told me that you grew up in a hippie community, somewhere rural, right? So you get it, it's not just about money and access, but the stability, not having to worry about certain things, even if you don't stay married it definitely doesn't hurt, right?

I nodded, slowly. "I guess not."

Iris got up quickly and started fumbling for her jacket. "I have to pick up Victoria from school. But let's talk again. Think about all of this, and feel free to call me anytime."

She offered to drop me at the subway, but I shook my head. "I want to walk," I said. "I want to look around and get a sense of the neighbourhood."

CHAPTER ELEVEN

I CALLED NAFTALI about ten minutes after I left his parents' house, as I walked through a neighbourhood filled with modern and Tudor style houses with front lawns overflowing with silver birch and sweeping willow trees, perfectly pruned hedges, little girls whose school uniform skirts went past their knees right up to their ankles, and their nannies, who were trailing behind them, talking on their cell phones. Among all the luxury cars, there was a bright yellow sports car, with a license plate that said ETROG.

Naftali laughed when I mentioned it. "Oh yeah, that's Tuvia's car. He's a friend of my parents. An etrog is a special kind of lemon we use on Sukkot, this big Jewish holiday in the fall. Apparently the car's had all kinds of problems since he bought it, so it's a joke. Have you seen his wife's plates?"

I stared at the black Jeep in their driveway and tried to read it out loud: ESHET CH18IL.

He laughed. "Eighteen is a lucky number in Judaism, in Hebrew it's pronounced Chai, which also means life. *Eishet Chayil* means woman of valour, and when I was a kid we used to sing it to my mom at Shabbat dinner. It celebrates all the great things she does."

"Wow. So did his wife choose the plates herself?"

He laughed again. "No, I think he got it for her, just wanting her and people who see it to know how great she is. There are two more good ones if you want to keep an eye out: there's a lady with four kids who drives a van whose license plate says AHSHAV, which means now in Hebrew. And there's another guy, an older rabbi who lives down the street, who drives a beaten-up nineties Cadillac with the license plate SH8NEZ. It's weird, but we're not allowed to wear clothes that are made of a mix of wool and linen, so this guy's job is to inspect people's clothes to make sure. It's called *Shatnez.*"

"That's so random. That's his whole job? Like, in life?"

Naftali laughed. "Yeah."

"Wait but, wool is a winter fabric, right? And linen is all light and summery. Why would you ever combine those two things?"

He laughed even harder. "That's a great question. No one knows for sure. I should take you on a tour sometime, show you all my favourite things. If you keep walking towards Bathurst, there's some good food, kosher restaurants and bakeries and stuff. My favourite is still Apollo. They have the best bagels and *kokosh,* which is this Hungarian chocolate cake. I have to get you some. If you walk in the other direction, there's a beautiful ravine and a walking trail. My siblings live nearby, too. Devorah's husband Max is originally a New Yorker, so he didn't want to buy a house, even though they could have. They own a double penthouse in a condo just off Bathurst. Their place is cool. He's really into scuba diving, so they have this giant tank in one of their living rooms with pet sharks. Avrumi and his wife, Shaindy, have a house right near the ravine. It's got all these huge pine trees around it, and it's set far back from the road, so it's not totally visible when you drive by, which is how he likes it. I want to take you to meet both of them and their families. I want to show you everything."

I took a breath. "Sure, yeah, that would be great. It was great to meet Iris, I really liked her."

"What's wrong?"

"Nothing, it's just a lot to take in. I'll call you later."

When we hung up, I decided to call Jillian. I was trying not to have a panic attack.

"I'll come pick you up," Jillian answered immediately. "Just text me the address so I know exactly where you are."

I wandered down a few side streets until I ended up on a Bathurst street corner. Bathurst was lined with faded cardboard brown brick buildings, full of porches glistening with kids' bikes and red plastic wagons. There were kids everywhere I looked. Little boys in button down shirts wearing yarmulkes decorated with Paw Patrol characters. On the corner I found Apollo's Baked Goods. A large, rusting air conditioning unit poked out of the upstairs window. Thick silver foil window covers blocked out most of the light, except for the window on the left that proudly showed Apollo's kosher certification. A big gold sign invited passersby to "Taste our Scrumptious Bagels, made fresh every hour." There was a bus stop right outside the bakery's automatic sliding doors, and next door was a Cash for Gold, a dry cleaner's and Pride of Palawan, a Filipino grocery store and remittance centre. I stepped inside Apollo's Baked Goods.

There were men with chest length beards, from Santa white to black and even red, wearing black coats, white shirts and black pants, and women in frumpy knee length skirts, with shoulder length brown or black hair which were obviously wigs. It was fascinating to see them up close.

I looked down at my fitted black pants that were like a neon sign screaming: Does not belong here! I distracted myself with pastries.

Behind the glass counters were trays of buttery cookies with green and red maraschino cherries, heavy rainbow sprinkles, or half dipped in dark chocolate. There were thick fruitcakes, heavy with syrupy cut kiwi slices, red grapes and oranges, stately seven-layer chocolate cakes, and dozens of tiny cupcakes in baby pinks, blues, and mint greens. I ordered two cupcakes, one pink and one green and waited outside for Jillian.

She showed up fifteen minutes later and, when I got into her car, I hugged her so hard that she yelped.

Jillian raised her eyebrows and grinned. "Wow, so was it worse than I thought it would be?"

I laughed and realized how tight my throat felt.

"It was intense." Jillian was blasting the Jill Scott song "How it Made You Feel."

Two Orthodox women stared and raised their eyebrows at us, and we laughed.

"Let's get out of here," Jillian said. "Let's go downtown and forget this whole day ever happened."

"I need a break from everything," I said.

Jillian grinned and put on Iggy Pop's "The Passenger." I liked sitting beside her, being driven around, not quite sure where she was taking me, but knowing something exciting was coming.

It started with drinks, first at a bar on Queen with a live mambo band playing in the background. Jillian ordered us mojitos. "There's nothing like fresh mint," she said, closing her eyes as she took a sip—and salsa, chips and guacamole, which she only picked at. My food and my drink disappeared faster than I expected it to, and Jillian immediately ordered more, with a Caipirinha to share. "Trust me, it tastes so fresh, you'll feel like you're sitting in the sun on a warm, tropical beach." The drink was sweet, full of sugar and lime, and I couldn't picture a beach, but I could imagine swaying in a hammock. I was startled when Jillian reached over and kissed me. "You just look so happy," she said, and I sighed and kissed her back. We left the bar. I was feeling slightly tipsy, my arm linked in Jillian's. "We need to go shopping," she said. "We need new outfits. I have this friend, Johnny, who's having a house party tonight. He's a painter, and he has all these artist friends. It's always amazing at his place, but we can't go like this."

She steered us into a makeup store a block away. Jillian picked out some gold and forest green glitter eye shadows, and ruby lipstick. We passed a vintage store and Jillian ran in, and came out holding two sequin tube tops, one silver and one gold.

We took turns changing in the backseat, blocking the window with our back for the one who was taking everything off.

Jillian chose the gold one. She gave my nipples quick squeeze. "You don't need a bra, trust me, you look great."

I rolled my eyes, took my bra off and pulled Jillian closer.

Johnny's party was in a huge loft. There were abstract and graffiti style paintings and sculptures, and hot people, some who looked like models, everywhere we looked.

Jillian caught my eyeballing everything, and grinned. "You're too young to be thinking about marrying a Goldwater. You haven't experienced enough of life to even know what you want yet."

I was still lightheaded from the drinks.

Jason, who had long blond hair and sleeve tattoos, grabbed Jillian's arm and pulled her into a hug. Jillian introduced us, and he put his arms around both of us. "Come join us on the patio," he said, his hair floating out behind him. "Come say hi to everyone and have a quick bump. We've got great edibles too."

Everyone was gathered around a wooden patio table.

I felt the familiar knot of fear and dread that disappeared the minute I took the straw he handed me and put it into my nose. I was instantly wired, delicious bursts of energy coursing through my blood stream. So what if I wasn't supposed to be doing this anymore? Wasn't I still young? Why was my life so complicated anyway? I couldn't help it, doing coke felt like going home.

I lost track of Jillian for a while, feeling like a cartoon bear with its paws stuck in a jar of the world's most delicious honey. I heard myself talking and laughing and I didn't know what I was saying but for the first time in a long time I honestly didn't care. Eventually I lay back on a cushioned lounge chair, my legs twitching, tiny, perfect fireworks firing in my synapses.

When I woke up, I found myself alone. The sun was up, so I realized that it must be the next day. I padded inside, my feet feeling oddly heavy. My head hurt and my nose felt almost dry enough to bleed. I used to carry nasal spray for just these occasions, but it had been too long, and I'd gotten sloppy. Jillian was stretched out like a cat on Jason's couch, still wearing her tube top and underwear, but no pants. I touched my face and realized I was sweating glitter. Gold was pouring out of the corners of my eyes, and red was dripping off my lips. We both smelled like cigarettes, Jillian's baby powder drug store deodorant, and probably more. I found my phone in Jillian's purse and pulled it out. It was 9:07 am. I had one missed call and four texts from Naftali.

"Come on," I said. "It's time to go."

Jillian groaned. "Not 'et," she said, she murmured. "It's too earrrly."

"Come on," I said, this time more firmly. "It's time."

Jillian found her pants, air kissed Johnny on our way out and insisted on stopping for coffee before we went home. It started raining as we drove, and I opened my window, letting the cool drops fall on my open hand.

We reached a side street with a Starbucks on one corner and a convenience store on another. I thought dreamily about getting more coke. I loosened my seatbelt as Jillian started driving faster. Jillian almost never wore hers. She screamed when the car turning hit us head on. Jillian was light as a bird, and she flew, through the glass windshield and onto the front engine of the car. I was thrown forward too, and my head broke through the glass, but my body hovered below me in the seat. I had this strange thought that it might look cool from the outside, that time had stopped for a few seconds, and I could just take out my phone and film everything.

When I opened my eyes, paramedics were standing over me. I tried to move my arms or my legs an inch or two, but I heard someone yelling, "Don't move, stay exactly where you are." Someone else told me not to open my eyes. They were going to use a special tweezer, she said, to remove the glass from the windshield that got into my eyes. Someone else stood in front of me, she had big feet and red sneakers on, and she wiped my fore-head which I suddenly realized was bleeding. She taped a thick piece of gauze to the spot.

"Don't worry, the head always bleeds a lot," she said. "You might not even have a concussion."

I had never ridden in the back of an ambulance. Growing up, everyone in the Tribe was against hospitals and vaccines and western medicine. When my mom be-came a nurse, she was all about preventing everything. I was fidgety, terrified of what could come next.

Jillian seemed oddly sanguine, even with a gash across her forehead that looked like a scene from a slasher movie. She filled out her forms quickly, with shaking hands, her eyes lighting up whenever one of the paramedics talked to her or asked her any questions. Even through my fog of headache and hangover, I could tell that Jillian was flirting with them, these guys in uni-forms whose faces and bodies she'd barely registered. I turned away and looked out of the window.

The waiting room was packed. The chairs were worn

but clean and the table next to me was full of a stack of old issues of *Chatelaine and Cosmopolitan*.

I saw Jillian go to the bathroom. She invited me to come with her, and I watched her wash her hands in the sink. She turned on the hot water and gripped the hot steel faucet until her hand burned. I watched the space between her thumb and her forefinger bleed. It was all like part of a strange movie I was watching half awake at three in the morning.

When Jillian went to the nurse's station to complain about the wait time, she bled three drops onto their white clipboard. Later they told her she had a broken wrist and needed two stitches in her arm. She also had third degree burns on her hand. I couldn't believe that she'd burned herself on purpose. I must have seen it wrong, I told myself. I was so out of it, or someone must have told her to do it. She cried a little from the pain. I stood with her like she asked me to when she got examined.

The doctor was young, early thirties maybe. He touched her hand softly when he examined it. He set her wrist tenderly. "Thank you so much Dr Weinberg," she said, and he smiled at her, his eyebrows furrowed with worry. She asked me if she should send him a thank you note.

I shrugged.

It turned out that I was mostly okay. I had mild whiplash and a deep scratch on my left cheek bone. I wondered if it would scar. The doctor used a tiny needle and gave me three small stitches in my forehead. I wasn't supposed to feel anything, but I felt a tug as he pulled on the sutures. I knew that it could have been worse.

Naftali arrived, looking tired and worried. He hugged me tightly. He even hugged Jillian.

"I'm so glad you guys are okay."

Jillian played it off like it was an uproarious best friend's gone wild misadventure from a movie.

It was only when Naftali drove us back to our apartment that Jillian admitted to me that her license had been suspended two years earlier. "I probably shouldn't be driving," she said quietly. "But I love it so much, I just can't give it up."

I thought about all the coke that I'd done. I knew I'd have to do it again.

"I get it," I found myself saying.

Later that night, after Jillian had gone to bed, Naftali lay on his back beside me. He kept asking me if I was okay, and I found it hard to hide my irritation.

I don't know, I wanted to say. None of it seems real yet and I don't know if it ever will.

My head hurt, but the throbbing, pulsing feeling in my body made me feel more alive.

"I'm fine," I said eventually. "It was scary, but it probably could have been a lot worse."

Naftali sat up and stared straight at me.

"I know you love Jillian, but what happened was scary. It's like she didn't even get it, like the danger didn't register. You guys could have died."

I knew that in some way I wanted them both, the excitement of someone I couldn't predict and the stability of someone else who would actually be there.

I don't know exactly what I told him, something about being happy that he cared, and grateful to be okay, and some kind of vague promise that I'd be more careful, and he seemed to accept that before we both fell asleep.

CHAPTER TWELVE

NAFTALI STARTED TRYING to teach me about Jewish culture. Instead of binge watching *The Walking Dead* or *Friends*, he started cueing up movies like *Little Jerusalem* and *Menashe*, which was in Yiddish with English subtitles. The closest I'd ever come to hearing Yiddish was hearing my father imitate his grandfather's accent. I was surprised by how comforting it sounded, even if I couldn't pick out a single word they were saying.

We watched TV shows like *Shtisel*, about an Ultra-Orthodox Jewish family living in Jerusalem. We both liked the Akiva character, a twenty something who was more interested in being an artist than being a rabbi. We even watched part of *Fiddler on the Roof* one night. I watched them like a cultural anthropologist, observing with as much neutrality as I could muster.

"You don't have to commit to anything, you just have to keep an open mind," he said. He set up a preliminary meeting with Rabbi Brown. "He'll explain to you what conversion involves and maybe give you some stuff to read and then you can decide. There's no pressure. I told him you were interested, but not exactly sure."

That put it mildly. I still wasn't sure I wanted to commit myself to him, let alone his religion and culture. But then I thought about the alternative: living indefinitely in Jillian's apartment, like a freeloader, waiting for her and her family to realize she could do better than me.

"I don't know much about even the basics of Judaism," I told him, and he sent me links to Orthodox educational websites like Aish HaTorah and Chabad. I started reading articles. As long as I didn't think about the future or myself, it was as interesting as learning about anything else.

"I know bits and pieces about Judaism from the way I grew up," I told him one day, "but it's hard to know how much of it was legitimate and how much of it was my dad's creative interpretation."

"I think you should just be honest with him. He helped Iris a lot. Ask her about him, I think he was good to her. He has an office in a synagogue that's pretty close to where my whole family lives."

"Are you going to come in with me to meet him?"

"I can if you want me to, but it might be easier for you to open up if I'm not sitting right there. You can trust him, I promise. I trust him."

Naftali said his other siblings wanted to meet me too. "Avrumi and his wife Shaindy love to host, and Devorah and Max live close by, and they'll want to drop in too. We can go by after the meeting. They figured tea or coffee or whatever would be less pressure than dinner. It'll be casual."

I asked Naftali if Iris would be there too. "I have no idea, call her and ask her."

Iris didn't seem surprised to hear from me.

"Look, I appreciate you asking," she said, "but Avrumi and I have been divorced for a long time. I mean, we try to get along for our daughter's sake, but I can't say I spend much time at his house unless I have to."

"What's Shaindy like, anyway?"

"She's exactly what you picture when you picture a very Orthodox young lady."

I thought about the women I saw walking around in the Goldwaters' neighbourhood.

"She's ... serious. She went to one of those all-girl religious schools where the goal was to get married at nineteen and start having kids. They all have standard go to answers for everything, everything is about the will of God and thanking Him."

"She sounds like the opposite of you."

Iris laughed. "You're not wrong. Avrumi and I were unhappy for a long time. I wanted a partner, and a best friend; he wanted someone who would unconditionally kiss his ass. When he became more religious, he wanted someone who was very serious about it, who looked like she belonged and always had. The optics were fine when he was a young successful doctor, trying to show what a man of the world he was. He'd have me wear a red Cheongsam to dinner with his friends, or had me cook traditional food, like cheong fun or bolo bau. I found it ridiculous, but I played along. Once he was sentenced though, he had to prove how serious he was about starting over and being a better person. He wanted a girl who was pure and naïve enough to believe he'd just accidentally made a mistake. The last thing he wanted was a woman who could pass as his kid's nanny."

I cringed. "Seriously?"

She shrugged. "It happened. I definitely experienced racism. At least a couple of times at Victoria's Jewish day school, a mom would start telling me about their kids' nanny and asked how I developed such a great bond with her and how her mom felt. You should have seen their faces when I told them I was her mom. Another time some random mom was complaining how her live-in nanny's English wasn't great, and I talked to the woman, who was great, and it turns out, Filipina. Then I realized that she thought I was also a nanny.

"Not everyone is like that, obviously, but it does exist. You know, the types who think that there's people like them and then there's everybody else. To be identified as Jewish by people like that. I'd have to really go out of my way to use *yeshivaish* words and dress even more modestly and make an effort that I wasn't sure I wanted to make.

"What matters most to Avrumi is how things look. So Shaindy's invited you over, and I'm sure she'll be nice to you, because it's a mitzvah to welcome guests into your home, and Avrumi wants the gossip, and she wants to make him happy. The truth is, she probably knows very few non-Jews and this whole thing probably makes her uncomfortable. I don't know if Naftali told you this or not, but Judaism is not a religion that tries to get people to convert. It's the opposite. They actually turn people away, three times sometimes, just to make sure they're serious about it and doing it for the right reasons."

I took this in. Naftali hadn't mentioned this at all.

"If you want to get along with them, and with the rabbi for that matter, don't make it sound like you're doing this for him. I made that mistake when I was with

Avrumi, and it set me back a lot. You seem like a sincere person, Hannah, so let that part of you show. Figure out why it matters to you, and that's your answer if they ask you why you want to do all of this."

That night I thought a lot about what Naftali had asked me. I thought about my dad and a handful of men who fathered hundreds of kids. The women were always pregnant and expecting more. Breastfeeding was a big part of it too. They believed in prolonging it until the kids were five or six. I didn't remember spending much time alone with my dad until I was five. We were sitting on a patch of grass outside the cabin. I was wearing a yellow and white polka dot dress that belonged to one of the other girls. I wanted to wear dresses every day, but my mother explained that they didn't have enough money. The yellow dress was my favourite. It had a big skirt that swirled around me when I spun in circles. A few days before, my mother had locked me out. I'd been having a tantrum and wouldn't stop crying. My mother picked me up and put me outside, and my stomach dropped when I heard the lock click on the door. I didn't believe it at first. I walked up to the doorknob, which I could just reach when I stood on my tip toes, and I pulled. It was really locked. I sat in the knee-high grass just outside the cabin. It felt like hours, but maybe it wasn't. It was hot and windy. I closed my eyes. The grass was soft. It felt like each blade was caressing my face. I fell asleep and woke up to find my dad carrying me inside. I looked at my father.

"I want mom," I said, and kicked at the dirt with my bare feet. "I want to nurse now. Where's mommy?"

He rolled his eyes. "She's with Jared." Jared was a

Cultivator. He mainly did manual labour, farming, and chopping wood. My father was always friendly to them, but I knew he liked the Advisors better. "At his cabin."

I started to cry again. My dad picked me up and held me to his chest. He often wore soft linen shirts, in white or cream, half unbuttoned. "I can nurse you too, you know."

I looked away and laughed. "You're so silly. Only mamas can."

He reached down and gently lifted my chin with his hand, so he was looking me in the eye. He smiled. "Of course I can. You just have to use your imagination, Hannah."

I closed my eyes. My mother was not an affectionate person. He put his nipple in my mouth. I imagined my mom. My mom holding me and hugging me. My mom telling me that I looked beautiful in my yellow dress.

After a few minutes he started moaning. He held his hand on the back of my neck so I couldn't move. I kicked and squirmed, but he held me until I felt something wet on the back of my leg. They were so strict about me not having accidents anymore.

"Daddy did you pee yourself?" I shrieked.

I touched it and it felt like the snot that dripped from my nose the last time I was sick.

He was gazing past me at the water and the mountains in the distance. He shook himself and looked me in the eye.

"Yes. Don't tell your mom."

"I'm going to go have a swim," I said, and he looked relieved.

My half-sister River, who was six and whose mom

was a beautiful woman named Maggie, told me that they'd been invited to a special celebration for our dad's birthday. The Tribe celebrated it every year together, but theirs was private. "We gave him a special massage," she said. "He told us to pull, like we were pulling a rope on a boat, and we were soaked with white water spray. He was so happy, and he gave us so many blessings."

I told her what happened to me when I was with our dad a few days before.

"You're so lucky," she said. "It was just you, all by yourself."

I nodded and smiled back at her even though I was scared.

Our half-sister Chantana, who was eight, told me how special dad was, but "he stops thinking we're special when we're ten and then only wants to spend time with us when we're much older." She showed me some drawings she'd made of our father, including one where he was naked. Her mom, Kohsoom, was a sculptor, and she showed me a small wooden sculpture she'd helped her make.

It looked like a penis. I felt sick and started to walk away.

"It's a Palad Khik," she yelled. "It's a Thai symbol of fertility. He thinks I'm going to have a lot of babies one day."

After that, I asked for it. I would go out of my way to track down my dad. I'd let him lift me up in the air and carry me around at Tribe events. I'd agree with my mother when she told people that I got jealous and didn't like to share him with his other kids. It could have happened to me less. I could have hidden, but I didn't.

I thought of telling Jillian, once, late at night, when we were in bed together. She always slept naked on her side, the knots on her spine like symmetrical, cool to the touch pearls.

I wanted to whisper it, just to keep getting it out of my body, like slowly draining a Poison Ivy blister. In a perfect world, Jillian would sleep through it, and I would know that I got it out without having to deal with her reaction.

But I was scared she wouldn't understand. Naftali was asking a lot of me, but if I wanted to tell him these kinds of details, I knew I could, and he wouldn't judge me.

"Okay," I told him later that day. "I'll try meeting the rabbi."

He smiled.

"But we have to take this one step at a time."

CHAPTER THIRTEEN

I EXPECTED TO have to wait a while for the appointment with a rabbi, but Naftali set it up a few days later. I'd never met a rabbi, and somehow I expected him to have the aura of a person whose feet didn't quite touch the ground, but he was just a regular man in a dark suit and a white button-down shirt. He could have been anyone who worked in an office, which made the whole thing feel anticlimactic.

He looked forty something, with a ginger beard and a friendly, if slightly guarded smile.

In the end, I convinced Naftali that I needed him to come with me. He parked the car while I got out to meet the rabbi.

"Remember, don't shake his hand," Naftali whispered. "Rabbis don't touch women unless it's their wife or daughter."

I nodded. I kept my hands glued to my sides when I first said hi to Rabbi Brown.

The synagogue itself was three large, converted houses. The outside was covered in beige Jerusalem limestone. It had big glass windows and a heavy wooden door. It was *called Mercaz Torah U'Tefillah*, which Naftali explained meant the centre of bible and prayers.

"I'm one of several rabbis at this shul," he explained.

We waited in the foyer for Naftali.

Rabbi Brown put an arm around him and clapped on his back. "So good to see you." He looked at me and smiled conspiratorially. "I've been trying to twist his arm to get to learn with us in our Kollel since he was in yeshiva. Maybe now I can finally get him in here."

Naftali's smile was tight and obviously fake. "*Bli neder*," he said, which he had explained to me before meant that he intended to but couldn't promise.

I thought about Jillian. The night before, she'd told me about her own religious explorations.

"In first year, I was strictly vegan, and I used to eat in this Hare Krishna temple downtown that had this amazing café. It was so delicious and so cheap, you could get a three-course vegan Indian meal for ten dollars. I loved the orange outfits, and these cupboards they had full of the most brightly coloured sequined dolls, you know how I feel about kitsch. So when this girl recommended I go with her that summer to India, I went, and we ended up in Auroville. It was wild, all these ideas about unity and connection and letting go of worldly things. It was like a cult-y kibbutz. I just wish you'd picked something more fun than Orthodox Judaism."

Jillian helped me pick out the right outfit that morning, a slate grey t-shirt with a high neck, a black button-down cardigan, and a black skirt I borrowed from her, with opaque grey tights so no part of my legs would be exposed. She even had me tie my hair up. It had been its natural ink black for a month now and without bright colours I didn't feel like myself.

Jillian had originally offered to drive me to the synagogue and even come in with me if I wanted, but she woke up and said was feeling really sick. She'd had endometriosis since she was a teenager, but lately the cramping and bleeding hurt more than ever, and the pills her doctors had given her had stopped working.

She was scared because her doctor had suggested surgery. I offered to go with her to her next appointment, but she wouldn't let me.

"I don't want you to see me like this," she said. "It's bad enough that my body is falling apart, I don't need a witness."

Naftali wanted things to go well, but he wanted to seem casual.

Rabbi Brown led them into his small office, his shelves decorated with volume after volume of leatherbound texts with Hebrew lettering. They sat down in chairs a small distance away from each other.

"So, Hannah," Rabbi Brown said, "Naftali tells me you've been keeping Shabbat for the last few months. That's wonderful."

I was taken aback. Not only had I been doing no such thing, I had only just started reading about Shabbat. I had to think on my feet.

"It's great," I said, "to have a designated day of rest."

I tried hard to remember what I was not supposed to be doing. "I especially like not being on my phone or being online. It's such a good mental break."

Naftali smiled and discreetly gave me a thumbs up from under his chair.

Rabbi Brown smiled. "I'd like to ask you a little bit about yourself, if you don't mind. Tell me, where does the attraction to Judaism come from? Do you have any Jewish roots?"

He took out a pad of lined paper to write down my answers.

I wanted to make a joke about this being like therapy, but I decided not to when I saw how serious both his and Naftali's faces were.

I looked away. "My dad is Jewish."

"Did you mother convert Conservative or Reform?"

I shook my head. "No. My mom is Catholic, though she doesn't really practice."

I felt my face getting hot.

"Is she upset that you're interested in Judaism?"

"No," I said, lying. The truth was I hadn't told her.

"So why are you interested in Judaism now?"

I thought about what Iris said, and I decided to try being honest.

"Growing up, my family was into spirituality in a way that felt chaotic and inconsistent. When other people talk about spiritual things, I'm almost jealous because I just can't feel it or tap into it. I feel like I'm missing something fundamental that everyone else innately understands. When I met my friend Jillian, I learned that she was raised Orthodox, and aside from the great food, and her family, she has a sense of confidence and belonging. I like what I've read about Judaism, specifically the rules about how to treat your fellow man. It's so specific, like a guide for how to be a good person in basically every situation."

Rabbi Brown stroked his beard and smiled. "Those

are good answers. I appreciate how deeply you've thought about all of this. There are lots of things that people find challenging, from not being able to eat in your favourite restaurants, to having to change all your clothes, the way you present yourself. There's still a lot for you to learn. I'm going to put you in touch with a tutor who works with us. Her name is Chaya. Her husband is another one of the rabbis of this shul. She's going to learn with you for an hour or two every week. She's going to teach you in more detail about what it means to keep mitzvot. She'll guide you.

"It was nice to meet you, Hannah. Once you've been keeping Shabbat for a few months longer, the senior Beit Din would like to meet you. We can formally start your conversion process then."

I kept telling myself that there was still time, that I didn't have to commit to anything.

Naftali waited until we were both in the car and driving onto the next street before reaching over and squeezing me into a hug.

"You did so well in there," he said.

"Thanks." I wanted to ask why he lied to them about what I'd been doing and tell him how saying that was like telling them I'd agreed to something, and really I still wasn't sure, but a part of me like being swept up in all of this.

"The meeting went much faster than I thought it would. Do you know we were only in there for fifteen minutes?"

I rolled down my window and sat back in my seat. "No, it felt way longer."

I needed to think about something else.

"If you want to reward all my hard work," I said, "you should know that I'm not wearing any underwear."

"What? You went commando to a meeting with a rabbi?"

I bit my bottom lip. "Oh, is that bad?"

He laughed. "No, it's kind of hot, I'm just glad you didn't tell me. It would have been so hard to concentrate."

By now we'd pulled up into his parents' driveway.

I climbed on top of him and straddled him in the driver's seat. "Too bad we can't just do it right here, right now."

He kissed me and pushed me back gently. "Well, aside from the very real possibility of either of my parents coming home, there's also the security cameras that are capturing all of this."

I laughed. "So, let's go inside already."

"That's my girl. We only have like fifteen minutes before we have to be at Avrumi's, so we have to make it really fast."

He gave my ass a quick squeeze and I moaned. "Perfect," I said, "that's just the way I like it."

CHAPTER FOURTEEN

WE STOOD SIDE by side in front of Naftali's full length closet mirror, in our underwear, fixing our hair and smoothing out the wrinkles in our clothes.

"The outfit you wore to meet the rabbi is perfect," he said, his tone reassuring and sweet. He tugged at my skirt to make sure it went all the way over my knees.

"Don't want anyone else to see the goods?" I teased.

"My brother is ... a special case. He needs everything in his life to be exactly the way he wants it. When you go to his house, you have to play by his rules, even though they're stupid, but he's a lot easier to deal with if you just play along."

I stared at him. "What do you mean, play along? And why would I want to do that if you think it's stupid?"

He exhaled sharply. "I don't know. You have to meet him and Shaindy at some point. They keep asking, since Iris has already met you. And since he became more religious, my parents respect him more and listen to him more. Don't worry, no one expects us to be close to him, it's not like my family doesn't know he's impossible. It's just a step."

I thought about it.

"So you want me to act like I did with the rabbi, answering like I'm trying to pass a test?"

Naftali reached down and kissed my neck. "Look, I don't want to stress you out. If you really don't want to go, we can cancel. Maybe seeing the rabbi was enough for one day."

I knew deep down that the smarter thing to do was to walk away. But for some reason, I wanted to prove that I could handle it.

"No, it's okay, I can do this."

"You sure?"

"Yeah. Let's just get it over with."

He smiled. "That's the spirit."

Avrumi's house looked like a Tudor style gingerbread house, with white lattice wood on every window. It was hidden from the street view by a wall of pine trees. I took a deep breath. It smelled like driving out to a Christmas Tree farm in the country with my stepfather. I hated how comforting it felt, and how perfect it looked.

When we pulled up, Naftali noticed that Devorah wasn't there yet. "Maybe it's better," he said, "less overwhelming if you meet my siblings one at a time."

I smiled at him and tried to hide my growing anxiety. "I have a feeling this is going to be fine," I said, but he was already kissing the large wooden mezuzah on the front door and ringing the doorbell.

Avrumi answered the door. He looked like a shorter, chubbier version of Naftali. He had the same angelic blonde hair and green eyes, but he had a fuller face and cheeks which were made fleshier by his full, white-blond beard. He was wearing a black suit and a button-down white shirt. His pot belly poked out of his two bottom shirt buttons.

A little girl popped her head out from between her father's legs. Naftali had told me some of his nieces' names, but they were hard to remember.

"Shoshi," Naftali said, grinning, and she jumped out and gave him a hug.

"Uncle Nafs!" She looked up at me and smiled shyly. "He's my favourite uncle," she said. Naftali reached into his pocket and pulled out a lollipop.

He leaned into me and said quietly, "Well, it's not hard when you know what their favourite treats are. Only blue raspberry flavour for this one."

And then, introducing me to both of them: "This is my friend, Hannah," he said.

Avrumi put his arm around Naftali.

"It's so good to see you, brother."

He nodded at me but didn't say hi.

Shaindy said hello from behind him and the baby she was wearing strapped to her in a sling started crying. "I gotta take care of this little guy," she said and walked away.

We followed Avrumi into the house and took off our shoes. There were wooden cabinets filled with Jewish books and texts, and a red colourful one filled with puzzles and children's books.

Avrumi looked near me without making direct eye contact. "I'd like you to meet my wife, Shaindy," he said, putting a hand on her elbow, "and our baby, Eliezer."

"It's so nice to meet you both," I said.

Shaindy was wearing a long sleeved loose grey shirt and a patchwork red and orange floor sweeping skirt.

Her hair was covered in a red paisley pashmina that was piled up in the back. She was make-up free except for some black eyeliner that was smeared around her brown eyes, top and bottom. She looked like a more stylish and cleaner version of the hippies I grew up with.

"Oh, I forgot to mention," he said, "we have a no electronics policy in our house. See that basket at the front door? That's where we ask people to leave their phones until they go home."

I raised my eyebrows and looked at Naftali, who shrugged, as if to say, see, I told you he was quirky. He took his phone out of his pocket, turned it off and threw it into the basket, then gestured for me to give him mine. I reached into my purse.

"Do you mind if I ask why?"

Avrumi snorted. "I would have thought Naftali would have explained this before bringing you here. To start with, we don't like smart phones and technology that exposes our kids to content that isn't kosher or is too mature or consumerist."

I nodded and tried to make my facial expression serious. "Okay."

"Secondly, and this is maybe even more important, there's obviously the issue of EMF's."

"EMFs?"

"Electromagnetic fields," He pronounced each word as if it had ten syllables.

"The radiofrequency of 5G phones has been declared a possible carcinogen, which means it could cause cancer. I don't practice medicine anymore, as you may have heard, but I take the responsibility of caring for my family's health very seriously. 5G can lead to DNA damage, oxidative stress, neurotoxicity, the list goes on and on. We're just very careful around here."

I looked up at Naftali. "I hear you," I said.

I turned my phone off and handed it to him.

I wondered if they were flat earthers too, if they questioned evolution or believed in Q-Anon.

We followed Avrumi and Shaindy to their kitchen, and we sat down at their big country style wooden table. Shaindy offered us green tea, and a variety of coffee alternatives, including Dandelion Coffee.

We both chose green tea.

"We have all kinds of food," Shaindy said, and opened the refrigerator. She came back with apple and orange slices on a tray—"all organic, of course"—dried dates, figs and almonds, and a sugar free, gluten free chocolate cake. "Devorah gave me this recipe. She's our family's health food expert."

"Oh, I almost forgot," I said. "I picked something small up on my way here to give you guys to thank you for having me."

Naftali smiled and reached for my hand. I pulled a small pot of small white and yellow daisies out of the plastic bag I was still holding. I put it on the table, but Avrumi waved it away.

"I'm allergic," he said and rubbed his eyes.

"I'm so sorry," Shaindy said. "This was so sweet of you, but we're going to have to get rid of these." She leaned in close to me and whispered: "He's allergic to everything, he breaks out in hives, it's a nightmare."

Shaindy grabbed the corner of my shirt and sniffed it. "Hannah," she asked so quietly only I could hear her, "what detergent do you use?"

I was still reeling from how invasively she'd grabbed me. "I don't know," I muttered.

"Tide, maybe."

Shaindy shook her head. "That's not good, Avrumi's allergic to Tide. Aren't you afraid of all the chemicals? There are studies that link those kinds of detergents to breast cancer."

Shaindy glanced down at my breasts, and I flinched.

"Wait, are you also wearing perfume?"

I nodded. "Yeah, I'm wearing Black Opium. Naftali bought it for me."

Shaindy pursed her lips into a tight, painful looking line. When she opened her mouth, I noticed how grey and jagged her teeth were.

"It's weird that he didn't tell you. It's okay, I'm going to take you upstairs and lend you some of my clothes."

Shaindy was as small and skinny as Jillian. Lately, Naftali and I had been eating out a lot, and I'd gained some weight.

"Oh, I know," she said, looking at me up and down.

"One of my maternity dresses would probably fit you. "Second or third trimester for sure."

I looked helplessly at Naftali, who was being monopolized by Avrumi. Avrumi was saying something about Trump moving the American embassy in Israel from Tel Aviv to Jerusalem.

"Even if people don't like him," Avrumi was saying, "you can't deny . . ."

I followed Shaindy as she opened a wooden baby gate and started walking up their cream carpeted stairs.

Shaindy led me down the hall. "This is my room," she said, and walked into her walk-in closet.

I looked around. It was nice, in a nondescript, furniture catalogue kind of way.

"Avrumi sleeps next door in the master bedroom. You know how it is, right? Orthodox Jewish couples have to obey the laws of Niddah, which means for two weeks out of every month we sleep in separate beds?"

I stared at her. "It's okay, you'll learn all about it if it becomes relevant. But basically, most couples look like they're sleeping in a large bed, but really it's two singles that come apart for half of the month. It's the laws of family purity. You don't touch the person or sleep in the same bed at certain times. It helps you miss and appreciate each other. A rabbi's wife teaches you all about it when you get engaged.

"Avrumi and I tried sleeping in the same room when we first got married, but he talks in his sleep, and he snores like a leaf blower. He also has restless leg syndrome so when we were in the same bed, he'd kick me all the time and I had bruises. This way, we spend a lot of time together during the day, but at night we actually get to sleep."

Shaindy pulled a long sleeved faded black dress out of her closet. It was floor length and smelled faintly of mold.

"See, it doesn't reek of artificial fragrances," she said, and I nodded.

"Do me a favour. Before you put it on. Rinse your neck or your wrists or wherever you sprayed yourself with the soap in the bathroom. Or use plain olive or coconut oil. We have them in the cabinet. I'll give you a bag for your stuff, and we can tie it up and leave it on our porch. I'd never been sensitive to scent before, but now that we live like this, your perfume and detergent bother me too."

She paused and looked at me.

"Thanks for understanding," she said, and I nodded again.

"I was raised around a lot of weirdly specific rules. My dad had a lot of unusual quirks too. I understand. Anyway, it's cool to finally meet you guys."

Shaindy raised her eyebrows. "What do you mean, finally? How long have you guys been friends?" she asked, using air quotes.

"A few months. But Naftali talks about you guys all the time, so I'm happy to meet you in person."

"Thanks. We were surprised when we heard about you." Her voice dropped. "You know, even with everything that's unusual about this family, Naftali is a huge catch. He could have any girl he wants."

Then so quietly, I wondered if I imagined it, she said: "You weren't what any of us were expecting."

We walked back downstairs to see Devorah and Max taking off their shoes and dropping their phones in the basket.

Devorah was tiny, with shoulder length golden blonde hair that looked too beautiful and real to be a wig. Even from a distance, she had perfect, doll like features, long eyelashes, and delicate red lips, big blue eyes and sculpted cheekbones. She was wearing a long, fitted lavender lace dress. She was the kind of girl my mother would say "belonged at the top of a Christmas tree."

She walked over to me and gave me a hug. It startled me, the contrast between Shaindy and Devorah, but it was also a relief.

"It's so nice to meet you," she said, her voice high and girly. "Nafs talks about you all the time."

She leaned in conspiratorially and whispered, "Sorry about the phone policy here. It's kind of mine and Max's fault. We came over for a birthday party once and forgot to turn our phones off. Avrumi swore that we gave him and one of his kids a migraine, and since then he's been extra careful. Don't worry, the rest of us aren't like that. You can use your phone anytime when you visit us."

I found myself hugging her back.

Shaindy invited us to come back and sit at the table. She offered us food, but Devorah waved her off. "We've actually just eaten," she said, and Avrumi rolled his eyes.

"My sister," he said, loudly, and looked at everyone. "Some of us are trying to change the world, to better ourselves, and our families, to elevate our *neshamas*. My sister is constantly trying to better her body. It takes discipline, I admit, to subsist all day every day on basically nothing."

I stared at Naftali, but Devorah laughed him off. "Please, Avrumi, it's not one or the other. You can have a life that's meaningful and also take care of yourself."

She stared at his stomach and reached over and poked his exposed flesh with her finger.

"Part of respecting God is taking care of the body he's given us."

She stepped back, leaned in towards Naftali and said, "you know what they say, you can never be too skinny or too rich."

I raised my eyebrows and Naftali laughed.

"I just realized the time," he said abruptly. "Hannah and I have to go. It was great seeing all of you."

Devorah squeezed each of our hands. "So great to see you both. Hannah, it was great to meet you."

"Thanks again for having us," Naftali said to Shaindy.

"Our pleasure," she answered, giving him a real smile. "We always love seeing you, Naftali."

"Your plant is just outside, if you want to take, it, Hannah," she said, and I reached down and picked it up awkwardly.

Naftali closed the door behind us.

I tossed the plant into their giant compost bin.

"Now do you see why I don't want to marry somebody who comes from my world?"

I could, but it didn't exactly convince me that I wanted to join it.

I thought about Naftali meeting my dad, and some of his girlfriends and followers, and I started laughing. Naftali stared at me like I was out of my mind because once I started laughing I couldn't stop. I was almost crying before I could choke any words out.

"Oh, God," I said, "I just pictured introducing you to my father. Trust me, it would be so much worse than this."

CHAPTER FIFTEEN

AFTALI OFFERED TO drive me home. I'd planned to stop along the way, to pick up some tabloids, Coke Zero, cigarettes, and peanut butter chocolate Häagen-Dazs, Jillian's four guilty pleasures, so he stopped at a Shoppers Drug Mart along the way.

When I got in, Jillian was sitting on Esmeralda, a hot water bottle on her lower stomach. She was watching a movie on her phone.

"Have you heard of *Tank Girl*?" she asked. "It's this weird cult female superhero movie from the 90's. Come watch with me."

I sat down beside her heavily, my thighs like dead weight I could finally unload.

I started to ask how she was, but she shook her head. "Same as before."

I stretched my legs out onto hers. I was dying to tell her everything.

"Okay," she said turning to me, turning her phone to silent, her brown eyes focused, "tell me all about him."

I'd forgotten how good it felt to get Jillian's full, undivided attention. It was like having a close, personal relationship with the sun. I tried to tell her what happened, how badly Avrumi and Shaindy had treated me, but I found myself stopping because it sounded crazy. What kind of people would demand that you give up so much —your phone, your clothes, your gift to them? What kind of people would talk about your relationship in air quotes and tell you that you weren't what they expected? I realized that if someone else told me this story I might not believe it. It reminded me of something my dad had said when I was a kid. "If you want to get away with something, don't go halfway. Let your imagination run so wild no one in their right mind would believe you."

"It's hard to explain," I finally said. "Devorah was nicer than Avrumi and his wife."

Jillian nodded. "Yeah, that makes sense. She's good at first impressions."

"I was surprised at how beautiful she was, to be honest. She's so tiny too, I can't believe she's had kids."

"Please," Jillian said, bristling. "She's so had so much work done it's not even funny."

"Like what?"

"She had her nose done when she was seventeen, and she didn't even try to hide it. She just walked into school a few days later, with a bandage on her face. I've creeped her a couple of times. She's definitely had Restylane and filler. She looks like she's had an eyebrow lift too, and who knows what else?"

"Huh. She seemed to know who I was though. She said she was happy to finally meet me."

"But let me guess, she didn't invite you over, or exchange contact info, or do anything to actually try to be your friend?"

I sighed. "Yeah, pretty much."

"Devorah is great at coming off as the good guy, while making the least possible effort. Some things never change.

"What does she even do now? Is she a professional mom and lady who lunches?"

I snorted. "Kind of. Apparently she's a nutritionist, and …" I stopped myself and giggled, "She's a life coach. She works in the same clinic as Max. She's like the face of their company."

"You're kidding."

I took out my phone and found her on Tik Tok and Instagram, Devorah Goldwater-Bensimon. She had over a hundred thousand followers.

There were soup and salad recipes, casually glamorous shots of Devorah, and photos of her kids in colour coordinated outfits, including one where they were all wearing blue and green outfits like a row of Madame Alexander dolls come to life.

Her most recent video was called *How to Break Out from Mom-notomy*. There was also *Devo-tionals*, where she talked about things she was grateful for, including sunshine, glass water bottles, and God.

"Did you meet her husband?"

I nodded. "Yeah, but only in passing. The way Avrumi set it up, the guys were on one side, him, Naftali and then Max, and Shaindy and I and then Devorah, were on the other side of the room. I barely interacted with him."

"Sounds very *frum*, keeping the men and women separate," she said.

"Is that what it was about?"

"I don't know, I wasn't there."

"I think I'm supposed to be deciding if I want this or not. It's weird but the way he needed to control every part of his environment really reminded me of my father."

She shrugged. "You could always go along with it, for now, and then ditch them and go on the road with me as soon as I'm better. You could do all my photos and videos and social media."

"I guess I could."

I opened my school email and, aside from the usual stuff, I had an email from my mom, and an email from Rabbi Brown. He wanted to connect me with Chaya, my study partner. I had no idea things would happen this quickly. Something about seeing it in an email made it feel real.

My mom's email had the usual stuff about the weather and her garden and my stepdad. It seemed like as good a time as any to tell her, so I replied and told her about school and my grades and mentioned briefly that I had a Jewish boyfriend and was considering the conversion process.

I didn't expect her to reply, but a couple of hours later, she did.

Hannah, I'm pleased to hear that school is going so well. A friend of your stepdad's had heard of your program and was impressed. Apparently the Gallagher Webb business program is quite elite. I told him you'd always been an excellent student. A lot of people explore things in their twenties— just don't lose sight of your own goals. As you know, I speak from experience. Stay warm this week. Love, mom

Her email filled me with fury. Like she knew what my goals were. Like she was ever around, like she had anything to do with whether I was a good student or not. All she ever did was let her husbands do whatever they wanted, from everything my dad did to my stepdad kicking me out of their house. She always acted so helpless, looking at me like she couldn't possibly give up what she had with them.

I'd spent the last three years waiting to hear them say they were proud of me, and I knew this was as close as my mom would get. Still, I felt like I was breathing fire. I plodded into the living room. Jillian was asleep on the chair. I turned off the light and draped a blanket over her. I started researching marketing stuff for a paper I had due in a week. I'd taken books out of the library days before, but I hadn't read them yet. I read and wrote for what felt like minutes, and I was startled to find it was 4:30 am when I checked the time. I checked my email one more time. I had folders for everything, including one for my mom, and I put it in there, knowing I would probably never reply.

There was one more email, in the folder marked Tribe from my dad. It was his sixth message in two years. I hadn't replied to any of them. I wanted to delete them without replying, but the lawyer I talked to about his case recommended that I keep them, just in case. My father wasn't supposed to be contacting any of us. Sometimes I had the restraint not to read them, but tonight I didn't.

I thought about how unimpressed my dad would be with my program. I thought about how much he'd hate the Goldwaters. He called interacting with affluent families like them "bobbing," as in "bobbing around the shallowest end of society's pool."

I pictured him writing it, slouching in a plastic chair in one of his moth-eaten plaid shirts, typing at one of the computers in the public library near his apartment. The sour stench of his body would turn the area into a men's locker room. He'd be oblivious, staring at the screen, laughing out loud at some obscure political commentary, baring his sharpie black, completely rotten front teeth. He called toothpaste hoax paste. Since being in jail, he refused to bathe more than once a week. Sometimes, in the later days of the Tribe, he'd refuse to leave the cabin for days, although people would visit him. Everyone would pretend to ignore the smell until eventually they stopped noticing it. My dad was an expert at getting people to doubt not just their thoughts but their senses. I opened the message.

> *My dear Daughter, he wrote. I am mystified and distressed by your choices. Completely avoiding me is inappropriate. Do you forget the Affinity we had for each other, the fondness? Who understands or knows you better than I? I'm thoroughly confused by what I heard from your mother this evening. What in the world would possess you to want to "officially" become Jewish? Am I not Jewish? Does the Torah not command you to honour your parents? Did we not have a beautiful and meaningful spiritual base for you in the Tribe? Do you not see how superfluous all of this is—these people, these empty, status obsessed people will never accept you, and they*

will certainly never love you. Why have you cut yourself off from the one person who truly loves you, who knows you best and values you most? Family and true connections are forever. When you come to your senses Hannah, trust that I will be here.

Your Father

My legs shook when I tried to stand up. I wondered how often my parents were talking now. As with everything else since the trial, I had to prove to myself that he was wrong about this too. I clicked on Rabbi Brown's email. I pressed reply and wrote the most enthusiastic response that I could think of.

CHAPTER SIXTEEN

A FEW DAYS later, Jillian, Naftali, and I were sitting around the apartment, doomscrolling. None of us could believe that a man who was famous for his catchphrase "you're fired," calling his daughter "a piece of ass," and advising Billy Bush, when it came to women, to "grab 'em by the pussy" was now the president of the US.

"He probably reeks of fake tanner, you know that sharp, yeasty smell?"

Naftali laughed. "Yeah."

We'd watched the debates together the night before. We cheered when Clinton responded that "when they go low, we go high."

"She kind of reminds me of your mom," Jillian said to Naftali.

He laughed. "Yeah, I could see that."

I was surprised by how deeply disappointed I was. It had been so obvious to all of us that she would have been great, that having a powerful female president would inspire so many girls and women.

"Do you know that the *Simpsons* predicted this?"

Jillian asked and pulled up an episode on her phone. "How bizarre is that?"

The last thing I felt like doing was putting on a modest, feminine dress and meeting someone who was going to lecture me about becoming a Jewish wife and mother. Rabbi Brown had emailed me back to let me know that I could get started with studying with Chaya, and I could meet her at her house later that day.

I hadn't expected things to move so quickly. I mentioned that to Naftali and he said: "For people like us, they do their best."

"What do you mean?"

"For families like mine, who are already religious and who contribute to the community."

He took my hand. "They can see that you're serious about everything."

"Of course, Hannah's serious." Jillian answered. "When she agrees to do something, she goes all in." She blew me a kiss. "It's one of the things I love most about you, Boo."

I laughed.

Naftali got suddenly serious.

"I told my mom about us. I figured it was better if she heard it from me." He sighed. "She said that they'd already gone through this with Iris, but they expected it because Avrumi challenged them from the day he was born. She said they expected more from me."

"What do you mean, more?"

"She said a lot of people start conversions and never finish them. If that happened to us, it would mean her grandchildren wouldn't be Jewish. She really laid on the guilt. She said: 'I can't believe it's you doing this, you, the angel who's always given us nothing but *nachas*.'"

"What kind of girl do you think she wanted you to be with? Someone like your sister?"

"Oh God, no. My mom's always going on about how superficial Devorah is. I think she just wanted to be part of the part of the process. She thought I'd take the matchmaker more seriously, and she'd meet all the girls, and we'd discuss everything. Like before university, we discussed the pros and cons of different schools and majors for hours. I think she always hoped I'd make simpler choices.

"My dad is okay with it, as long you convert. He was always supportive of Iris, even in the beginning."

"There's a lot of drama with your family," Jillian said, her eyes laser focused on Naftali.

"I don't know, every family has drama. We offer a lot too."

Jillian shrugged.

"You know what they say, '*Marbeh Nehasim Marbeh Da'agah*.'"

Naftali raised his eyebrows. "Are you quoting *Pirkei Avot*?"

Jillian laughed. "As a matter of fact, I am."

"What the hell are you guys talking about?"

"There are these books, *Ethics of Our Fathers*. She quoted a good verse."

He looked at me, and said more gently: "It means, the more possessions a person has, the more anxiety."

Jillian grinned. "My favourite part was always "*Marbeh basar marbeh reemah*."

Naftali shuddered. "It means the more flesh, the more worms. Gross."

"Yeah, but I like the same things in Judaism as I like in art. I like when things are direct, when they're not afraid to tell you exactly how it is. Think about how many movies we see or how much we listen to, or how many books we read. Things that are disturbing are memorable."

"I guess so," I said.

"I'm impressed, Jillian. I thought Hannah said that you weren't religious anymore."

Jillian loosened the tight ponytail her hair was in, and shook it out, thick black hair spraying around her face like a shampoo ad.

"I'm not, but I'm still spiritual. I was raised so religious that I can't forget things even if I want to. It's like a reflex, the other day, I bought this new sweater"—she looked at me—"the purple one, and I immediately found myself muttering the blessing for new clothes, like before I could stop myself. But when people look at me, they don't think religious."

Naftali smiled. "You're an insider and an outsider. Sometimes I feel like that too." He took my hand. "It's too bad we can't just have Jillian tutor you."

I dropped his hand and stood up.

Jillian stared at me with huge eyes and Naftali followed me out into the hallway.

"Hannah," he said eventually, "what's wrong?"

"It's just, everyone eventually falls in love with Jillian. She's scintillating and intense and she finds a way to connect with everyone. And she knows all these things about Judaism I couldn't possibly know, and she's travelled so much, and seen and done so much with her life already, there's just no way to compete. And she knows it."

Naftali exhaled. "Jillian is great. She's smart and she's interesting and I'm glad to be her friend, since she's so important to you, but I'm in love with you. And by the way, not everyone falls in love with Jillian. Just ask my sister."

I let a small laugh that sounded like a squeak.

"So do you still want me to take you to meet Chaya? I'm sure we could reschedule if you want to."

I nodded. "Yeah, I think we should just get it over with."

Naftali was careful to drop me half a block away.

Chaya looked much younger than I expected. She wore a chin length, coffee brown wig that was clearly not her real hair. Her voice was soothing, and she had a dimple in her left cheek. She told me she had three kids under the age of four. Her job, she explained to me, was not just to teach me the Jewish laws, but to help people like me fit into the Jewish community.

"I do outreach," she said, "along with my husband. In Hebrew the word is *Kiruv*. It means to bring people closer."

She asked me if I knew how to read Hebrew. I shook my head.

"So when you go to synagogue, do you find yourself a little lost, trying to follow where everyone is? I want to teach you to read Hebrew, but in the meantime, here is a little gift."

It was wrapped in white paper, and when I opened it, it was made of baby pink leather.

It was a transliterated prayer book, which she called a Siddur, which had every Hebrew word written out phonetically in English, instead of using Hebrew characters. It also had a line-by-line English translation.

I wondered if she had a whole series of *Judaism for Dummies* books.

"Thank you," I said.

"Now, you can go to any Orthodox synagogue, and follow along, even sing along to the songs," she said.

"Great."

"So, let me ask you something," she said. "We could learn here in my house, or I can take you down the street to buy some essentials for this process. What do you say? Do you want to go shopping? If you want to be part of our community, you have to share our values, and that includes dressing modestly like us. There are some great stores around here that sell kosher clothing, you'll see."

The first store I followed her into was called She Sells These Shells.

A shell, she explained, was a thin polyester long sleeve shirt that could be worn under a tank top, or dress, or t-shirt. The store also sold modesty dresses, which were dress length shells to go underneath dresses that were too short, or too revealing, and skirt extenders, to make sure that skirts went over the knee.

"Basically, we have to make sure that, aside from the obvious areas, your collarbones, elbows, and knees are covered. I brought you here first because I don't think you have to necessarily get rid of your clothes. These layers can make almost anything appropriate.

"Choose colours that will blend and match the clothing you already have. If you have a pink dress from before, say it's low cut or has spaghetti straps, you can find a similar or even identical shade here to wear underneath."

She pointed to rack of shells that ranged from the palest ballet pink to salmon and dusty pink.

"There's nothing worse than a girl wearing a bright white shell underneath say, a red halter dress. It's an eyesore, and it marks her immediately as either newly religious or newly converted. We want you to look like you've been dressing like this your whole life."

I chose long sleeved and three-quarter length shells in navy blue, olive green, and black.

I went into the fitting room to try them on. They were all skintight. My arms felt like sausages in casing. I was sweating already. I came out of the fitting room wearing a three-quarter length sleeved black one.

Chaya put a hand on my shoulder approvingly. "Changing the way you dress is hard. People see clothing as a way to express themselves, and anything that changes the way we conceive of ourselves is complicated."

She tapped my shoulder before I walked back into the dressing room. "I always go at least one size bigger than my normal size when I buy shells. Don't worry if you're buying one or even two sizes bigger than what you usually wear, this is about being modest."

I nodded and she offered to get me bigger sizes.

"I know there are women who say it's empowering to wear whatever they want," Chaya said. "I know about body confidence and ..."—she dropped her voice several octaves—"I've heard the term slut shaming. But I want you to know that the spirit of the commandment is not about not looking or feeling beautiful.

"We believe in outer and inner beauty. Judaism believes that women have *binah*, which is a unique type of intelligence and insight. We believe that every woman deserves to be appreciated for her intellect, her intuition, who she is on a deeper level.

"Sometimes everyone wants to feel pretty and attractive and free to do whatever they want. But if you're a woman, freedom isn't always free. Every woman has some story about men making them uncomfortable, saying inappropriate things, catcalling them, even God forbid, touching them inappropriately. The way we dress, and more than that, the way we hold ourselves, is an extra layer of protection."

I wanted to tell her that what she was saying was wrong, that things happened no matter what you wore, or didn't wear, or what you wanted, or didn't want. I wanted to tell her that I wished that things were that simple, that if dressing a certain way was enough to guarantee protection, a lot more women would do it. But I didn't say anything. My past moved inside my throat and chest like a heavy, knotted rope.

She paused and looked me up and down.

"You're a very pretty girl, Hannah. Look at your dark eyes. You kind of look Jewish. I know you're involved"—she took a deep breath—"with a well-known family, but even if you weren't, if you went through with the conversion, you'd have no trouble finding a husband."

I almost laughed. "Thanks, I guess."

I had to stop myself from making jokes about goats and factories or whatever modern dowries are made of.

Chaya leaned in close. "I'm not supposed to say anything, but if you change your mind as you go deeper into this conversation, I can help you. The Goldwaters might be powerful, but they're also not"—she paused—"well, I'm sure you know their reputation. If you decide for any reason that this isn't what you want, I think we'll be able to find you another match."

I took that in.

"I'll support you, of course no matter what you decide. It's just my job as a mentor to take care of you. Next time, we'll actually start our studies."

I nodded. "Sure, that sounds good."

In a strange way, Chaya's honesty convinced me that maybe I was being too judgemental of the Goldwaters. I thought about what my stepdad had told me once, how there was a hierarchy even in prison, that child molesters were the lowest, the ones most likely to be beaten up. It turned out to be true, which somehow garnered my dad even more support from his followers.

A family that was too good or too pure would never be okay with my family's past.

When I saw Naftali later, I didn't mention what we'd talked about.

It was nice to think that Chaya was looking out for me.

CHAPTER SEVENTEEN

IT WAS EASIER to make progress in the conversion process than I'd anticipated. I just had to play by the rules, which everyone was only too happy to constantly spell out. I liked the feeling of people being happy with me for working hard. It wasn't so different from being at Webb, except there was no competition, just praise, that was intended towards my very character. I half expected Chaya to give me a gold star sometimes, and if she had, I probably would've accepted it. I went to her house twice a week, for an hour each time to study.

She was always encouraging me, telling me how smart I was, and I entertained the fantasy a little.

From an early age, my dad decided who among us was exceptional, who had true imagination, who was a math mastermind or a whiz at languages. I started reading when I was four and a half. I knew the prodigies like him could all read by the time they were three, but I loved being able to read. My first book was *Cinderella*. One of the moms who read us all bedtime stories told my dad how impressed she was with me, and I felt good for a second, until he shook his head. "She's good at memorizing and following the rules. She's not much of a thinker or an innovator."

Being with Chaya and her family made me fantasize about growing up in a different family. Every time Chaya told me she was proud of me she touched a tender nerve I didn't know I had. She printed off Hebrew alphabet worksheets for me. They were clearly made for kids, with bubble letters and line breaks large enough to use crayons. I imagined being five and colouring them in at school and having Chaya as my mom telling me that they were beautiful and that she wanted to display them on our fridge for everyone to see.

She always told me I asked great questions, like when I wanted to know the difference between the two Hebrew S's, the samech and the shin. She told me how impressed she was that I was paying such close attention. I wondered how different my life could have been if I'd had people believing in me when I was little. Maybe I was more of a hard worker than an innovative thinker, but so what? What if I'd just been allowed to feel good about that?

I started attending synagogue regularly. There was no driving on Shabbat, so I had to either stay with Chaya or with Jillian and her family, to be in walking distance of an Orthodox synagogue. Men and women sat in separate sections, so even when Naftali said he wanted to join me and he walked to Chaya's synagogue from his parents', we could only peek at each other through the dividing wall until after. After, there was a small gathering called a *Kiddush*, where people lingered and socialized and drank pop or sweet wine, and ate foods I'd never had before, from potato kugel to cholent, to herring with Tim Tam crackers. I wasn't a fan of any of it.

When Chaya saw other people she knew, she left me standing there awkwardly. I wished it wasn't Shabbat so I could do something with my hands, so I could busy myself with filming or taking pictures of all of it. All I got was the occasional hi or a mumbled Good Shabbos. In those moments, I felt like a fly that got stuck to the side of a five-tiered wedding cake, just waiting to be swatted away.

Jillian's family was warm and inclusive, and they explained that the differences in singing style, the collective chanting for example, instead of lots of singing, was cultural, that theirs was a Sephardic synagogue for Jews whose families originated in North Africa and the Middle East.

Chaya and her synagogue were Ashkenazi.

"Totally different cultures," they said, "with a completely different approach."

I asked Jillian one day what parts of Judaism she actually liked.

"I like going to shul. There's something amazing about looking around and realizing that everyone around you is there because they need something, health, or the health of their family, or success, to find a partner, or have kids. It's beautiful how open and vulnerable they're being, like our fundamental needs are all the same, and we're all in it together.

"Listen, forget coming on Shabbat. Shavuot is next week, come stay with my family for the whole holiday. It's a more intense, meaningful experience."

Chaya gave me some handouts on Shavuot or the Feast of Weeks. "You're lucky you're staying with them," she said. "Sephardic food is the greatest."

On the first day of the two-day holiday, we both slept in. Jillian woke me, and we got dressed and speed walked to her parents' synagogue.

We snuck into the back of the women's section.

"Oh good, we didn't miss it," she said.

"Miss what?"

"There's a special prayer during the Amidah."

Chaya had taught me that the Amidah, which meant standing, was the core of Jewish prayer. First, the person praying praised God, then they asked for what they needed, then they thanked Him. I was often moved when I thought about the meaning of the prayers.

"There's a small group of men, called Kohanim, and they give the congregation a special blessing on holidays. They do this special chanting before they start that always gives me goosebumps. They say something very beautiful too, '*hamevarech at amo Yisrael b'ahava.*' It means that it's literally their job to bless the congregation with love and pure hearts."

"Wow."

"I remember being a kid and being told, explicitly that I was not allowed to look up when they were doing their blessing. And normally if you tell me not to do something, it's the first thing I do. But somehow, I knew not to. I was genuinely afraid to look, afraid to disturb the feeling of completely believing. You have to experience it to understand.

"There's also something special we read, about dreams. In between the chanting, there's time to read it

124

quickly. It adds this extra layer of mysticism. It's a prayer to God that says I had a dream, but I don't know what it means. If it was a good dream, please confirm and reinforce it, and if it was bad, heal the person or transform the dream into something good for me."

She looked at me. "I figured you'd like it, I know you're into dreams."

I nodded.

The Kohanim shuffled to the front of the room. The Arc that held the Torah was open.

Jillian reached for my hand. "Close your eyes," she whispered.

I close my eyes.

There is someone holding my elbow, so gently I almost didn't feel it, but I turn to see, and it was a man, with a long silver beard and white linen clothing lined with gold, like the God I'd pictured as a child when my father had laughed at me

"Are you God?" I whisper.

A small smile and faint glow light up his face.

"I wish. Actually, I don't. I'm one of His messengers. You'd call me an angel, I suppose."

I reach for his hand which surprises me, and he holds it, his skin rougher than I expected.

"So God is a man?"

"God is the original they/them. Humans seem to relate better to God as a man, some of you anyway. Some of you understand completely. I like your generation. You're in touch with what feels right, and you have the confidence to follow that instinct."

Mahler's "I've Become Lost to the World" is playing

and the finale of Tchaikovsky's sixth symphony, but they're being drowned out by the sound of a mom singing lullabies, her throat all ragged and raw, and another mom in a different corner. It sounds like she's singing in Hebrew.

There's someone playing guitar, singing a song about ducks, and there's the sound of a TV, the *Sesame Street* theme song is playing, the unmistakable *boom chicka wah wah* of porn.

My dad's voice is crackling out of a speaker right beside me, tinny sounding, cartoonish even, and it's being garbled by other voices, other men other women, and I can only catch every third word, but I feel like my dad is standing right there, and a chill runs through my arms.

I see my mom in the distance, holding the yellow and pink blanket she crocheted for me as a baby up to her face, breathing in my baby scent. She looks around me, everywhere around me, but not at me, then she disappears.

There is the crying muffled and clear, the struggle to breathe, the muttering, the struggle to try to tell someone or understand what had happened, to put it into words.

There is someone telling herself, re-enacting it on her Barbies or her younger sister or maybe it was her brother who did the re-enacting.

Someone else on herself in front of the mirror.

The yelling back, the sounds of hands being tied the smell of rope burn.

The tearing of skin the knife a gunshot.

I can't take any more, I turn to the angel.

"Where are we?"

"Between worlds. The place where souls depart, and new souls enter. A holding area. I think your mother would call it purgatory. There isn't an exact word for it in Judaism, but you understand, right?"

I nod.

"Who are they?"

"They're the kids like you, the kids who were cajoled and tricked, the kids that were forced, with words or limbs, the ones who were discarded immediately after, the ones whose tears lined their eternal resting place. There was too much trauma, too much unresolved. They don't trust adults anymore, Hannah. They're afraid to go anywhere. Some of them prayed, and God didn't answer, God did nothing to stop any of it, so how can they believe now?"

"There are a lot of kids who've lived what you have, Hannah. More than you can imagine. It's commendable that you're learning how to trust."

I want to leave, but my heels are glued to the floor. The sounds make my body hurt. Can I have noise cancelling headphones?

He shakes his head. "You need to hear this. You need to remember because very soon you too will be bringing new souls into the world. You must learn to face your fears. You must learn how to name things, how to ask the right questions if you plan to protect your children."

I want to vomit. "I don't know if I can go through with this, I say. I don't know if I can be a mom, if I'm good enough, if I'd be able to protect them from everything."

He puts a finger to my mouth to stop me from continuing. "Shh."

"I'll see you again when you're in labour. I'll meet your child."

I feel the sweep of a feather across my forehead. "You're working hard, Hannah. We see you."

I open my eyes to see women starting to sit down, men folding up their prayer shawls, and Jillian looking at me, her eyes barely concealing a sense of awe.

There are tears running down my cheeks.

"It really moved you."

"I feel like I just woke up," I whisper, like I'd woken up from something that was between a dream and a nightmare, that was also transformative, even if it hadn't happened in the way I'd imagined.

"Wow, that's amazing, a genuine spiritual experience."

I nod. "Thanks to you."

We link arms and stay in our seats for a few more minutes. "Come on, let's get out of here," she says. "Nothing could possibly top this."

"I think I'm ready," I say quietly, "to actually start converting."

CHAPTER EIGHTEEN

WITHIN A WEEK, Chaya called me to tell me it was time for my first meeting with the Beit Din.

"I think you're ready," she said, and it felt like a wispy veil of clouds was parting in my head.

"Thank you," I said. "I hope you're right."

She drove us to a large red brick synagogue half an hour north of where we were. Inside, it had a big open space, with leather chairs that we were invited to sit in while we waited to enter one of the conference rooms.

I waited for just over an hour. I wished I'd brought my camera to capture the bizarre mundaneness of it all. I tried to read an article on my phone, but the words blurred together into an endless watery sentence.

When I was finally called inside, I saw three rabbis sitting in a row behind a long table. I looked at the rabbi who was sitting in the centre. Chaya had told me that he was chief rabbi of the court.

My first thought was that he looked like Gandalf the White from the *Lord of the Rings* movies.

He had a chest length white beard and a kind expression.

He smiled at me, as if he had a clean view of my past and my present and an even clearer view of everything I could still be. I could feel the sun from the window behind him blanketing me.

I wanted to close my eyes.

There was, of course, no small talk.

"It's really nice to meet all of you," I said, but they just nodded.

The rabbis asked similar questions to Rabbi Brown. "Do you keep kosher?" one of the others asked, and I nodded vigorously.

"As of this year, yes."

I was startled when one of them used Yiddish words.

"Do you mix the *milchik* food *mit* de *fleishik?*" the rabbi sitting to the left of Gandalf asked me.

I looked at him blankly. I felt the minutes ticking by, and I froze.

I looked at Rabbi Brown, begging silently for his help.

"It means do you mix meat and dairy foods together," he said after what felt like an hour.

"No, of course not. I wait six hours in between," I said quickly, before they could ask.

"Is all your clothing kosher?" The rabbi to his right asked her, gesturing to what I was wearing.

"Yes, Chaya took me shopping."

"Very good," Rabbi Brown said, smiling approvingly.

The chief Rabbi asked me only one question. "Are you absolutely certain that this is what you want?"

His eyes were the calm grey blue of my childhood lake in Nelson. He reminded me of my mom's father.

"Yes," I said, knowing that he could sense the full range of my uncertainty and insecurity, and hoping that it would still be okay.

CHAPTER NINETEEN

AFTER THAT MEETING, I stopped wanting to stay over at Naftali's. The seriousness of all of it had entered my heart and I couldn't shake it. I felt guilty every time we slept together.

Chaya's most recent lesson had been awkward. She gave me a book called *A Woman's Guide to the Laws of Niddah*, which she said was about family purity.

"Usually," she said, "we wouldn't talk about any of this until you were engaged, which often happens shortly after conversion. We have bridal classes, where we talk about marital relations in more depth. But you're dating someone, and standards for dating in the world are different to the way we are expected to date. I saw him kiss you once when he picked you up from here. He should know better. This is just the basics, but I want to give you an idea."

It wasn't about dressing modestly or saving yourself for marriage. It was about not having sex when you had your period because it was considered ritually unclean.

I was shocked when I realized that fourteen days out of the month a married couple weren't allowed to have sex. There was other horrifying stuff that ranged from sending your underwear to a rabbi whose specialty was examining discharge to let you know if you were good to go or not, to avoiding any physical contact in that time, including accidentally brushing up against each other at the breakfast table. The book swore that the time apart kept things fresh and exciting, but it sounded like a dystopian satire.

He came over two nights after I'd read the book. We kissed and he led me straight into my room, and we flopped down on my unmade bed. His hand slipped below my waist, slowly onto the top of my underwear. He slid a finger down further, and I flinched.

"I just started my period, babe."

"So?"

I stared at him like it was obvious, and he looked back at me like he was trying to solve a puzzle.

"Oh, does it hurt? Do you have cramps?"

He kissed my cheek.

"No, no, it's my first day. It's not even that heavy yet. It's just, aren't we not supposed to be doing this? I'm reading this book." I got up and grabbed it from my dresser drawer.

"Ugh, seriously?" He rolled his eyes. "First of all, we're not married yet, so this doesn't even apply. But even if it did, is this how you want to live your life?"

"What do you mean? Isn't this how we have to live our lives?"

"Who's going to know? It's what happens in the privacy of our bedroom."

"But Chaya says you can't just pick and choose; you have to keep all the mitzvot."

"Hannah, come on."

"What?"

"Everyone picks and chooses. Everyone chooses what resonates with them. And if this is important to you, we can talk about it, but do you really want to go half of every month not having sex?"

I shook my head.

"I think it's hard enough to stay committed to one person your whole life, and if your sex life is so pre-scribed, it's even harder. Not to mention my mom has railed against this so many times, so maybe I've thought about it too much, but doesn't it bother you that women's bodies are considered dirty? Having your period is a normal thing."

"I like this feminist side of you."

He grinned. "Listen, I'm not trying to sound super woke, but if it scores me extra points with you ..."

I smiled back. "A little. And I agree with you. I just didn't think rejecting it was an option."

"It can be for us."

He reached over and touched my thigh.

"We've done it lots of times when you've had your period. We'll just put that dark blue towel down."

He grinned at me wolfishly, and the pure desire made me feel sexy in a way I couldn't control.

"Okay, yeah, grab the towel."

He pulled my shirt off and got up to find it in our bathroom. I took everything else off and waited for him. When he got back, he closed the door behind him. He took off his pants and his boxers.

"Listen," he whispered. "Since you're on the pill, and the only people in this relationship are us, do you want to not use a condom tonight?"

I pulled him down on top of me, put my arms around his neck and kissed him before I could change my mind. The next morning I woke up before he did. He was lying on the other side of the bed, almost at the edge. I was more anxious than usual. I got up and rolled over, and he looked at me bleary eyed, his blonde hair a sea of waves on my pillow.

"Hey babe," he said, and inched closer.

"I've never done that before, what we did last night."

"Me either. Now I get why people say condoms are like having sex with snowpants on."

I laughed. "Yeah. It was a lot more intense."

"Hannah, do you want meet my mom?"

"Really?"

"Yeah, I think she'd like you. This weekend my dad is away, and my siblings are all doing their own things. You could stay with Chaya again and just come over for Friday night dinner. It'll be low key, just the three of us."

"What about Iris?" I asked.

"Oh she's away too, with my dad. Goldwater business stuff."

"Oh," I said, "that's too bad. I like Iris. But sure."

Jillian lent me an outfit that was both modest and stylish.

"No shells," she said, "they look ridiculous on everyone."

She lent me a knee length silver dress with three quarter sleeves and silver shoes. She lent me big bracelets to hide the tattoos near my wrist. She even blow dried my hair and did my make up for me.

"You look beautiful," she said. "My mom bought

this for me a while ago, and let's be honest, I'm never going to wear it."

It was tighter on me than it was on her, but Jillian insisted it was modest enough.

Naftali's eyes bulged when he saw me. He picked me up off the ground and kissed me.

"You look so hot," he said.

I grinned. "Thanks, but am I ..."

"*Tznius* enough? Yes."

I laughed. "Perfect."

He drove me first to Chaya's to drop off my stuff.

I could see the disapproval on Chaya's face, the way her lips curled down at the corners. I could tell she didn't think my outfit was modest enough, and it bothered her that Naftali and I were still spending so much time together. We pulled up to his parents' house fifteen minutes later.

I took in more details from the main entrance—the forest green and dusty pink swirling marble floors which looked like a bird's eye view of a flowering countryside from the window seat on a plane. There was a giant sky light that made the foyer seem bright and inviting, and a maid in grey scrubs at the door, who took our jackets and shoes. There was a large orange and white painting of two doves kissing.

"This is beautiful," I said and turned around to find Malka Goldwater right behind me.

She was smaller than I expected, taller than Devorah but just as slight. She was wearing a fitted long sleeved black dress, a heavy set of pearls, and a light brown chin length wig that made her look like a cross between Anna

Wintour and Audrey Hepburn. Her makeup was minimal, and her skin was glowing. She could have passed for a woman in her thirties.

She reached out a hand, and I was surprised by the firmness of her grip, her red nails digging slightly into my palm.

"It's nice to meet you," I said.

She nodded. "I see you like the Kadishman. You've got good taste, but we knew that already."

"The Kadishman?" I mouthed at Naftali.

"Menashe Kadishman," he said. "The artist who painted the doves."

I nodded. We followed Malka into one of the living rooms. There were three living rooms that I could see, one with a fireplace and velvet couches, another with gold silk couches and foot stools, and a third with more art, a huge screen TV, and leather couches. She chose the one with the gold couches, and we sat down across from her.

"We have one more guest who's joining us tonight."

"Is that Naomi, Mom?"

Malka frowned. "No, she's not coming until tomorrow. Guess who called to say she'll be in town just this weekend? Penny. So I had to invite her to stay here and eat with us."

"Of course," Naftali said, and rolled his eyes.

We heard laughter coming from the next room.

"Hi, Naftali!"

Malka got up to see her and Naftali leaned in.

"Mom is obsessed with doctors. Max's sister had an allergic reaction to walnut oil at Devorah and Max's wedding, and Penny ran in and started treating her and gave her an EpiPen, before we even had time to call

Hatzolah. Mom's loved her ever since. I'm sorry, I had no idea she was going to be here."

Penny came running over. She was rail thin with a dark aquiline nose and a big white toothed smile.

"Naftali," she said, squealing, "it's so great to see you. I hear business school is going really well."

"It's pretty good, yeah. How's the world of medicine?"

"Great, thank God, just super busy."

Malka stepped out from behind them.

"This is Naftali's friend, Hannah. Hannah is converting to Judaism, and Naftali's helping her out."

"Um mom," Naftali said, "that's not exactly ..."

"Oh, that's so nice." Penny gushed. "You've always been so generous, Naftali. I'm sure I can help your friend too. After Shabbat, I'll give you my phone number or Naftali can give it to you. Any friend of the Goldwaters is a friend of mine."

"Thanks," I said. "What kind of doctor are you?"

"Well, I'm still doing my specialization. I was thinking of pediatrics for a while, I love kids so much, but it's so hard to see them sick, especially if their conditions can't be cured."

She pouted. "It was too heartbreaking, after even a few weeks I was getting too attached. So I'm studying to be an OB-GYN."

"Wow, that's really cool."

"Penny is going to be the most amazing OB GYN," Malka said emphatically. "She has great instincts."

Malka led us to the dining room. We passed a giant mirror on the way, and Penny turned to survey herself.

"You look great," Naftali said quickly, and I looked away.

We found ourselves in the dining room, and Malka seated us. The table could have easily hosted twenty more people. Malka sat down at the head of the table, with Penny on one side and Naftali on the other. Naftali invited me to sit beside him.

Naftali made Kiddush, and we did the ritual hand washing and he said the blessing over the challah bread.

Malka nodded to the maid who was standing off to the side to start serving. Naturally, she served the talented doctor first, then Naftali, then herself.

I looked at Penny.

"Is Penny short for Penelope?"

"No silly, it's Penina. It means Pearl in Hebrew. I'm named after my Bubby."

She reached over and rolled back my bracelet.

"I thought I saw something poking out of there."

On my right wrist I had a tattoo of the Selkirk Mountains. I saw them from a distance almost every day when I was in the Tribe. They were so beautiful, snow dusted in the winter and dry and dusty in the summer, but always like a billboard advertising all the beauty that existed in the world, beyond the community and my dad. I always promised myself that I'd hike them when I left, but when my mom and I left in a blind panic there was no time. It was something I still wanted to do one day. The other tattoo, below it, was a tiny camera, like the one my grandparents had given me when I visited them as a kid.

"They're so cool. Tell me what they mean."

I shook my head. "It's kind of a long story. They're personal."

"I always thought if I wasn't born Jewish, a tattoo is

the first thing I'd get. That and eating lobster. You're so lucky, Hannah, that you get to choose."

I didn't know what to say to that.

The maid finally brought me my bowl of matzo ball soup. It had two carrot circles floating in it.

I put my spoon in and tasted it. It was a little salty and cold.

Naftali looked at me and started eating. Penny and Malka were almost finished their food.

The maid started bringing out more food, roast chicken and green beans, brisket and onions, and tiny potato kugels made in muffin cups.

"Wait," Penny said. "Will the rabbis even let you convert if you have a tattoo? They always used to warn us, as kids, if you get a tattoo, you can't be buried in a Jewish cemetery."

An uncomfortable silence settled over the table.

I didn't know the answer to either of those questions.

I got up. "I think I'm going to go to the washroom."

Naftali glared at her.

"Can we not like, plan for her death? Also, you know it not true, lots of non-religious Jews get buried in Jewish cemeteries, tattoos and all."

"Relax, Naftali, I'm just trying to get to know your friend a little better."

Naftali clenched his jaw. "She's my girlfriend, obviously, whatever my mother tells people. Anyway, why do you care?"

I walked away after he'd pointed to the direction of the nearest bathroom. It was steps away.

Naftali had told me that there were nine washrooms in the house. It had a blue marble sink, and a bar of soap that looked like it was full of gold glitter, and as Jillian had promised, it had a large letter G in the middle of it, as did the hand towel.

I could still hear every word of their conversation.

"Let's try to calm down. I've never seen you so worked up." I heard Penny say. "You forget how long we've known each other. I consider you my friend, too."

I heard Naftali sigh. "Okay."

"I know your family has been through a lot. And I know how important Iris is to all of you. But don't you think you're making your own life harder by making the same choices as Avrumi?"

"I'm not doing anything like Avrumi. The fact that you'd even say that shows how little you know about me."

"Okay. I just, I don't know about this girl. You should have seen the look she gave me from the second I met her."

I heard him sigh again, this time more deeply. "What look?"

"Like narrow eyes, all suspicious and then irritated that I was here, like I was the one imposing on her. Your mom is amazing, and we talk about everything. She told me about her, and I was curious. The timing just worked out well."

He sighed. "That's great, Penny."

"Your mom loves you, Naftali. She just wants you to have every option available to you . . ."

I came out of the bathroom and walked back up to the table.

Naftali smiled at me. "I'm glad you're back," he said. He moved down a couple of chairs. "Come sit beside me."

He reached for my hand.

The maid handed each of us a bencher, a thin book where the Grace After Meals was printed. Unlike at Chaya's, where they read each verse out loud, and sang out loud together, everyone read them silently. I opened mine to find it had only Hebrew words printed in it, no English and no transliteration.

I tried to read a page, struggled and gave up after a few minutes. I looked at the cover instead. It said Bar Mitzvah of Avraham Michael Goldwater in gold cursive font.

Penina looked up at me and smirked.

I hated that she was enjoying watching me struggle. I wanted to tell her that I wanted this, that I was working hard, but my lips felt fused together. What bothered me most was the feeling that she might be right; that someone born into this life would just know these things, and that it would be easier for Naftali if the person he was dating could be a real partner and not his student.

Naftali pulled out his chair.

"It's getting late, and I have to walk Hannah back to where she's staying tonight. Good Shabbos, Penny."

The maid brought us our coats and our shoes.

I struggled with Jillian's ankle boots and their ridiculously thin leather laces.

I heard Penny come up behind us.

"It was good to see you," she said to Naftali.

"Thanks," he answered quietly.

"I have to ask," she said even more quietly, "are you sure this is what you want?"

I watched him nod his head definitively.

"That's great. It's just, I want you to know that I'm always here if you need to talk, about anything. If you need support, if you need a friend, if …" She dropped her voice an octave. "If you change your mind …"

He didn't answer her.

Malka showed up just behind us.

She surveyed me head to toe, like an eagle eyeing a rodent from a distance, trying to decide if I was worth the trouble of hunting. I found myself wanting to say something to appease her, even though I could still feel the tension of the night building at the back of my head.

"Thank you so much for having me. It was so nice to meet you."

Her gaze softened slightly. "My son is a very deliberate person. There must be more than what first meets the eye."

"I … I hope so. Hopefully we'll get to know each other more in time."

"I look forward to that," she said, and Naftali raised his eyebrows at me.

He squeezed my hand as we walked back to the rabbi's house.

"Ugh, I can't stand Penny. She used to date one of my best friends, who used to live on the street, so she was around a lot, like on Shabbat and stuff. She and my mom got along really well."

"I overheard your conversation," I said quietly.

"Yeah, I figured, sound really travels on the main floor."

"Do you think Penny's into you?"

He shook his head. "Not like that. She just really likes my mom. She wants to do what she thinks my mom wants her to do. They have tea together, where they sit around talking about all the things that are wrong with the orthodox world, but also all the things they love and find comforting about it. Penny's not close to her mom and my mom and Devorah have always fought."

"About what?"

"You know how some kids, they just want to fit in and be normal? Devorah is still like that, but as our mom gets older, she just gives less fucks." He cleared his throat. "They don't spend much time, just the two of them."

He looked at the watch he wore on Shabbat when he couldn't use his cell phone.

"It's actually early, it's only 9. What time did you tell them you were coming back?"

I shrugged. "I didn't tell them anything."

He looked at me and grinned. "Do you think we have time for a detour?"

"They gave me a key, and there's a separate entrance to their basement anyway. But I really don't want to get caught."

"There's this field kind of on our way there, near the running track. It's pretty quiet at night."

I dropped my arm around his waist. "Okay," I said, eager to shake off all the tension, to let things go, to just stop thinking. "Let's go."

CHAPTER TWENTY

IRIS CALLED ME a few days later, when I was at home and Jillian was testing me on conversion questions. I'd spent half the day writing my last paper for one of my business classes, and now I had to cram. Jillian had never offered to study with me before, and I was excited.

"So, I heard dinner went well on Friday," Iris said.

"Is that a joke?"

"No, not at all. I hear you really held your own with Malka. That's the trick, by the way, never let her see you sweat or get emotional. Honest to God, she seemed to like you."

I laughed and told her what had happened with Penina.

"Look, you're going to have to face it, Naftali is a very in demand bachelor. Lots of girls would kill to marry him, even girls who aren't into guys."

"What?"

"I mean, obviously, what did you think her and Malka talked about?"

"So why would Malka want them to get together?"

"I mean, I can't pretend to understand Malka, but I guess she wants Naftali to have his options open."

"What do you mean?"

"Like, I don't know. What if he does want to date men? Or what if he has problems staying faithful to one person or wants to have something more open? Naftali is a guy who likes freedom, and no one understands that better than her. On paper, someone like Penny makes sense for him. They both grew up religious in the same community, same schools. They both grew up wealthy. Look, you can't be intimidated by girls like her. You have to carry yourself like you belong. Fake it 'til you make it, baby. It worked for me."

"I'll try," I said quietly after she hung up the phone.

"Hey," Jillian asked me suddenly, "have you thought about the Hebrew name you're going to take on when you're done converting?"

Chaya had explained that at the end, I'd get to dunk in a ritual bath called a *mikveh,* where they would officially announce my Hebrew name.

"Yeah, of course. Chaya wants me to use the Hebrew version of Hannah. Chana, I guess. Apparently she willed herself to have a kid through the power of prayer?"

Jillian snorted. "Is that what she told you? I mean, I guess that's right, whenever women have trouble conceiving they use her as inspiration. She gave birth to the prophet Samuel. The only thing I like about Chana for you is the meaning of the name. It means grace, which suits you."

I blushed a little. "Thanks. I mean, it's going to be impossible to pronounce for people like my mom."

She laughed. "Good."

"I was thinking, for my middle name, maybe if it's okay with you, I'll use Miriam. The other day Chaya was teaching me about how Miriam led the people in the Song of the Sea, and it made me think of you. You're my inspiration, Jill. You're the one who introduced me to Judaism, and you've taught me so much."

Jillian got up suddenly and glared at me. "Miriam is not my name. I hate it, and I hate the idea that you think you're doing me some kind of favour."

I stared at her.

"I thought this was an experiment," she said. "I had no idea you planned to go through with becoming Orthodox, and I thought I could be supportive, but I can't. The Jewish community is great, if you want people to tell you exactly how to live your life down to the most minute detail, but if you're weird and unique like us, it's wrong. It's not a place for people like us."

She spoke more gently now. "Trust me. You're going to get rejected, over and over. What you told Iris about that girl at dinner? It's just the tip of the iceberg. Why would you want to put yourself through that?"

I felt tears hot on my cheeks as I tried to get words out. I didn't know how to explain that it made sense to me that I had to prove myself.

"You have the best life," I said quietly. "Your parents are still together; they love you and your sister. Your mom cooks for you and gives you furniture and her blessing to be a musician and take time off school. You have more money than you know what to do with. You don't have to work; you don't have student loans. When you think about the future, you think about being or doing anything you want. There are no limits. Before I met you, when I thought about the future, I thought, I hope I survive. I hope I accomplish the most minimal things.

I dream of having your confidence when you walk into a room, and part of that is where you come from."

Jillian walked towards me and the next thing I felt was her nails digging into my arms.

She pushed me backwards across the room and out the door.

"Get out," she said, hissing. "Get the fuck out of my apartment."

She slammed the door behind her. I stood there, stunned, and noticed that my left arm was bleeding, but just a little bit.

I stood outside for twenty minutes, waiting for her to come and join me, or relent and let me in, but she started blasting Pantera and I felt like I was going deaf.

I sat on the hallway carpet for a few more minutes.

My purse was inside but I was still holding my phone.

I texted Naftali. He asked if I wanted him to say anything to her, but I told him not to.

He offered to come pick me up, and I waited for him outside.

"You could unofficially move in with me," he said. "We haven't been seeing each other as much lately, and I've missed you."

"Maybe." I tried to smile. I really didn't want to live anywhere else.

A couple of hours later, Jillian's mother called me.

"I'm so sorry that you and Miriam had a fight," she said. "I know how fond she is of you. We all are, Hannah. Just give her time. She's had issues since she was younger, maybe she told you. It's hard when someone you love is sick. She's been having a rough time lately, I don't know how much she's shared with you, but nothing like when she was a teenager, Thank God. I'm hoping you can forgive her. You mean so much to her, she's just been ... unsettled lately."

"Thanks for calling," I said. I put my fingers in the corners of my eyes to stop myself from crying again. "She means a lot to me too."

"Motek, it'll blow over. It always does with her."

Later that night, when I was sitting on Naftali's couch, pretending to read, Jillian texted me.

" *Feel bad about before. hope you're OK. Did my mom tell you about my health stuff? that's the reason. I have a lot to tell you. Call me.*"

I showed Naftali and he shook his head. "Are you going to call her?"

"Maybe tomorrow," I said, but I knew I was lying.

An hour later, he was lying on his side, snoring lightly, and I was still tossing and turning, so I walked into the living room and called her.

She'd been asleep, I could hear it in her voice, and that startled me because it was 12:45 a.m., which was early for her.

"I'm sorry," she said. "I've just been going through so much lately, and you've been so busy, I didn't know how to tell you."

"Tell me what?"

"It's not just the endometriosis. I mean, it started with that, I've had it since I was fourteen. It's just so fucked up. I started being sexually active when I was fifteen, which obviously would have been a big deal to my family, so I didn't tell them. My sex drive was high, I knew I was into girls, but I didn't know basic things like where to meet anyone, so aside from two girls, I slept with a bunch of a guys. When I was sixteen, I got HPV. Tons of people get it without getting sick, and I didn't get the warts right away, so I didn't know. I didn't tell anyone for a long time, and when I finally did, my parents acted like it was a punishment from God. In my community, everyone knows everyone, including my Orthodox Jewish doctor, so they didn't want anyone to know. By the time I was seventeen, I'd lost a lot of weight, I was coughing and short of breath all the time, I couldn't sing. It turned out I had cancer on my ovaries. They call it endometrioid cancer. It was only stage two, and the doctors were very positive about my recovery because of my age and my health, but my family was really depressed and thought I was going to die, which is why we never talk about it."

"Oh my God, Jill."

"Yeah. Lately, I haven't been feeling so good. I just remember how I felt before, and I feel similar, but I've been too scared to go to a doctor."

I let the words sink in. How self-absorbed had I been to have missed this? I'd been annoyed with her for not being more involved in my life.

"Let me go with you, please."

"Maybe. I just keep telling myself I'm a survivor. I survived before and I'll survive again."

"Of course you will."

"I'm sorry, I know I was really unfair to you earlier. It's just, my parents aren't that great if you know them.

They let things get so bad that I was almost dying. To this day they can't even say the word cancer."

"Yeah. Your mom seemed really worried about you, but she didn't say anything explicitly."

"AHHH. I know. It's so frustrating. How does she expect me to be able to face it head on, if she can't even name it?"

"I can help. I can say cancer, we can talk about everything, I can go with you. I can be there Jill, if you'll let me."

I heard her crying on the other end of the phone.

"I love you, Hannah," she said.

"I love you, too. And I'm here for you."

"No matter what?"

"No matter what," I said, feeling like I'd just agreed to marry her too.

"Hey, Hannah," she said, before she hung up the phone. "Don't take my Hebrew name. Take my mom's. She loves you, and she really lives that life and loves it."

"Okay," I said, if you're sure that's what you want."

"It is," she said. "Chana Esther sounds really good together."

CHAPTER TWENTY-ONE

A T MY NEXT study session with Chaya, she said she had a surprise for me. She was booking an organized trip to Israel, for women only, for ten days, and at the last minute, someone had cancelled, and she had an extra spot.

"Do you want to come with? It'll be an unprecedented opportunity to learn and experience things from Jerusalem to the other holy cities, to meet other families and make new friends. It's a really hands-on, meaningful experience."

I took a few minutes to answer.

"How much does it cost? Is it expensive?"

"Well not as much as it would be normally. It's highly subsidized by a couple of Jewish organizations."

"How much is it?"

"Well, normally the flights, roundtrip are around $1500. If you factor in hotels and accommodations and food, you're looking at around $3000. We offer this trip for $1250, everything included."

I did the mental math while trying my hardest to keep a neutral expression on my face.

Conversion was expensive. Aside from this trip, there was the new clothes, the kosher food which cost double what regular food cost, the books, the fact that between this and school, I now had no time for a job, aside from a few social media gigs.

"Can I think about it?" I asked.

"Sure, but not for too long, okay? We're leaving next Monday, so I need to know in the next couple of days."

I called Iris to ask her what she thought of the idea.

Iris laughed. "It's not like you're going to Vegas. If anything, it makes you look even more serious. I think you should go."

"Have you ever been to Israel?"

"Yeah, I've been twice. Once before I converted and once after, when Victoria was younger."

"What did you think?"

"It's an interesting place. I liked Jerusalem. You're going to have a very different experience to me anyway. You could pass for Jewish. I'll always be foreign and other to them."

"That's awful."

"I still think it's worth seeing. I understood the Jewish community better after being there."

"Hmm. If I decide to go, I have to figure out how I'm going to pay for it."

"Naftali didn't offer?"

"I haven't told him yet."

"You should ask him."

"No, I feel weird about it."

"You know," she said, and I heard excitement creeping into her voice, "Jack often donates to these Israel trips and sponsors people. I can mention it to him if you want. I know how expensive these things are, and if he's going to do it anyway, it might as well be for his future daughter in law. I can let you know what he says."

"Wow, you'd do that for me? Thanks, Iris."

"Anytime. When I was growing up, I always wanted a sister, but I don't exactly have anything in common with Devorah and Shaindy. I mean, you've met them, you get it."

"Yeah. I haven't met Jack yet, what's he like?"

"He's great. He's always been so supportive of me. He admires people who are ambitious, who change their lives if they decide that's what they want. He admires converts, which is not common, even though it should be. He'll appreciate how serious you are about everything. He and Naftali aren't close, but he wants to change that. Naftali and Malka, they'll look at each and laugh at the same jokes or get annoyed by the same people. I think no matter who he ended up with, the change would have been hard for her."

"How was she to you?"

"Polite. I wouldn't call her warm, but I wasn't dating her favourite kid. Oh, until you're married, call her Mrs. Goldwater. She's not a call her by her first name type until you're actually family."

"Thanks, Iris."

"Anytime, Sister."

Naftali called me an hour later, and I told him.

"That sounds awesome, babe. You should go."

I mentioned my conversation with Iris and her offer to talk to his dad.

"You know, she's right, it's a great idea. He's probably sponsoring someone on the trip anyway. I'll talk to

Iris, but maybe we'll drop by tonight or tomorrow, and you can meet him and thank him."

"Okay," I said, "if you really want me to go."

"I think you'll have a good time," he said.

I called Chaya, who seemed excited.

"When we go to Jerusalem, everyone stays with different families for Shabbat. I already talked to my friend Ilana. She and her husband Ze'ev are amazing, and they would love to have you stay with them and show you around.

"That sounds good," I said.

"And if you love it there," Chaya said, "which I think you will, because everyone always does, after you convert and get married, you and your husband can go back together. There are amazing programs for newly married couples."

Naftali snorted when I mentioned it to him. "Good one."

"I didn't promise her we would or anything."

"Good, because once this is over, you owe her nothing."

That night we dropped in on his parents.

They stood on opposite ends of the foyer, his mother with her hands on her hips, his father smiling.

Jack looked like a more distinguished and cavalier version of Naftali. It was like looking in one of those fun house mirrors. Everything was slightly exaggerated, but the resemblance was undeniable. He was also tall, with wavy blond hair that was greying at his temples. He had a red paisley and gold pocket square in his black suit jacket, and a matching tie. Instead of walking languidly, like Naftali did, he strutted with purpose, as if every step could be potentially life changing.

"Hannah," he said, taking a few big steps towards me. "It's so nice to meet you."

"It's so nice to meet you too," I said, and then I looked over at Malka.

"Nice to see you again, Mrs. Goldwater."

She gave me the thinnest of smiles. "Hi, Hannah."

We stood in silence for what felt like an hour.

Jack's gaze was like standing next to an open fire.

"Hannah, I realized we know so little about you. Your family is from out west, right?"

I nodded. "My mom lives near Hamilton now."

"And your dad?"

"Stouffville. He lives with his partner and some friends."

"What do your parents do?"

"My mom is a nurse practitioner. She's married to my stepdad, who's a pharmacist. He owns a bunch of drugs stores in that area. My dad is ..." I paused. "Retired."

"Oh, what did he used to do?"

I'd practiced my answers with Jillian.

"He was a teacher of world religions and philosophy. He used to teach at a rural school out west."

Naftali rolled his eyes at me, but he smiled.

"I hear you've been very committed to the conversion process." Jack said.

I was surprised when Naftali answered for me.

"She's been working so hard at everything. When I met her, more than a year ago, I knew she was special, I felt it in my gut, and I was right. She's so committed to everything she does, including becoming Jewish. I'm glad you had a chance to meet her tonight."

"So, I hear you'll be taking a women's trip to Israel," Malka said.

"It leaves in three days, I'm really excited."

"I'm sure you'll find Israel very stimulating," she said more gently. "We have lots of relatives there, you'll have to meet them next time."

"That would be great. Thank you both again, for everything."

Jack winked at me on our way out the door. "Iris thinks very highly of you too. Enjoy the trip. We'll see you when you get back."

Naftali hugged me when the door closed behind us.

"You always do so well with them," he said. "It's such a relief."

I laughed. "I just think of how confident Jillian is in every situation, and I try to channel that."

"Speaking of Jillian, philosophy teacher?"

"Yeah, that was her. You have to admit, it's much better than crazy cult leader."

We both laughed.

"I'm going to miss you so much," he said.

I had never left the country. I had a passport that my mom insisted I get a few years back, and it sat in a plastic sleeve, pristine and untouched.

"You don't even know," I said and leaned my body into his, "how nervous I am. I wish you were coming with me."

CHAPTER TWENTY-TWO

STOOD SQUINTING in the midday sun next to the hand washing station next to the Kotel in Jerusalem. It was so hot I could see the air move in tiny waves in front of me. My plastic sandals were melting into the hot stones under my feet, and I could feel my mascara dripping into small black pools under my eyes. I wondered how all the religious people around me could handle all the layers they had to wear. The flight was thirteen hours long, and most of the other fifteen women in my group were very religious. There was one girl, Ella, whom I clicked with immediately. She had brown hair that looked like it had been dusted with gold. It framed her face like a lion's. She was a chef, living a completely secular life despite her upbringing. Her parents begged her to take this trip and paid for it so that she'd go.

Jillian had given me some prescription sleeping pills, plus a pack of homeopathic pills called No Jet Lag. I split everything with Ella. When Chaya let us know the schedule for the day we arrived, Ella rolled her dark brown eyes. "I'm excited for all the free pockets of time."

"Why?"

She looked away. "My parents are in denial about my beliefs. I've been anti-Zionist for years."

"What do you mean?"

"I mean, I don't think Israel should exist, especially the way it does now."

"What?"

She sighed. "It started when I lived here. I was still religious, and I was studying in a seminary for a year. Once you see what life is like here for other people who aren't Jewish, once you see East Jerusalem or Hebron, once you experience the checkpoints, once you make friends who've lived a wildly different life to you, you can't unsee it."

I wasn't sure what to say, but it was interesting.

She added, "You're becoming religious, connecting with the culture, and everyone around you loves Israel so much, right? But you have to see the whole picture. There are all these Jewish values, like *Tikkun Olam*, fixing the world, and I want to live by them, you know? Maybe not in the way the community I was raised in wants me to be, but I still believe in these things. I care so much."

I thought about what my mom said to me the day before, when I called her to tell her I was coming. I didn't expect her to be enthusiastic, but I was taken aback when she repeated the word Israel with the kind of disgust she usually saved for her patients' venereal diseases. She reminded me that living there had been a dream of my dad's.

"He worked on a kibbutz there for a few months after he finished high school," she said. "They had him pick melons, and he still had fungus under his fingernails when I knew him. I think it's where his idea for The Tribe came from. Think how much better off we all would have been if he'd never been there."

Before I hung up, she mentioned her cousin Tara, who lived there and worked with an NGO in Khan Younis.

"She was shaken by the conditions people were living in. If you have time, I want you to reach out to her. Make sure you see other places, the ones that aren't on your itinerary," she said. "Make sure you keep a genuinely open mind."

"This trip will give me a chance to visit places I've always wanted to see," Ella said.

"Like what?"

"I've volunteered as a chef in Aida before, and I'm going to stay for an extra week to do that again. There are so many amazing people, thousands of women and kids whose lives have been affected this way for decades."

Her voice broke. "Aside from the important things, I want to see art and culture. There's a new museum that just opened in Birzheit called the Palestinian Museum. I've heard their exhibits are beautiful. I want to go back to the Darwish museum in Ramallah. I've only been once, but it was amazing. His poetry is so beautiful. I also want to finally see some of the Banksys, like the Walled Off Hotel in Bethlehem, you know with the little girl holding a bunch of balloons? I don't know that I'll get to do all of this, it's complicated to get to these places, but I really want to try. You're welcome to come with me, if you want to. Just let me know in advance so I can organize it."

I didn't know what to say, so I nodded. Her words affected me deeply, but I didn't know what to do with them. I fell asleep for the rest of the flight and dreamed that Jillian had come on the trip instead.

Jillian insisted I pack a few fun, non-religious outfits, including shorts and a bikini, and I hid them at the bottom of my bag, along with flip flops and two tank tops. She also gave me thirty-six dollars and asked me to give charity in her name at the Kotel.

"Ask them to pray for my health. My full Hebrew name is Miriam bat Esther Aliza. If they give you a red string, bring it back for me."

"Of course," I said. She found out that she had a major doctor's appointment while I was away, and she promised to call me as soon as she knew anything.

We checked into a beautiful hotel, the Waldorf Astoria, whose marble lobby reminded me of the Goldwaters' house. For the rest of the trip, Chaya explained, we'd be staying in less opulent settings, but Jerusalem was special, so they wanted us to stay in a special place.

I was instantly taken with the city; the snaking streets filled with apartment buildings and bright grassy parks, the chalky beige stone walls of the old city. It was jarring to walk through the Mamilla mall, to see the glowing store signs of the Gap and Aroma coming out of buildings made of cracking, ancient stones. The mix of the ancient past and my possible future made me feel slightly feverish.

Walking through the Old City, I realized I had never seen so many stray cats or so many children wandering around without their parents, aside from in my time in the Tribe. A little blond boy with a light blue velvet *kippah* who couldn't have been more than three asked me to pick him up, so he could press the buzzer outside of a stone walled building.

I looked at a couple of the girls in the group, and they shrugged. "Go ahead and help him, it's a normal thing here."

He even gave me a hug when I put him down. I passed a father singing to a pair of twins in a stroller. "*Hamalach hagoel oti mikol rah.*" I felt like I was dreaming. My dad had sung it to me when I was sick when I was little. I had a fever that wouldn't break, it was over a hundred, and my mom was angry that he wouldn't get me Tylenol or Advil, but I loved the song. It was about an angel protecting children from harm. I remembered him telling me about his grandfather singing it to him with a heavy Yiddish accent. "*Hamlach hagoy-yell osi,*" my dad had pronounced it. He'd laughed but I could hear tears in his throat. Tears pricked the sides of my eyes. I wondered, for the first time in years, if my dad would be happy if I called him to tell him I was here.

By the time we got to the Kotel, everyone in the group was excited. I walked closer to the wall. Aside from our group, there were about twenty other women in the women's section. Some wore long dresses, and they had their hair covered in scarves, and some wore jeans and t-shirts and took pictures with their phones.

I hadn't expected to feel anything at all, but there was something primal that was stirred in me, a deep connection. I couldn't control my tears. My body shook.

A woman standing next to me reached over and gave me a hug. I sobbed harder. She reached into her purse and handed me a tissue.

"Siddur?" she asked me. She gestured to a cart of prayer books a few feet away. "They have more over there."

"I can't read Hebrew."

The woman looked me in the eye. "It's okay. You don't need to. God will read what's in your heart."

I walked closer to the wall. I touched the stone and felt a vibration that echoed through my body. I felt the push of a woman's body into my back. Everyone wanted the chance to get close to it. I stepped back and sat down at a white plastic table a few feet behind. Chaya explained that there was a long-standing tradition of writing notes, of expressing what we wanted or prayed for most from God and sliding them into an available crack in the wall. I looked and saw that the cracks were overflowing with requests. Chaya handed out pens and tiny scraps of paper. I wasn't sure what to ask for.

Please help me find the place where I belong. Please help me to reconcile all the different parts of myself, to feel happy and safe, to live a good life, to help people.

Please let my friend Jillian, Miriam Dina bat Esther Aliza, have a full and complete recovery

Please let this be a world where everyone knows peace and safety, happiness and security.

Please help me to do the right things, to know what they are, and to do them

In the tiniest print I could manage, at the bottom I added, *please help me become the kind of person who deserves the things I want.*

I squeezed it into an opening and then walked backwards, as Chaya had instructed us to, so that my back was never to the wall. I found an older woman peddling red strings for charity a few steps later. Her eyes widened when she saw the dollars, and she repeated the blessing and gave me enough red strings to give the whole group. Chaya led everyone to the different meeting spots to meet the families who were hosting them for Shabbat.

"You'll like Ze'ev. He grew up in the States, totally not religious, but he's been Orthodox for twenty-five years now. I'm sure he'll tell you his story."

Ze'ev startled me by coming up behind her. He had salt and pepper beard, and blue and white knitted kippah. "Chana?"

It took me a minute to realize that he was talking to me.

"Hi," I said. "It's nice to meet you."

He led me to his family's apartment about a twenty-minute walk away. The Old City was full of steep hills and streets that were packed with ancient looking beige brick apartment buildings. We cut through the market, and I was overwhelmed by the sights and smells of cardamom and hookah smoke, zaatar and fresh fish, piles of bruised mangos and soft dark cherries, lavender and rosewater, and soot and fresh jasmine.

I reached into my bag for the cold bottle of water I'd bought just twenty minutes earlier, but it had turned piss warm. I emptied it out on a hibiscus bush in the front of his building. They were on the fifth floor, but thankfully the lobby was air-conditioned.

His wife wore a giant turquoise head scarf on her head that was pinned with a shiny sequined orange flower brooch. She looked much younger than her husband.

"Hi," she said, her voice rising above all the kitchen sounds. "I'm Ilana. We're so excited to have you."

Their living room was a mess of baby dolls and

stuffed animals, plastic beads and strings of wool, and piles of Lego. I tripped over a copy of the *Very Hungry Caterpillar*.

"We wanted to clean up before you came," Ilana said. "But it's so hard with Shabbat starting so early."

I rubbed my ankle and tried to smile. "I totally understand. Here, let me help you clean up." I bent down and started picking up Lego pieces.

"Oh, that's great, thank you," Ilana said. "I just have to run back to the kitchen to finish cooking but come join me as soon as you're finished."

I put everything away as fast as I could. Ilana hadn't told me where I'd be staying, so I left my bag beside their worn red cotton couch and walked into the kitchen to find her frantically chopping carrots. It smelled like freshly baked challah.

"Here, you can help chop onions," she said. "And then I'll fry them."

I cut up potatoes and cauliflower and put them on aluminum trays she gave me to roast in the oven.

"You're amazing," Ilana said. "Thank you so much for all your help."

"Thanks for having me. I've only been in Jerusalem for a few hours, but I feel it deeply already. How long have you guys lived here?"

"Oh, about fifteen years. Ze'ev's been here longer. I came here to study in seminary after high school. I was only supposed to be here for six months, but I never went back."

"Are you from Toronto?"

Ilana shook her head. "No, New York. I met Chaya

here in Israel. Is this your first time here? Have you thought of studying here?"

"I would never have before, but now that I'm here, I can see why people do it."

Ilana nodded. "You have no idea. Tonight, at dinner, you'll meet our niece Leora. She's studying at Midreshet Rosenbaum. You can ask her all about it."

Ilana showed me to my room, which looked like a tiny, converted walk in closet, and advised me to start getting ready for Shabbat. "If you want to shower before Shabbat starts, now's the time," she said. "We have eight people in this house right now and only two bathrooms."

I stepped into a bathtub filled with orange, green and yellow rubber ducks and two plastic boats. For the first time, I let myself imagine having a kid of my own. I felt anxiety rising in my chest, along with a new feeling of inevitability. I wondered what kind of dad Naftali would be, if he'd be the kind to buy rubber ducks and bath crayons, if he'd want to bathe his own kid, or expect me to do everything. I wondered, if given my own childhood, I'd even know what normal was supposed to look like. He was beautiful though. A kid who looked like him, golden and angelic, who had confidence like him and Jillian, would be amazing.

A memory of my father in the lake flitted into my head, and I jumped out with a cold splash.

I took my time getting dressed. By the time I got to the kitchen it was almost candle lighting time. I was touched that Ilana had set up two candles for me. I had memorized the blessing for the candles. I was ready.

At dinner, the men sat at one end of the long dining

room table, and the women and little girls sat at the other. They started singing Shabbat songs, and Ze'ev invited the whole group to his side of the table for *Kiddush*. After the blessing, I sipped from my tiny cup of wine. It was the best kosher wine I'd ever had. It wasn't cloyingly sweet, or too dry. It went down like velvet. After we washed our hands and said the blessing on the bread, Ze'ev left the bottle of wine on the men's side of the table and brought another full one to the women's side.

Ilana poured herself half a glass and then leaned over to me to ask if I wanted more. I nodded and got up and poured myself another glass.

Ze'ev stared at me uncomfortably. "Hannah," he said quietly, "are you sure you want to do that?"

I laughed. "I'm not much of a drinker," I said. "This is just so good."

"Stay here for a second," Ze'ev whispered to me, and he gestured to Ilana.

"Make sure no one else has any more wine," he said quietly. "It's not kosher anymore."

He leaned into Ilana: "The girl is a *ger*. She's in the middle of *giyur*."

Ilana looked panicked. "She helped me cook."

Ilana walked into the kitchen with me trailing behind her. She picked up the tray of potatoes and cauliflower that I'd cut up and dumped them into the garbage. "What a waste," she said and glared at me. "What a terrible waste."

I wanted to cry. "Ilana, I don't understand. Why are you throwing the food away?"

"I forgot that you're converting, Hannah," she said, almost apologetically. "Chaya did tell me, but you look and act so Jewish, I honestly forgot. There's a rule called *Bishul Nochri*. We're not supposed to eaten certain foods if they're cooked by a non-Jew, and on Shabbat no less."

I was shocked. I knew I couldn't go back to the table with everyone staring at me. I walked past the dining room and into the room I was staying in. I threw the clothes that I'd unpacked into my bag as fast as I could. I walked to the door. Ilana followed me.

"I'm really sorry," I said, staring at the cream tiles in her foyer. "I honestly didn't know. Thank you so much for having me."

Ilana's lip quivered. "Don't apologize. I'm sorry, Hannah. I completely forgot what your situation was. You're more than welcome to stay."

I shook my head. "I don't think I can now but thank you."

"Hannah wait." Ilana grabbed my arm.

"Our *Shabbos goy* is away this weekend, and I know as a part of conversion you're supposed to break Shabbat every week, so would you mind helping us before you go?

"Can you turn on the light in the other bathroom? And in the hallway, right here? And do you mind checking that all our appliances in the kitchen are off? We forgot to check before Shabbat."

I was incredulous. "No," I said, spluttering, and turned away. "I'm supposed to be keeping Shabbat too. You're supposed to teach me and help me fit in. I'm here because I'm supposed to learn from you."

I tore down the stairs, hearing my shoes clack against the concrete with every loud step. I wasn't sure where to go or how to get back to the hotel. Every street looked the same, and they were all named after biblical figures or Israeli heroes I'd never heard of. Chaya had mentioned that two women were staying there this Shabbat, and that everyone's rooms were reserved for them just in case. If these people want to make it so hard for me, I thought, if they wanted to go out of their way to make sure I was clear that I wasn't one of them, maybe I shouldn't bother trying so hard anymore. My cheeks were hot with sweat and tears. It was 10:30 p.m. Maybe I would break Shabbat. I reached for my cell phone, first to check Waze to figure out where the hell I was and how to get out of there and called a cab. A young-looking guy with gelled hair and silver aviator sunglasses pulled up beside me. Sitting in the back of the car, I tried to calculate the time in Toronto. I needed to speak to Jillian.

"I miss you," I wrote. "Having the worst night ever."

I was about to turn my phone off, when I saw the three dots, a forming text bubble from Jillian.

I expected her to be surprised that I was texting on Shabbat, but she didn't mention it.

> ☹ *Had some blood work done, and I got the results today.*
> *Will find out for sure at that appointment next week. But I'm not crazy, the Dr is worried too. The fuck am I going to do if the cancer's back?*

I felt sick. Before I could respond, Jillian wrote more.

> *Too* 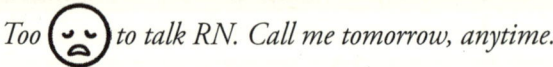 *to talk RN. Call me tomorrow, anytime.*

I bent over and threw up all over the floor of the cab.

CHAPTER TWENTY-THREE

THE NEXT MORNING, I called Jillian, but she didn't pick up. She usually picked up or at least called-back right way. I wondered where she was, if she was at home alone in pain, or if she'd gone out with friends.

After trying three times, I started texting. She didn't respond. Cold sweat poured down the back of my neck. I contemplated flying home. I checked but there were no available flights until Monday morning. I'd either have to go into my overdraft or borrow money from Naftali to get back.

I decided to leave the hotel room. I put on a black cotton t-shirt dress and my sandals. I walked downstairs to the lobby.

Chaya had mentioned that there were in-house prayer services. I wondered what exactly they'd tell her, if they'd feel bad or be angry with her for sending me.

I wanted to go because of what Chaya had taught me about the *Mi'Sheberach* prayer, the Jewish prayer for the sick. At a specific point in the service, the rabbi asked people for the names of their sick friends or relatives and then prayed for all of them.

The prayer service space was more casual than I was used to. Instead of a partition separating the men's and women's sections, there was a row of tall plants, and everyone was sitting on white folding chairs. I grabbed a seat in the back row, beside an older woman with white hair who was wearing a long black dress. A large gold star of David hung around her heavily lined neck. She smiled at me. "My name's Marlene," she said. "I'm here from Cincinnati for my grandson's bar mitzvah."

"I'm Hannah," I said. "It's my first time in Israel."

"How lovely." She smoothed out a wrinkle in her dress and mouthed along to a song they were singing.

I turned to my siddur, but Marlene was talking to me again five minutes later.

She looked at my wrist. "Tell me, what's a nice girl like you doing with a tattoo?"

"I ... I don't know," I said. "It was meaningful to me at the time, and I guess, it still is."

Marlene's jaw clenched. She rolled up her sleeve to just above her elbow. There was a thin line of fading black numbers. 120 403.

"You ever seen a tattoo from Auschwitz before?"

I shook my head.

Marlene looked at me and asked more gently, "What do you know about the *Shoah*?"

"Not enough. My dad's parents were survivors, but they lived across the country, so I never really knew them."

"If you want, I can tell you my story," Marlene said.

I told her I wanted to hear it.

She told me about growing up in Frankfurt. Her family were intellectuals, she said, and not religious. They were wealthy and had lived in Germany for six generations. They never believed that they were in danger.

"They moved us around. First to a ghetto in Poland, then by trains to Auschwitz. I lost my whole family, except for my father. I survived because I could play violin. I played in an orchestra right next to the crematorium. Happy music, Mozart, Brahms, Wagner, of course. I couldn't listen to any of it for years. I'd hear songs on the radio, and I could smell the oily, burning flesh. I never played again, you know. Not a single note."

I swiped at a tear with the back of my palm and reached over and held Marlene's bony hand with the other.

"I'm sorry about my tattoos," I said quietly. "I usually cover them." I took a deep breath. "I'm converting to Judaism. My dad is Jewish, but my mom isn't. I've been learning a lot about Jewish laws, but I haven't learned nearly enough about Jewish history."

"It's good that you want to learn," she said carefully. "And it doesn't matter if you're fully Jewish or not. Back then, just having one Jewish grandparent would have been enough to send you to the camps."

"I didn't know that."

"Well, now you know. Don't worry," she said, squeezing my hand. "You have a lifetime to learn all of this."

When the service was over, Marlene invited me to meet her family, but I told her I had to go.

"Thanks for sharing your story with me and for teaching me. It meant so much."

Marlene nodded. "God bless you," she said quietly. "May God bless you and protect you."

"You too," I said, and she smiled.

I was in desperate need of a change of scenery.

I didn't want to stay at the hotel, or anywhere around here in case I ran into anyone from the trip. I went back to my room and checked my phone. I still hadn't heard from Jillian, but I remembered her telling me that her favourite beach, Gordon Beach, was in Tel Aviv. I called myself a cab but sent it to an address that was a couple of blocks away, according to the map.

The sea was bright and glittering and the sand was overrun with people. I was amazed by how many languages I heard: French, Russian, Spanish, and Amharic, along with Australian and American English. The air was heavy and salty. Just in front of me the sand was packed with women in orange, blue and gold bikinis sprawled out on beach chairs, dripping with tanning oil.

I felt a rush of envy. There were all these people who weren't keeping Shabbat, who seemed perfectly happy. They also seemed so comfortable in their own skin. Even when I was little, when all the kids in the Tribe skinny dipped, my instinct was to go as deep into the water as I could.

I walked along the boardwalk, past some steep rocks and a sign that in English said, The Bathing is Adjective Forbidden, and a block later, another one that said Parents, Keep Your Golden. I took photos and wondered how I'd explain them to Naftali.

I took off my shoes, walked right up to the water, and put my feet in. The Mediterranean Sea was deliciously cold. A clear plastic bag floated past me, and a man behind me yanked me by the arm and pulled me out of the way.

I jumped and turned around. What the hell, I thought.

He pointed at the bag. "*Meduza*," he said.

"What?"

"Jelly feesh," his friend behind him said.

"Ohhh, jellyfish. Do they bite?"

The guy shook his head. "Not bite, sting. Ow, ow." He pointed to his foot and pretended to jump up and down.

He leaned forward, and his hair bounced. It was long and curly and subdued by a grey cotton hairband. I'd never seen a man wear one before, but looking around, it was clearly Israeli fashion. He had beautiful white teeth and olive skin.

"B'kef," he said. "Zis is your first time in Tel Aviv?"

"My first time in Israel."

"Wow. You want someone to, ehm, show you around?"

"I'm okay thanks. I'm here with a group of people." I pointed randomly at a crowd just behind them. "See, that's my group."

The first guy turned to the second guy and said something in Hebrew.

"What?" I asked.

The second guy answered. "He said for sure you have a boyfriend, or you're married."

I laughed. "I have a boyfriend."

The first guy looked at me and said something in Hebrew. The second guy rolled his eyes and translated. "We have this saying 'a boyfriend is not a wall.'"

I had no idea what that meant. For some reason, I kept talking. "We have talked about marriage, but we're not engaged. It's kind of a weird story. My dad is technically Jewish, but not exactly practicing, and my mom is Catholic. I'm in the process of converting to Judaism, but I still don't know that this is what I actually want."

"What, to be Jewish?"

"I don't know. Any of it." I thought of Naftali's collection of photographs. "Do you know of any cool places that sell photo prints, and art? Or places that are good to photograph?"

The first guy said that there was an artist's market in Nachalat Binyamin, right beside the regular market. "You must come back on a Tuesday or a Friday morning."

The second guy named a few art galleries in South Tel Aviv.

"There's cool graffiti all around here," he said. "A lot of Israeli artists. There's this guy, Adam Yekutieli, he goes by the name Know Hope, his graffiti and installations are all over the city. He also has a show at the gallery on Gordon."

They offered to drive me to the Tel Aviv Museum of Art. They dropped me by the main entrance. I walked around mesmerized by seeing Cartier-Bresson's and Weegee's photography up close, not to mention the paintings and photos of the local artists.

I decided to try calling Jillian one more time. I was so happy when she picked up right away.

"I feel like you're stalking me," she said, then laughed like that's what she wanted me to do.

"I've been so worried about you. Do you want me to come home?"

"No, don't do that. I'm going to New York tomorrow to see some doctor friend of my parents who's a specialist. They think I should get a second opinion."

"Who's going with you? Do you want me to come back?"

"No, don't worry, my sister is coming. Listen, do me a favour, if you do go home early, don't say anything to my mom. She's a wreck as it is, and I promised her I wouldn't tell anyone this time until we knew for sure. I told her as far as anyone knows, it's a music trip. Trust me, it's better this way. My mom's not good at talking about complicated things."

"Okay, I won't say anything. Whatever you want."

"And Hannah? Let's not panic until we know, okay? Let's try to stay calm. If you're calm, it'll help me. Hopefully it will be okay. Have fun there for me. Israel is such a fun place. I wish I was with you."

"Me too," I said, and turned off the phone.

The rest of the trip passed in a blur. We saw more than I could remember, holy cities like Tzfat, which were full of turquoise doorways and paintings, Tiberius, which was full of famous rabbis' graves, and the Sea of Galilee, hiking Masada, which was like walking in a postcard, and swimming in a waterfall in Ein Gedi. Ella ended up leaving the group after a few days, and she texted me photos of the kids and women, of the art, and even parts of Darwish poems, which made me cry. My favourite line was "So who am I? I am no I in ascension's presence."

Back in Jerusalem we visited Yad Vashem, the Holocaust Museum, and I thought of Marlene, and wished I could tell her. One of the most interesting sites was Amuka, the grave of Rabbi Yonatan Ben Uziel. It was at the top of a mountain, in a forest. Amuka, we were told, was the most auspicious place to pray for a soulmate. On our way out, Chaya handed me a gold keychain, shaped like a key with Hebrew writing on it. "Give this to Naftali when you get home. May you be married *B'shaa tova*, at the right time."

"Thanks," I said and asked for a second one, which I told her was just in case I lost it or it broke. I wanted to make sure I had one to give to Jillian too.

CHAPTER TWENTY-FOUR

'D BEEN HOME for a day, jet lagged and out of it, when I found a note on my door in pencil crayon from Jillian, telling me to come to her room. I figured that she'd gotten in late, when I was asleep, and the thought of her going out was reassuring. She looked washed out, and skinnier than ever, which I knew she'd take as a compliment. She hugged me tightly.

"I can't believe you're back," she said.

"Of course," I said, "did you think I was going to stay there?"

"How was Israel?"

"How was New York?"

We both started laughing.

"You go first," I said.

"New York was good. I love the city. I've always wanted to live there, did I tell you?"

I shook my head.

"Such a great music scene, just so stimulating and inspiring. I really missed you though. I wrote you a song."

"You did?"

"Yeah. The doctor's news wasn't the greatest, but I'm still going to see another specialist here."

"Tell me what he said."

"She. And not now. I want to play you the song first. There's no way I could get through this, or anything without you. It's called 'Haven.'"

She took out her acoustic guitar and handed me a piece of paper with the lyrics written out in lime green and pink pencil crayons.

"I know you like to read them," she said.

Her voice was softer and sweeter than I'd ever heard it.

> *I was walking around this city*
> *Drowning in self pity*
> *And then I thought of you*
> *I thought I'd built myself a haven*
> *But I was just a slave to*
> *The life that I wish I had*
>
> *Chorus: There's so much I collected*
> *But all I did was resurrect*
> *A past I would rather leave behind*
>
> *You're my haven*
> *And you've been saving*
> *Me from the moment you moved in*
>
> *I used to be so sentimental*
> *But now I try to be more gentle*
> *We give each other freedom*
> *But all my fears, you can see them*
> *And you know how to be right here when I need you*
> *Chorus*

Oh, I miss you when you're far away
I wish that you could stay here always
I know there's things you need to see and do
But I need you too
And together we can conquer anything
Chorus

I couldn't stop myself from crying.

"No one's ever written me a song before," I said.

She came over and sat beside me on her floor. She put her arm around me.

"Well, no one's ever loved you this much."

I laughed and gave her the keychain from Amuka.

She examined it and looked at me. "Aren't you supposed to give this to Naftali?"

"Don't worry, I have one for him too."

She snorted. "And they knew this on the trip?"

"No, I just told them I needed an extra one just in case. They didn't ask any questions."

Jillian laughed. I took out my phone and captured her, hear head thrown back, one of her eyeteeth caught in her bottom lip. She was so magnetic.

"I haven't filmed you in so long," I said. "Why don't I make a video for this song?"

"I have a better idea," she said grinning. "I have this artist friend, Johnny. He's a guitarist too. He has this tattoo place on Queen West, and he does such beautiful, fine line stuff, all delicate like Winter Stone. We can get the word 'haven' tattooed."

"Really small? And in a place no one could see it?"

"Maybe we could do it on our ribs. It's supposed to be painful but it's a beautiful, easily hidden place."

I didn't answer, and the next thing I knew she was texting Johnny.

She jumped up. "He says he has some free time, but we have to leave right now."

I stayed sitting her on carpet. "Look, let's just check it out, okay? Worst comes to the worst, we won't do it. You've been so focused on all of this conversion stuff and school, and this trip to Israel sounded like it was intense. It sounds like it's brought up a lot of complicated feelings."

"It has," I said and got up reluctantly.

Johnny was tall, with shoulder length dark hair, blue eyes, and a dimple in his chin.

He had colourful, full sleeve tattoos on his pale, marble looking skin. He was wearing a Ramones t-shirt with the sleeves cut off, and when I told him I loved them, he asked me what my favourite song of theirs was.

"'I Don't Want to Grow Up'," I said, and he gave me a big smile.

"I like her," he said to Jillian, who waved her finger at him.

"Careful, she's about to get engaged," she said.

He gave me a half smile. "Well, call me if that ever changes."

"Let's just look at some of your designs," I said, and he brought out his book.

Jillian chose our font quickly, a delicate, looping dark purple cursive. We both got it on our left sides, because Jillian said, it was closer to our hearts.

"You're so cheesy," I said, rolling my eyes, but I was secretly touched.

He gave us the instructions for after care, and a

small bottle of aloe vera and witch hazel and sent us on our way.

Not long after we got home, Rabbi Brown called. My tattoo felt like it was burning my skin, so I walked to the freezer and grabbed a piece of ice and told myself I was being ridiculous.

I had a meeting with the rabbis in three days, he said. I thanked him and wrote down the date and time.

A few minutes later, Chaya called me squealing. "We're almost there," she said.

I felt like there was a balloon overfilling in my chest, and one more emotion would tip me into explosion.

I tried to tell Chaya what happened at her friend's house. I tried to give her specifics, but she gave me a lesson about *Lashon Hara* or evil speech. We were not allowed to gossip or slander anyone, even if what we were saying was true, and both of us were responsible if we did, she explained, both the teller and the listener.

I touched the bandage on my ribs gingerly.

She offered to drive me to the meeting, but I told her that Naftali would. She seemed surprised but she accepted it.

There was no wait this time.

Rabbi Brown led me into their room, and they all looked at me this time when I said hi.

They started with basic questions, what blessing do you say on watermelon and challah bread, and what I would do if I accidentally said the wrong blessing.

The rabbi who looked like Gandalf smiled at me.

"So, what did you think of Israel?"

"I felt it deeply. I saw and experienced a lot. Jerusalem felt otherworldly. It brought up feelings I didn't expect, like hearing someone sing 'Hamalach Hagoel Oti,' which reminded me of my father, and this beautiful, pure moment we once had. I don't know how much you know about my father," I said, choking on the words. "His real name is Aubrey ..."

Gandalf's blue eyes zeroed in on me.

"Of course we know who he is."

"It's hard when something positive comes up. I normally block those kinds of memories because if I don't, I'll talk to him again, I'll be that person who's so desperate for his attention and love that I'll do anything."

I looked down at my shoes and told them about Marlene and my tattoos.

"I felt so stupid that I didn't know. It's wrong that I have them, isn't it?"

Gandalf's eyes were now soft and grandfatherly.

"In the book of Vayikra, which is one of the five books of the Torah, it says that you cannot make any marks on yourself. This is something that even Jewish children know."

"The human body is God's creation," the rabbi sitting next to him said. "God is the original artist, so we try to protect it rather than damaging it in any way or mutilating it."

"You weren't born Jewish," Gandalf said, "so the laws that govern your life now didn't apply before. But, if you choose this life now, you have to live according to them. That means, that going forward, you are not to get any more."

I stared at him, and I wondered how he knew.

"I wish they were meaningless. They feel like they're part of who I am, but I feel guilty about that."

He looked at me. "Hannah," he said, gently, "we know who you are. It's not about being ashamed. These are parts of your body that you would have to cover now regardless.

"What you feel is tremendous conscience. This genuine feeling is a great gift. As Jewish people, we have the responsibility to be a light onto the nations. Don't forget this once you become Jewish."

They asked me to step outside for what felt like an hour and then told me to come back.

Rabbi Brown smiled at me on my way out. "You're ready for the test," he said. "Our secretary will contact you to set up a time."

I stepped outside the synagogue, my vision blurry.

"It's almost over," I told Naftali. "I just have to write the test."

He picked me up and swung me around the parking lot.

"I knew you could do it, babe. I'm so proud of you."

I felt dizzy. "You wouldn't believe how generous and kind they were to me."

"I totally would. They're the best at reading character, and they could see you. That's what I davened for this morning, by the way. I davened for them to see you like I see you, to see the real you, and how pure your intentions are."

I started crying.

I texted Jillian.

"So apparently it's almost time for my bat mitzvah."

MAZEL TOV she texted back

I'd heard rumours of the conversion test being hundreds of pages long.

I texted Chaya later to tell her, but she was not a great help when I asked her about it.

"I'm not allowed to tell you," was her answer whenever I tried to get a specific sense of what I should be studying.

I texted Iris and she texted me back right away.

> *I'll deny it if anyone ever asks me, but I checked and I do still have a copy. Someone else sent me theirs, so it's the least I could do. I'm afraid to forward it to you in case it gets traced to me. Come over tomorrow night. Avrumi will have Victoria and I can print it for you, all eighty-five pages.*

The test was to be written in the same synagogue that I met the rabbis in, and it was open book, which meant that I could use any of the prayer books or Torah translations that were available.

"You know that the test is just a formality, right? If you're writing it, you're as good as in."

"If that's true, it's a ridiculously long formality," I said, and she shrugged.

"Hey, no one said they make it easy. But you know what they say, anything worth having ..."

"Yeah, yeah, yeah."

She hugged me and told me she was proud of me, and I almost cried again.

"The conversion process is long, but it will be worth it, trust me."

That night she sent me a text that said: *Don't get frustrated. It's going to happen, and soon, I promise you. You got this, sister.*

I showed it to Naftali.

"That's so sweet," he said. "She must really love you."

"I love her," I said. "I've always wanted a sister."

He bent down and kissed me. "Everything is going to start happening now. Are you ready?"

"I think so," I said, and felt myself smiling tentatively.

"Good," he said, grinning. "I've been ready for a while."

CHAPTER TWENTY-FIVE

I STOOD NERVOUSLY pacing outside the changing room belonging to the *mikveh*. I'd followed all the instructions that Chaya had emailed me. It helped with the endless worry that I was making a mistake, that I wasn't good enough for the world I wanted to be part of.

I'd scrubbed the nail polish off my finger and toenails and checked that there wasn't even a tiny piece remaining. "Nothing," Chaya had written, "should separate your body from the holiness of the experience." I'd washed my hair with a mild shampoo so that there would be no soap residue. I brushed the knots out of my hair and made sure there was no extra body hair sticking to me. I even used a Q-tip with peroxide on my ears and bellybutton. I wasn't wearing any make up or jewellery. I took out my contact lenses, so everything was a little blurry, which seemed right somehow. I was wrapped in a large, worn blue towel. I expected Chaya to inspect me but instead she just waved me in.

"Come on," she whispered. "We don't want to keep the rabbis waiting."

Chaya led me into the *mikveh* room. The bath itself was below, down a very short flight of stairs. The rabbis stood at a distance, on a platform a floor above that was surrounded by a railing. They had their backs to me, but I still looked up at them. "Hi."

The head rabbi answered me.

"Do you know the rewards and punishments for all the different mitzvot?"

"I think so."

"Do you understand that once you do this, you'll be Jewish, and the rest of your life will be different?" He paused. "Do you understand everything that means?

"I think so."

"Do you promise to give your children a Jewish education?"

"Yes."

"When you go into the *mikveh*," he said slowly, "you will dunk once, come up and say a *bracha*, the *bracha* for immersing. It's right there on the wall in Hebrew, and if you need, in English. You will dunk again and then say a different blessing, this time *shehichiyanu* because you are experiencing something new. After that you will dunk a third time. Are you ready, Hannah?"

My legs were shaking.

"I'm ready."

The rabbis turned their backs, and I stood with my feet close to the edge, still wearing my towel.

"Don't worry," Chaya whispered. "Their backs will be turned the whole time. They just have to check that your head is fully immersed." And then, she repeated: "Don't worry." Her smile was lopsided.

I looked up at the rabbis and saw the head rabbi putting on a thin black belt that he wrapped around his waist. A *gartel*, I remembered from something I'd read.

I inched in slowly, dropping my towel right by the edge. The water was surprisingly deep and warm. It was rainwater. I tried to drop in deep enough that every part of my body was covered.

My thoughts drifted to my childhood. There was no running water in the cabin so in the summer we bathed in the lake. We used handmade bars of soap that smelled like peppermint and rosemary. I loved swimming and staying submerged until my lungs hurt.

I didn't want to come up now. I bobbed slowly to the surface. I had memorized the *bracha, al hatvila*, on immersion. I whispered it at first, then said it loudly enough for everyone to hear.

"Again," I heard Chaya say.

I held my breath and submerged myself again. I felt my calves touching the mosaic bottom of the pool. Relief filled my muscles. I gasped when I burst through the surface of the water. I said the second *bracha*, this time with more confidence.

"Go on," Chaya said. "One more dunk."

I kept my eyes open this time. I wanted to remember what the pool looked like. I wanted to tell Naftali and Jillian. I counted to sixty and came up. I sputtered a little and asked Chaya to bring me the towel. It was over.

Chaya was smiling more brightly than I'd ever seen.

She led me back to the change room. I started to put on the black dress I'd been wearing before, but Chaya shook her head. "You need to wear new clothes."

I took out a second dress, a dark green one out of my bag. It had long sleeves and was covered in tiny white flowers. I'd been waiting for the right situation to wear it. Chaya led me to the rabbi's office. "They're going to give you your Hebrew name now."

I'd thought about this all night. Chana Esther was what Jillian and I had discussed, but I thought about my father, who had taught me a little about Judaism in his own strange way. I thought about my artist great grandmother, and how I felt when I was in Jerusalem. Her name was Brocha, which was the Yiddish pronunciation of *bracha*. I knew I wouldn't tell my father.

"Can I choose three names?" I asked them.

"You can choose as many names as you want."

"Chana Esther Brocha," I said, and I felt the room vibrate with warmth as they gave me my new name.

"*Mazel tov*," Chaya shouted and gave me a big hug.

I looked at the rabbis and tried to absorb all the love and care I was feeling.

Naftali came to pick me up, and he squeezed my hand. "How are you feeling?"

"I don't feel like a different person," I said slowly. "I feel like parts of myself that were always there, but were undefined have come together, like tiny beads that were scattered under my skin have all floated to the surface. Now I can make a necklace that everyone can see, but I always knew it was in me. I hope in time, it'll feel more real than it does right now."

He nodded. "I'm sure it's a lot to absorb."

He put his hand on my lower back and led me to his car.

We sat side by side in the front seats.

He reached over and kissed me, right there in the parking lot.

I pulled back and started singing MC Hammer's "Can't Touch This."

He stared at me. "Are you serious?"

I arranged my face into the most neutral expression I could.

"I mean, of course, I'm a bas Yisrael now . . ."

He took a deep breath. "Okay, I respect that . . .

I laughed. "I'm kidding. Well, technically I am, but I don't actually know. I want to be able to kiss you in public and not worry. I want to do other things too . . ."

He smiled.

When we got to his building's underground parking, he found a spot that was in a dark corner.

"Should we wait and go all the way upstairs? Or do you want to just go into the backseat?"

I kissed him. "Right here, obviously."

"Don't worry about anyone driving or walking in, it's 2 in the afternoon, and I have a feeling I'll be really fast."

"I'm a lucky woman," I said and peeled off my tights.

He was fast, less than five minutes I guessed, but he spent twenty minutes going down on me which made up for it. My heart was racing, and I was trying to be as quiet as possible in case someone heard us.

"That was so amazing," I said.

"Good, but don't worry, we're just getting started with the celebrating."

He moved back into the front seat and took out a package of wet wipes. He wiped his hands and face. "Just getting cleaned up for what's coming next."

I pulled the mirror down so I could put on some eyeliner and lipstick. My hair was still damp from the *mikveh* so I ran my fingers through it to try to make it dry faster.

He led me inside, past the lobby, and into the elevator.

We walked up to his front door and he got down on one knee.

"Hannah, I knew I loved you way before I was brave enough to tell you."

He pulled a ring out of his pocket.

"Wait, is this happening right now? In the hallway?"

He laughed. "Why wait anymore? This one is the one from my family. The stone is an heirloom, it belonged to my Bubby."

It was a platinum ring with a big, shiny square shaped diamond in the middle.

"It's beautiful," I said, staring at it.

"I asked Jillian to help me with the design. She knows your taste."

"Wait, Jillian knew and didn't tell me? How long ago was this?"

"A couple of months ago. Turns out, she's good at keeping a secret."

I thought about Jillian's health and cringed.

"Oh, I'm supposed to say yes now, aren't I?"

He laughed. "Only if you want to."

"I want to," I said, and kissed him.

He kissed me back.

He started opening his front door. "There's some people inside that want to celebrate with us."

CHAPTER TWENTY-SIX

NAFTALI BURST THROUGH the door, holding my hand.

"She said yes," he said, and there were shouts of *mazel tovs*. I scanned the living room, slowly, taking in who was there.

Jillian ran up to me first and squeezed me into a hug that reminded me of an episode of *Power Puff* girls we watched one night when we got high. She was wearing a lime green dress that was swimming on her, even with a belt cinched tightly across her waist. She had dark circles under her eyes, and her cheeks were flushed. Her hands felt hot when I held them, and I wondered if she had a fever. Her eyes had a wild, slightly glazed look, and I was tempted to blow off the party to take her home.

Iris came up to me next. "I'm so happy for you, and I'm so proud of you for getting through this," she said, and I realized that I couldn't leave but I held onto to Jillian with my left hand.

"I couldn't have done it without you," I told Iris.

"Please, it's what family does. Very soon, we'll be family for real."

Her daughter Victoria stood shyly behind her. I still

hadn't met her, and I got emotional when I hugged her, and she called me "Auntie Hannah."

She was tall and beautiful, a perfect mix of Iris and Avrumi. She smiled with her lips closed, and when she talked, I noticed she had bright pink braces.

Devorah, Max, and their oldest daughter Aidy and oldest son Shmuel came to say *mazel tov* next. Max and Shmuel's blue ties matched Devorah and Aidy's blue dresses, and they all had big smiles and said *mazel tov* in unison.

In the corner, stood Shaindy, who was holding her baby, and Avrumi, who was staring out the back window. Jack stood close to him, but he was facing us. He waved and smiled. I saw Malka, standing next to a woman I'd never met before. Naftali took my arm, and we walked over to them. He introduced us quickly.

Malka was more relaxed than I'd ever seen her. Naomi, he said, was his mother's closest friend. I told her I was happy to finally meet her. Naomi was tall, with short silver hair. She was wearing a long, shiny plum coloured jacket over shiny matching pants.

"We're a family full of outliers," she told me. "You'll fit in great."

She hugged me, and they both looked emotional. Just behind them was a slim woman wearing a navy dress. I felt dizzy when I realized it was my mother. I pulled Naftali close and whispered through gritted teeth. "You invited my mom?"

He looked panicked.

"Jillian did. I know she knows more about those things than I do, and she seemed to think it was a good idea, so …"

I hadn't seen her in almost two years.

My mother was standing beside the living room table. There were fruit salads, tea sandwiches, and mini quiches, muffins, crackers, and cheese and drinks that included Perrier, iced tea, and a few bottles of white wine.

My mother had put exactly one whole wheat cracker and two cheese cubes on a plate, and she had one of the bottles of wine beside her.

"Do you want me to get you a corkscrew, Mom?"

Naftali introduced himself before she could answer. "Mrs. McKillop," he said, "it's so nice to finally meet you."

I saw my mom's eyebrows arch and her eyelashes flutter when he told her I was beautiful, and he couldn't believe how much I looked like her. She'd always gotten along better with men, and when it came to women, Naftali could turn a glacier into the tiniest, softest ice cube.

"We're so happy you could make it," he said.

He led me into the kitchen.

"That wasn't so bad, right?"

Devorah popped out from behind us. "I just came to get some water," she said. And then in a sing song voice: "Ooh, and while I'm here, show me the ring." I held out my hand. "Oh Nafs, it's so beautiful. Bubby would have loved this."

Naftali smiled and looked at me. "I think she would have loved Hannah too. Right, D?"

Devorah hesitated. "Uh huh," she said brightly, and when he turned around to talk to Aidy, she leaned in and said: "My grandmother was a very conservative woman. Naftali could do no wrong, and neither could Avrumi, at least before he married Iris and then the whole scandal happened. She was a lot more critical of women. She would have been tugging your skirts down over your knees or grilling you about your background. But yeah, I guess aside from that, she would have liked you."

Devorah turned to Shaindy and wrapped her in a tight hug, and Shaindy mouthed *mazel tov* to me, then turned to Devorah and started talking to her.

A few minutes later Shaindy asked if she could use Naftali's bedroom to nurse her baby.

Naftali looked nervous.

"You know what, it's such a disaster in there, I'm just going to organize things a little. Why don't you wait a second, and Hannah will come get you, okay?"

"Okay," Shaindy answered, but she didn't look happy.

I walked up to the bedroom, Naftali trailing close behind me. I wondered what he was afraid of Shaindy seeing, condom wrappers in the garbage? Dirty underwear on the floor?

When I saw my father sitting on the bed, I thought I was hallucinating.

He looked like a mad prophet from an ancient oil painting.

He smelled exactly the same, a mix of body odour, tiger balm, and weed. His long, sandy blond hair and beard had patches of grey and white. He was wearing a worn navy gingham shirt unbuttoned so that the top of his chest was showing. There was a thumb sized moth hole just below the pocket. A younger woman sat behind him. She had short blond hair, cut into a bowl style bob, like a five-year-old's, and her face was covered in freckles. She was wearing a long flowing pink sari skirt that tied in a knot on her hip, and a white tank top that stopped just above her belly button. Her pink nipples poked through the thin fabric.

I started backing away, out of the room, but Naftali's hand was on my shoulder.

"I'm Mel," she said and turned to Naftali to hug him first. I was aware of Mel's nipples pressed up against Naftali's thin shirt. She hugged me, not nearly as closely, and then got up and sat in my father's lap. He slipped his arm across her waist casually while Naftali looked away. I kept staring.

My dad was holding a photo in his left hand and murmuring something about precious memories.

"Hi, Daddy," I said tentatively, and I realized that my hands were shaking. Naftali looked worried.

My father nodded at me and then avoided eye contact.

"I found this the other day. Your mother must have taken it. You know how I feel about photos. You were darling then and now look at you, all grown up."

He held up the photo so I could see it.

I was sitting on a purple plastic potty, completely naked except for a giant pink straw hat that had belonged to my grandmother. I must have been two.

I snatched it from him and held it against my chest.

"You have spiders in here," he said a few minutes later. "A grey one with a handful of babies. Seems appropriate, doesn't it? Marriage leading to nurturing. Nature is always the best teacher."

He held up his small broccoli quiche, then stabbed at it with one of the gold plastic forks. "See this?" he said, turning to Mel. "This is a broccolini, a hybrid of broccoli and Chinese kale. These people are supposed to keep kosher."

"Of course it's kosher," Naftali said quickly, "we ordered it from a kosher restaurant."

My dad laughed. "This is a clear example of *kilayim*, a forbidden mixture." He looked at Naftali with a smug smile. "My daughter likely doesn't know what it is, but I expect that you would."

Naftali shook his head. "She did say you were a philosopher. I'm not sure this qualifies as *kilayim*, but that's interesting."

"I've been learning for years," my father said, his voice rising with indignation. "Longer than you've been alive. I used to have to drive across BC for the community for hours, listening to cassette tapes of rabbis learning. I spent all my time in jail reading the Torah and the Talmud, regretting the time I spent on other religions."

I felt my body temperature rise. I wanted to sit down, but not here. I started backing out of the room.

Mel caught my eye. "He said you wouldn't stay long," she said, and I turned away and kept walking.

Melissa Jonas, I realized a few minutes later. Her family had been part of the Tribe, and she was around five years younger than me, which made her sixteen or seventeen now. I thought about the way her hair was cut, the way she didn't wear a bra. I could feel the vomit rising in my throat.

"We have to go outside," I whispered to Naftali.

We were quiet in the elevator until we got to the lobby.

"Let's go for a walk."

He took my hand. "Whatever you want," he said, and we started walking. A block later I found myself sitting on the sidewalk, and Naftali stopped and sat down heavily beside me.

"Do you know my father used to give lectures, in his Friday night men's series, about things like Ancient Greek culture and how back then it was normal to have sex with underage kids? My half-brother, Jason, who used to go with some of the teenage boys, told me about it just before he and his mom left the Tribe. Our dad questioned why the age of consent is seventeen or eighteen, when in some places it's twelve or thirteen. He asked them why it matters how old a person is, biologically, because what matters is how adult they are in their souls. He told them that people who call themselves victims are manipulative, that if you enjoy it, it can't be bad. And he told them he always knew how to judge that."

"Wow ... that's unbelievable," he said, shaking his head.

"Naftali," I said, my voice breaking, "everybody knew what he was doing. Everyone there knew what was happening to us, and no one did anything. I know the women were victims too, but they weren't little kids. My mom refused to have more kids with him, which I guess is better than some of these other women who kept giving him more, but she didn't protect me. The only reason the police got involved was because a couple of women died after childbirth. My dad was a big believer in natural birth, and my mom and the other Nurturers acted like midwives even though they didn't know what the fuck they were doing. My dad had all these natural 'cures' like olive oil and apple cider enemas and having them squat while they were in labour over a pot of hot coffee, while they drank castor oil, but it didn't get too crazy until he started performing what he said were emergency C sections himself. Within a week two women and one of the babies died. Suddenly the police and then children's services were everywhere, and my mom and I ran away."

I couldn't stop talking. I didn't feel better, but I hoped I would when I got it all out of my system.

"My mom pretended that she didn't know anything. I think she convinced herself too. I remember once, we saw this guy, who was like thirteen or fourteen, and this girl who was my age, maybe seven at the time, doing some pretty sexual stuff. We also saw some young boys together, some girl and her dolls, and the girl was saying things that sounded like my dad. I was a kid, I couldn't have done anything, but she could have."

I felt my voice break. "At the trial, she refused to come with me. I had to go alone, with my crown appointed attorney because she and my stepdad refused to pay for a private one. She wasn't there physically or mentally. I had to go to court and give answers on the stand, get examined and cross examined. They start out friendly at first, they ask you about your hobbies, ask you gentle questions about the Tribe and your life, and then you start doubting yourself. Did you remember right? Are you exaggerating? Are you lying because you're angry with someone? Was it really as bad as everyone said? Where were the adults? I think my mom knew that this was all going to become a matter of public record. Some of the people she knew growing up knew she moved to BC, but they didn't know she'd gotten involved with him. I think she was embarrassed for people to know that she was one of his followers. Maybe she was worried she'd be tried or found guilty too, of being complicit, like an accessory or something. The judge ruled that the women were victims too, but she couldn't have known that. I just don't understand these women who give up everything, their kids, their friends, everyone in their lives, just to keep supporting him. It makes me so angry."

I took a deep breath. "He can't be at our wedding."

"Of course. I'm sorry he was here today."

"In his world, he is never guilty or wrong. He'll be asking you for money and guilting you into giving it to him. If we ever had a kid, he'd be telling everyone that he's a grandfather, telling us how great he is with kids. I've seen him do it. You either have a relationship with him, where you believe everything he says, or you don't. I've spent the last three years trying to get his voice out of my head, and now even if I sometimes miss the concept of having a dad, I can't, I don't want to."

"Okay, we'll make sure he's nowhere near us. Not just at the wedding."

"Good. But right now, you need to get them out of the apartment. It's our bedroom and just picturing him there ..."

"Yeah. Of course, I'll take care of it."

"How?"

"Don't worry about it. Let's just go back, unless you want to wait here, and I can come get you after they've left."

"Yeah," I said quietly, "I'll wait here."

I thought about Jillian. I'd spent the last two nights at Chaya's house, and both nights Jillian had had seizures. It was a side effect of one of the new medications she was given in New York.

One night she found her sheets and pajamas soaked with urine.

"It was so embarrassing," she said. "And cold."

The next night, she woke up on the floor, with bruises or cuts on her face or arms from her bedside table, with her lamp and tons of pencils falling on her. They both started with a cramping in her throat and stomach. She felt the muscles in her throat clench, like knots she couldn't untie.

It felt like I'd been sucker punched when she told me. I couldn't believe it happened when I wasn't there.

I texted her now.

> *How are u? Still here? How are u feeling?*
> *where else would I be?*
> *I'm worried, I wrote back. How are u feeling now?*
> *Like I don't want to steal your*
> *Ur not. This is insane. I'm worried. U look beautiful but sick .*
> *Sounds about right.*
> *Where are you?*
> *Don't ask. Coming back upstairs in 5.*
> *K*

I heard my phone beep. Naftali was texting me.

> *Babe, you OK? He wrote. Don't worry, they left, w/out a scene. Just told them the party was getting bigger and moving over to my parents' house. Figured they wouldn't want to come.*

Good, I texted back.

I was still sitting on the sidewalk when he came to get me, and he pulled me up slowly.

"It was my worst nightmare having him here, in our room." I said quietly.

He looked down. "I'm sorry."

"It's not your fault. I don't know if I told you enough about how badly he'd behave. If we ever …"

He smiled a little. "What, have kids of our own?"

"Yeah. I mean, I'm still scared to, but I might want to, one day. And if we do …"

"Of course, he won't go anywhere near them. We'll get a restraining order if we have to, which probably wouldn't be hard. I'll protect you. I'll do whatever you need me to do."

We started walking and he looked at me.

"We're getting married," he said, as if the weight of it had just dawned on him.

"I know," I said, trying to let the weight of everything fully sink in.

CHAPTER TWENTY-SEVEN

THE GOLDWATERS WANTED a fast engagement. We were both graduating from our program, with our last classes at the end of April, and Naftali wanted to have the wedding in May.

"Oh yeah, that's totally normal," Jillian said. "Three months is about average, six months at most. I know some very religious types who do it in three or four weeks."

Ever since I told Naftali about her seizures, he insisted that she sleep on our fold out couch.

During the day, she either went home or to the studio to work on her music or to her doctors' appointments downtown.

On her second night, we woke up to the thud of her falling off the bed. We saw her arms thrashing and her head smash against the floor. I ran over to her and held her and put my hand under her head. Naftali gently held her legs which were starting to thrash. I stroked her forehead. Her eyes rolled back in her head, and her eyelashes flickered like centipede legs.

She came to a few minutes later, pale and struggling to sit up. For a few more minutes she didn't know where she was, and she didn't recognize us.

We helped her up, and I helped her change into dry pajamas while Naftali changed her sheets.

Her body looked so fragile. I promised her I would go with her to her next appointment, and she finally agreed to let me. She also promised she'd keep staying with us.

I called Esther, and she said that they were worried about her too, but she was relieved that she had such great friends. "We keep asking her to stay here," she said, "but she doesn't want to. May God bless you and Naftali for your generosity."

I'd never felt so powerless.

Naftali surprised me by asking if his mom and Naomi could come by that afternoon to visit us.

I mentioned it to Jillian, and she finally agreed to go visit her parents.

Malka and Naomi came over an hour early, while we were still cleaning up. Naftali had two garbage bags in his hands when they walked up to the door.

Malka was wearing a long sleeved white and black Breton shirt and a knee length black jean skirt. Her hair was tied back in a ponytail, and she was wearing a Raptor's hat.

She laughed when she noticed me staring. "I found this at the house, I think it was Naftali's. I'm more of a Knicks' fan. I wanted to check on something at the factory, so we were here, anyway."

Naftali offered to make us tea, and I arranged some dried fruit, nuts and crackers on a tray.

Malka waved them away. "We've just eaten, don't worry. We just wanted to talk to both of you. And have a cigarette, if that's okay."

"Of course, mom." Naftali got up and brought out a heavy, crystal ashtray.

"You don't mind, Hannah?"

I shook my head, knowing that it didn't matter if I did.

"We're so happy for both of you," Naomi said. "Hannah, I know we've just met, but I've known Naftali and Devorah and Avrumi all their lives. It makes me emotional to see how much you both love each other. It's evident to everyone."

"That's really lovely to hear," I said.

"We just wanted to ask," Naomi said gently, "if it would be all right with both of you if I attended the wedding with Malka."

"Of course," I said, "why wouldn't it be?"

"I haven't told her any details," Naftali said.

Malka shook her head. "My son, so predictable. Anything to avoid complication."

"It's okay, Mrs. Goldwater. I understand. Of course, I'd want you both at our wedding."

Malka looked at me intensely. "You can call me Malka, dear. And I appreciate it. Neither my other son, nor my daughter wanted Naomi at their weddings."

Naomi leaned forward. "Not true. I was at Avrumi's first wedding. Neither he nor Iris seemed to mind then."

Malka snorted. "A lot of good that does us now."

Naftali laughed. "Sometimes life is weird. You just never know."

"Would it cause problems with Jack, if you were there together?"

Malka shook her head. "You really have told her nothing, haven't you?"

He shrugged. "I told you."

He turned to me. "My parents were never in love with each other. My mom grew up in New York with a very religious and wealthy family. To get her inheritance, they expected her to marry and have kids. She and Naomi met in seminary, but there was no question in their community that they couldn't be out. My mom turned twenty-five, which for the community back then, was like forty-five, and she finally agreed to marry my dad. She was always open with him about what the situation was, and he was okay with it, because it came with wealth, and the chance to be in other relationships as long he was private about it."

He stopped. "Am I leaving anything out, mom?"

Malka smiled. "No, not at all."

"My dad was from Toronto, so they moved here. Naomi got married too, but they still visited each other every year and stayed in each other's houses. Naomi got divorced a few years ago, but for some reason, my mom stays married to my dad."

"What do you mean for some reason? First of all, I stayed with your dad for too long. Now he's entitled to a lot of my assets, and if I left him, I'd lose money. Second, just because I've never been interested in him doesn't make him a bad guy. He's actually a pretty decent father."

Naftali looked at me and almost laughed. "I guess it depends on whom you compare him to."

I rolled my eyes and pretended to punch him. "Well, if you compare him to my dad, I bet he starts looking really good."

I looked at Malka and Naomi. "Sorry about my father the other night. I didn't invite him. I wouldn't have."

Malka waved me away again. "Hannah, you have nothing to be sorry for. We're not responsible for who our parents are. Besides, I think your bodyguard did a pretty good job of getting him out of here."

I looked at Naftali with pride. "Yeah, he did, while I had a meltdown outside. I had no idea my dad was here. We're not planning to see him again. I don't even want him at our wedding."

Malka nodded. "Good."

"It's your decision to make," Naomi started to say, but Malka shook her head.

"It's the right decision. Why should we encourage her to do anything else?"

On their way out, I hugged them both. "Thank you both for wanting to be at our wedding."

Malka looked at me approvingly. "Marriage can be a great thing, Hannah, if it's based in love and partnership. But once you get in, it's harder than you can imagine to get out, so you have to be sure. A million years ago, when Naomi and I were still young, it wasn't legally an option for us. The truth is, I do think about divorce now. Now that my youngest is getting married, and there'll be no one at home, it's starting to feel possible, if still complicated because of the Orthodox community."

"Anyway, if you don't mind, look over the prenup before you sign it. If I'd been smarter, I would have made Jack sign one. But this isn't just about protecting Naftali. It's about protecting you too, and if you have them, your future children."

Naftali looked at me nervously as he closed the door behind them.

I sat down on the couch, and he stood beside me.

"How do you feel about a prenup?"

"I don't know. Okay, I think. It makes sense. I get why she has regrets. Thanks for getting them to open up to me. Your mom is a different person when Naomi's around."

He nodded. "Yeah, she is. She's so much happier. It's never bothered me, except for the fact that she's unhappy whenever they're not together."

"Thanks for letting me talk about my dad so much," I said. "I hate talking about it, but I needed to. I've never talked to anyone else the way I talk to you."

He put his arms around my waist. "Good thing we're getting married, huh?"

I smiled. "Yeah, probably."

"Probably?"

"Definitely. A hundred percent."

I walked to the kitchen and poured myself a glass of water.

"Hey, Nafs?"

"Yeah, babe?"

"Don't tell anyone about my dad."

"I would never. To be honest, my dad loves to research people, and we always joked that he should have been a private investigator. It's possible that he knows, after seeing your dad in real life, but knowing him, he'd never tell anyone, and he'd only respect you more for how much you've overcome. My mom has sharp instincts, but I can tell she doesn't know the half of it. My parents don't really talk to each other, so if he does know, he wouldn't have told her. The only person he might have told is Iris, but she can keep a secret. You can tell them one day, if you want to, but you never have to."

He kissed my forehead.

"Okay," I said, knowing full well I would never.

CHAPTER TWENTY-EIGHT

W E GOT MARRIED quickly, even by Goldwater standards. When you were a Goldwater, people stopped time. They changed their schedules. They worked through the night for you.

My dress was floor length and made of white silk. The sleeves, which were added by Malka's dressmaker, had tiny crystal stars and flowers embroidered into them. The veil was long and matched the sleeves. The Hebrew words, *Ani L'Dodi V'Dodi Li*, I am to my beloved, as my beloved is to me, were embroidered right down the centre.

For a few nights after I got engaged, Jillian and I watched episodes of *Say Yes to the Dress*. It was the magical thinking that I was addicted to the most, that something as simple as finding the right ball gown could lead to self-acceptance and better relationships with everyone in the bride's life.

I didn't get to choose my own dress. It was gifted to me by all the Goldwater women at a special engagement tea they threw for me.

We sat in their gold living room, holding antique teacups and picking at low carb biscotti when they told me they had a surprise for me, and their dressmaker wheeled it out on a mannequin. "Of course, we'll have to fit it on you," she said, and I was whisked off, half expecting mice with needles and threads and tape measures to jump out from somewhere behind her.

Malka offered to lend me some family heirlooms, including an heirloom hair clip with two small lilies, decorated with tiny diamonds and white pearls, and the delicate diamond and sapphire tiara that both Iris and Devorah had worn on their wedding days. I sent a selfie to Jillian of myself in the pinned dress, wearing both the tiara and the clip, and a heavy pearl necklace with a diamond clasp.

!!!!! she texted back.

> *You look beautiful. It is a lot though. You need a sceptre and some cake to throw at peasants. Oh there's gonna be a massive cake,* I texted back. *They actually want my opinion on that.*

In the end, we decided to have a massive croquembouche, which worked for the Goldwaters who loved all things French. I hated cake, especially when they told me that it had to be dairy free, because they were serving meat at the meal.

Malka chose the venue, a decadent banquet hall in Thornhill, where Avrumi and Devorah had gotten married, which could hold more than five hundred people.

I struggled to imagine more than ten people I wanted to invite, but everyone kept telling me that weddings were for the family.

All Naftali said was that he didn't want to have it in a synagogue.

"We won't be able to dance together," he said, "because you can't have mixed male and female dancing in an Orthodox shul. Plus if Jillian is well enough to sing, it would be a problem because of *Kol Isha*, you know, the rule that Orthodox men aren't supposed to hear women singing."

Jillian had promised to write us a love song, to sing Haven and Etta James' "At Last" and Rachel Platten's song "Speechless" as our first dance together.

"Are the men in your family going to have a problem if she sings?"

He shrugged. "My dad won't care. Max won't care. The only person it'll bother is Avrumi, and someone can warn him ahead of time so he can go outside. The mixed dancing will bother him too. Knowing him, he'll probably leave as soon as he can. That's why I asked Rabbi Brown to marry us. The last thing I want is for Avrumi to offer. Imagine how awkward it would be."

I almost laughed trying to imagine it. I nodded.

Malka and Naomi offered to organize all the food. They mentioned a lot of things and I nodded along, from centrepieces to benchers and parting gifts for guests.

The chuppah itself was going to be covered, floor to ceiling in white flowers, roses, baby's breath, and lilies. They wanted to do smaller versions at the tables.

Naftali gently elbowed me in the ribs. "You're sure you're okay with everything?"

"Of course."

I thought about Shaindy, who'd told me a few days before that Avrumi had planned their entire wedding in two weeks. "The food, the guest list, the flowers," she said, checking them off on her unpolished fingernails. "I didn't have to do a thing. He chose classic stuff, you know, white tulips, people from our community, grilled organic chicken and grassfed steak. I never liked the idea of having all that attention on me. You know that moment, when you walk to the chuppah with your mom and dad, and everyone stands and looks at you? It's my idea of a nightmare. I just bought the first dress I tried on. You're so lucky that Malka had your dress made for you."

"The truth is, I was never a little girl who dreamed about my wedding. All of these things are wonderful, but they're just details. I'm actually excited to get married."

Devorah dropped by with a pair of shoes that she wanted me to wear on my wedding day. Even the box looked expensive, with embossed silver writing.

"They're Louboutin, darling. If you're going to become a Goldwater, you might as well look like us."

They were white leather and high, with swirls and patterns and even two tiny hearts cut into the leather.

"Does your mom like them? Does she think they match with the dress?"

She laughed. "Who do you think designed the dress in the first place? My mom hates all this stuff."

I shrugged. "She always seems well dressed to me."

"Ask her, trust me. She'll give you a lecture on the difference between being a femme and feminine, if you're interested in hearing it."

"I am interested."

"Well, good for you," she said. "Listen, I saw the shoes, and they reminded me of you. The salesgirl called them luxurious hippie, like Florence Welsh, and they really are, both boho and ornate."

Jillian loved Florence Welsh.

"It's so generous of you," I said carefully.

I sat down and tried them on. They pinched my toes instantly, but they were beautiful. I was scared to look at the price.

"Devorah," I asked before she left. "Why does your mom's lifestyle bother you so much?"

She sighed. "It's not just me. It bothers a lot of people. It's like, there's a lot of things we're forbidden to do, but some are more tempting to some people than others. So one perspective is my mom is very progressive for living her truth. But another is that she's being lazy. We're all tempted to do all kinds of things, but some of us can control ourselves. She's our mom, she's our example. She should too."

I wanted to tell her that I knew about her and Jillian, but I didn't. I felt sad for her and the feeling surprised me.

"If her partner was a man, would you be happier?"

She sighed. "Maybe. It was hard growing up, seeing both of my parents with other people in private but acting like a happy, normal couple in public. It's exhausting to have to pretend. If you don't mind, I'd rather not talk about this anymore."

"Of course," I said. "Thanks again for the shoes. I just hope I'll be able to walk in them."

She laughed. "I'll help you practice. There's a strap up top here, see, that'll make it easier. And now we can move on to other things, like hair and makeup. I was thinking bronze, glowing skin, plump light pink lips, and soft pink cheeks. Like, natural, but better, you know?"

I nodded slowly.

"And an updo. Something chic to show off the tiara."

"I wanted to wear my hair down," I said, "since I'm going to have to cover it from now on."

"Trust me," she said, "this will look much more beautiful and appropriate."

I didn't trust her, but I knew I didn't have a choice but to pretend.

CHAPTER TWENTY-NINE

DEVORAH AND **S**HAINDY convinced me to fast on my wedding day. It was just a custom, Naftali said, but they convinced me, insisting that it added to the spiritual experience of the day.

I had bridal classes with Chaya, and he had a groom class with the Rabbi. Naftali called me after his class, and we secretly met in the ravine not far from his parents' house. It was 9:30 at night.

We made out for ten minutes, and he then he stopped. "I have to tell you what the rabbi taught me today."

"What?"

"It's a woman's right," he said, "and a husband's obligation to pleasure his wife. It's right in the Talmud. If a man doesn't perform his duties in a loving and satisfying way, the woman can divorce him."

"Seriously? I had to learn about the laws of Niddah in even more detail, and you got to learn about orgasms?"

"But your orgasms. Mine don't matter."

We both laughed.

It would be weird to wait until our wedding night.

"It's a bit of a conundrum," he said grinning, "because we want to wait, but I'm not supposed to waste any seed."

I offered to go down on him, but he shook his head. "As hard as that is to resist, I think we should. Besides, it's all about you, remember?"

"Oh, I remember."

The next day, Devorah took me shopping for wigs. We went into a women's basement store. She had wigs from all over the world, for thousands of dollars apiece.

"We can dye them anyway you want, from highlights to lowlights to full colour changes," she said. "We can also cut and style them for you."

She took a long, sandy brown wig and put it on me. Then she braided a piece from the front and pinned it to the top of my hair and took a curling iron and waved the bottom pieces.

She brought me a mirror, and I had to admit, it looked really good.

"A great *sheitel*," Devorah told me, "doesn't just perfectly match your natural hair colour and texture, it improves on it, so you looked better than ever. The idea is that no one can tell, it moves and looks and feels like regular hair, so people just think you look beautiful and marriage agrees with you."

She bought me two.

On the day of the wedding, I felt giddy and a little dazed from fasting.

Today, Chaya had told me, the gates of heaven were open to my prayers. Devorah had opened up her social media accounts so that everyone she knew could give me lists of people to pray for, people who were sick, people who wanted to find partners or have children, people who were struggling financially.

I didn't care anymore about what was supposed to

be done, the only person I wanted to pray for was Jillian. We knew for sure now that the cancer had come back. Jillian looked so tiny and exhausted, so stripped of her usual magic. Her skin was the colour of clay before it was fired in a kiln. The night before, she slept over at the Goldwaters'. Officially, she was my *shomeret*, the person who was supposed to guard me and protect me on my wedding day. Really though, we both knew that I was hers.

"I wish I'd never told my family," she said. "They always want to hear how I'm feeling or how I'm getting through it. The truth is, I don't know. I'm sitting and waiting for the next thing that the doctors tell me, these specialists who poke me and prod me in the most invasive ways."

I reached for her hand and all I felt was bone.

"When's your next radiation treatment?"

Jillian sighed and played with a cuticle on her thumb. "The day after the wedding."

"What's it like to get radiation?"

"It's always first thing in the morning, when it's still dark outside. All of us patients know each other by sight. I never remember their names. We have our own waiting area. Like an airport lounge, except instead of a great destination, you get to go to a treatment instead. Then you go inside these heavy steel doors. Every damn time they ask me for my ID. I feel like Reese Witherspoon when she got pulled over for drunk driving, like don't you know who I am?"

I didn't want to be able to laugh, but I did.

"The radiation itself is pretty fast. I get on the table and then they raise it. I close my eyes. My skin is marked with ink x's, and they use lasers. There are two techs in the room, and they're pretty efficient. They blast the cancer, I guess. Sometimes there's background music on. I like it better when it's quiet. I try not to think about what they're doing."

I saw her lips start to tremble. "When they lower the table, I feel like a kid, swinging my feet off a jungle gym. I just want to be a kid sometimes. Or a regular person in her twenties. I'm still so young, you know, what the fuck?"

"Do you want me to come with you?"

Jillian shook her head. "Yeah, right, I think you and Naftali will have other things to do."

"I know," I said "But you're just as important to me. He'll understand."

"No, don't worry. My mom will come or my sister. If you see me like that, I'll have to start seeing myself as a cancer patient and not as me. I don't want anyone to have to see me like this," she said a little more forcefully. "Tomorrow is your wedding. Tomorrow you're going to walk down the aisle, and I'm going to walk behind you and cry, and then later I'll sing "At Last," and you and Naftali are going to look at each other, all in love, and you're going to be so beautiful, and everyone is going to cry and be so happy for both of you."

"And you are going to get better," I told her just as forcefully. "Because you're my best friend and I need you. I don't want to do any of this without you."

She smiled at me. "I love you," she said.

"I love you more," I answered and watched her toss and turn for hours, talking quietly in her sleep.

The next day, when I woke up, I started praying.

Frida, the family's makeup artist, got to work on me when we got to the venue.

I blinked when I saw myself when she was finished.

"You look beautiful," Jillian said.

She was wearing a bright red dress and bronzer and almost looked like herself again.

Malka re-pinned a tiny piece of my hair that had come loose. Devorah yanked and then straightened a crease in the bottom of my dress.

"You look like a different person," Shaindy said, and Jillian glared at her.

Devorah put her arm around me. We stood side by side in front of the mirror.

"You're going to be great today," she said. She grabbed a tissue and dabbed underneath her eye. "I can't believe my little brother is getting married."

My mother suddenly burst into the room. "Hannah," she said, "turn around, I want to see your dress."

I felt self-conscious but did a small twirl.

"You look lovely, if a little overdone."

"I think she looks quite natural and very elegant," Malka said, and I smiled.

"Thanks, Malka."

I sat down and my mother sat down beside me. Somehow she'd found a bottle of kosher white wine, and she took out some plastic champagne flutes.

"Do you want something to drink?"

I shook my head.

"Oh, that's right, I read that Orthodox Jewish women fast on their wedding day."

She leaned in closer but didn't lower her volume. "I

read on the internet about a girl who fasted on her wedding and only ate right after the ceremony. She was a tiny slip of a girl, like your friend Jillian over there, and they gave her some fancy finger food, and she vomited all over herself and her dress. It was incredibly expensive too, and of course, she had nothing else to wear."

Iris and Victoria walked in. "*Mazel tov, Kallah*," Iris said, and gave me a huge hug. "I can't wait to dance with you."

Victoria looked at me with wide eyes.

"You're the most beautiful bride I've ever seen." she said.

I finally saw Naftali for the first time during the *Bedeken*. I was sitting on a gold chair, surrounded by all the women, and he danced over to me, surrounded by all the Goldwater men singing Hebrew wedding songs. My face was covered in my beautiful but thick lace veil. He lifted it up, as per the custom, to make sure he was getting the bride he wanted. Tears swam in his blue green eyes.

Devorah and Malka lead me into the hall where the ceremony was held. Malka and Jack walked Naftali down the aisle, and my mom walked with me, Jillian standing on my other side.

The ceremony was all in Hebrew. The rabbi made a blessing on the wine and passed the wine glass between Naftali's mom and my mom who was supposed to pass it to us almost took a sip. The rabbi looked alarmed, and I grabbed the glass away quickly and drank some. Then he gave us the seven special wedding blessings and told Naftali to place the ring on my index finger. When the ceremony was over, no one said "you can kiss the bride," so I stood there like an idiot until Naftali grabbed me and kissed me.

We were led down the hall into the *Cheder Yichud*, a special room for the bride and groom to be alone. We heard the door click locked behind us. We sat together on a black leather couch surrounded by plates of appetizers and bottles of water.

He kissed me again. "You look beautiful," he said.

He was wearing a navy suit with a white shirt. "You look pretty great yourself," I said.

He poured me a glass of water. "Here, drink something, you look a little faint."

I gulped down the whole bottle and asked for another.

"Go easy," he said gently and kissed me again.

"You know, a lot of people consummate their marriages in the Yichud room."

"Really?"

"Yeah. I mean if you want to. It's just we won't be alone again until the end of the night, you know with all the dinner and the dancing."

I wondered if I'd be able to take off my own dress. It felt like it had been sewn onto my skin. I thought about what my mother said. I imagined tearing it or staining it.

He reached over and kissed me. "Let's just make out," he said, and I kissed him back.

After a few minutes, he passed me a mini burger from the tray.

"Should we eat some of this?"

I nodded. "But first I want to give you something. I made it last week."

I pulled out my phone and showed him a video I'd made, a collage of images and conversations and moments in our relationship that I'd collected, some without him knowing.

"I want us to always be able to remember these things," I told him, and he looked emotional.

The rest of the night was a blur of dancing, speeches I could barely remember, including Naftali's and talking to guests.

My mom and stepdad made polite small talk and even danced a little.

I danced so wildly with Jillian and Iris that my hair came out of its updo. Naftali and I danced together and posed for pictures and walked around thanking people for coming. I lost track of Jillian for a while, and we found her, at the end of the night, smoking weed outside, her body limp and slumped against the railing.

"It's medicinal," she said, and I hugged her.

"Don't worry, you just need to rest," I said gently. "I'll call you an Uber."

Our room was full of champagne and white chocolate covered strawberries and mini cupcakes.

We took off our clothes and lay side by side on our backs on the plush king-sized bed.

"I'm worried about Jillian," I said quietly, and he nodded.

"I know, I was too. She doesn't look good."

"What are we going to do?"

"I'm sure my parents know specialists she hasn't seen. We can help; we just have to figure out how."

I reached over and kissed him. "I love you," I said. "Today was amazing."

He flashed his big smile, which was so full of love and genuine happiness.

"I love you," he said. "I think it was even better than I expected it to be."

"Do you mind if we just sleep?" I asked him.

"No, of course not, today was a huge day."

I checked my phone, to make sure that Jillian got home okay. I checked my email and found that my father had messaged me from a new address.

Dear Daughter,

> *I assume that my invitation got lost in the mail.*
>
> *I spoke with your mother, who seemed equally perplexed at the oversight. But be that as it may, I wanted to share with you my thoughts on getting married.*
>
> *There are many different kinds of connection. There is the romantic connection which you and this young man profess to feel, and I pray that the Divine Being blesses your union.*
>
> *There is the connection with your parents, and the connection with strangers among us, the ger, it says in the Torah, which means non-Jews. They add so much value, and it is well known that they are the superior choice of partner. If you don't know it now, you will find out. As Jews, we are commanded to honour our mothers and fathers. This commandment, the fifth of ten, comes right after the commandment to keep Shabbat because they are linked. It's hypocritical to keep Shabbat if you can't properly honour your parents. All things must be done in the right*

order. I wish you abundant blessings, Hannah.
Marriage leads to children, and there is no
greater gift than being a parent, even those who
resist giving me the honour I deserve. May you
merit to receive even a quarter of the connection
and admiration I've had.

I wanted to scream. It was so predictable, but there it was. Everything, including my wedding day was about him, even if he wasn't invited. I paced up and down until I was tired. I lay back down and curled up next to Naftali. I closed my eyes and tried to forget.

CHAPTER THIRTY

THE DAYS AFTER the wedding were a blur of *sheva brachot* and thank you notes. The tradition was to have dinner parties for six days after the wedding, where the seven wedding blessings were read out loud, and the couple was celebrated. The best blessing was the seventh one, where the guests wished love and friendship, companionship and harmony. I was touched when Jillian's mom offered to host one. She had Moroccan caftans for all of us to wear, including a white bridal one with gold beads for me and a white groom's one for Naftali.

Jillian was there too, pale but smiling, bringing us tea with fresh mint grown in her parents' garden. She told us that she'd helped her mom make us a special Moroccan marzipan dessert that their family only made for weddings and when children were born. My favourite was the one shaped like two lovebirds that they placed in the centre of the table. Naftali put it on his nightstand, and we took small bites of it when we got into bed that night. It tasted nutty and sweet, like candy with a fine, grainy texture.

Chaya and her husband hosted one, as did Moshe and his wife, who were friends of Naftali's, Malka and

Jack Goldwater, Devorah and Max, and finally, Avrumi and Shaindy. Avrumi as it turned out didn't show up to our wedding. They hosted a simple final party at their house with takeout from a local kosher shawarma restaurant with salads that Shaindy had made. The day after our wedding, Avrumi had texted Naftali a picture of the food he was eating, which it turned out was snuck out to him in a set of Tupperware by Shaindy, who left early because she said she had to take care of her kids. "Thank you for a meal fit for a king," he'd written.

Naftali had laughed so hard. "Sorry, I'm just picturing my mom's face, or oh God, Devorah's face, when they saw Shaindy sneaking out of there at 9 with a bunch of Tupperware. Iris told me that Shaindy took one of the centrepieces home, and her expression, rolling her eyes with her lip curled up, like she was wondering how she could have ever married him."

"What was his and Shaindy's wedding like?"

"Very small. They had it in an old synagogue, and he wouldn't let my mom decorate because 'God's beauty doesn't need extra splendour.' There was no dancing at all, not separate or mixed. He gave a long speech, and then we went to a kosher restaurant."

"That doesn't sound so festive."

"It wasn't."

We arrived just as people were starting to eat. They needed ten men to make the Sheva Brachot blessing, and Avrumi had exactly ten including Naftali.

He put his arm around Naftali and introduced him to his Rabbi and yeshiva friends, and it felt like being at a birthday party for him, like an adult bar mitzvah.

Shaindy talked to me a little. She apologized for

leaving the wedding early, and said she had a present for me. She handed me a bag with two books. *The Surrendered Wife* by Laura Doyle, and *A Jewish Women's Guide to Childbirth* by Aviva Rapaport. I stared at the second book, and she squeezed my arm.

"Soon by you," she said. I stared back at her.

I flipped through the first book. There was a chapter on the "myth of equality" and another on using the words "I can't" and "Whatever you think." I wanted to vomit.

The inscription read:

> *Dear Chana,*
>
> *We welcome you to the family. This is just a little bit of advice that was recommended to me. It's a reminder to know yourself and choose the right things.*
>
> *May you build a Bayis Ne'eman b'Yisroel.*
> *Much love,*
> *Shaindy*

I reread the note and felt dazed.

Naftali managed to break free of Avrumi and his friends, and he walked over.

I showed him the books and flipped through the first one again. "Do you think they really live like this?"

He looked too. "Oh, yeah. Avrumi's biggest complaint about Iris was how into her career she was. He swore if he ever remarried, he'd choose a girl he had a hundred percent control over."

"Seriously?"

"Yup."

"Well, that's disturbing."

He shrugged. "I agree."

When Naftali went to the bathroom, I tried to talk to Avrumi.

"I'm sorry you couldn't be with us at the wedding," I said, "but it's nice of you to host us now."

He grunted. "Thanks. I see that Shaindy's given you our gift. We have one more book for you, the one I wrote last year."

"Um, thanks," I said. Naftali had mentioned it; it was a book about Jewish halacha that Avrumi had self-published.

He signed it in front of me, "To Hannah with best wishes."

We looked it over on the path on our way to the car, and I noticed he'd underlined ten pages about virtue and family purity. At the bottom of one of the pages, he'd written FYI.

"Let me see that," Naftali said and ran back towards the house. I wondered if he was planning to confront him, but he did something better. He found one of Avrumi's outside recycling bins and threw it in.

"Hey, you want to throw in those other two books too?"

I nodded and he threw them in as hard as he could.

We left for our honeymoon a few days later. Naftali booked us a week in Miami. We stayed in South Beach, at a fancy hotel called the Fountain Bleu where we were steps from the beach in one direction and the Orthodox Jewish community in the other. There was a million times more variety and better-quality kosher food on 41st street, which Naftali called "Bathurst by the sea."

Every night I texted Jillian to see how she was feeling.

She asked me to send her photos from the trip to cheer her up, and everywhere we went, I picked up small gifts for her. She gave me two small jars to fill with sand from the beach, and I bought her sunglasses and kitschy keychains and t-shirts from Miami, because I knew she'd love that.

She waited until we got back to tell us the news: she had stage three endometrial cancer. She weighed ninety-eight pounds. She'd started taking sleeping pills in the mornings after the pain kept her up at night. She told me her sister was taking her to all of her doctor's appointments, so I brought her food that she hardly touched, anything she said she wanted, from popcorn to saffron rice. I brought her books about music and art that remained where I left them and celebrity magazines that I could see she flipped through, so I'd buy five at a time and drop them off.

It had been five weeks since I'd last had my period, and before I told Naftali, I found myself telling her. It was way too soon. I couldn't say anything to him because I knew that I wasn't ready. I thought it was just the stress of the wedding that had thrown things off, but now it was weeks later and still nothing.

I bought a test and told her I was going to take it in her bathroom. I peed on the stick and stared at her rhinestone dick pic art as I waited for three minutes to pass.

My hands shook when I showed it to her. It was positive.

I was surprised to see a spark of real emotion in her eyes.

"Wow, Hannah," she whispered. "A new life, a beautiful little person, to join our world."

I stared at her. "What?"

"All this stuff that's happening to me right now kind of just puts things into perspective." She took both of my hands. "When you first met Naftali and then decided to go through with all of this, I found it hard to understand. It's hard enough to understand Jewish stuff when you're born into it, but to choose it, voluntarily, I thought you were out of your mind. And I was afraid of losing you. You're the best friend I've ever had. I was jealous of all the time it took up. But now ..."

Jillian's voice caught in her throat. "I want you to be happy. I want you to have everything you want. And I want to be there. I want to live to see everything. I want to meet this kid. She's going to need a crazy aunt."

I felt like I was going to cry. "How do you know it's going to be a girl?"

She smiled. "I know, trust me, watch and see."

"It's too soon. We just got married. It's new, and I'm just getting my head around everything. My childhood was fucked up. I'm probably not even capable of being a parent."

I picked at a cuticle on my finger. Iris had recommended a shellac manicure before my honeymoon, and it was peeling off in little pink strips.

"When I first saw my dad at my engagement party, do you know what I thought? How familiar he looked and smelled. I thought that's my dad, and in some primal way, I wanted to erase the past or pretend it never happened and just have him tell me he loves me or something. But isn't that fucked up? I'm supposed to hate him. I'm supposed to make sure he stays far away. How am I supposed to protect my child when I can't even protect myself from being hurt by him?"

Jillian touched my shoulder.

"Hannah," she said gently. "Naftali knows the story, he's in this with you, and so am I. No matter what happened before, you're here right now. You're alive and healthy, and you have people who love you. His family may be complicated, but they care about you. They'll probably hire you a fleet of nannies, so you won't have to do the child raising alone."

I snorted. "I guess."

"My cousins in Israel all have kids," she said, "and I've seen how they do it. Babies don't have complicated needs: they eat, they wet or shit their diapers, they sleep. They don't have existential crises. In time you figure out how to guess what they need, like you would with anyone else. I think you're going to be great, but you should tell Naftali. You said he's good with kids, right?"

Naftali was so excited that his smile cracked the tops of his cheekbones. "I can't believe this," he said and kissed me.

"It's amazing," he kept saying, over and over.

I tried to get into the spirit of things. We decided to wait a full three months before telling his family. We decided not to tell my mom, since it was clear, no matter what she promised, that she would tell my father.

At first, I had an aversion to certain smells. I couldn't wear any perfume or put cumin or paprika on my food or eat even a bite of avocado or onions without a wave of nausea so heavy, I'd sweat and have to run to the bathroom to vomit. The term morning sickness, I learned, was a misnomer. Within two months I was vomiting around the clock, morning, noon, and night. I emptied my stomach until all I could retch was water. It got better when my obstetrician told me I had hyperemesis gravidarum and prescribed strong anti-nausea pills and gave me a vitamin IV drip.

Within two months of my pregnancy, both Shaindy and Devorah were pregnant again. Unlike me, they were glowing and swanning around fashionably dressed, gaining such a small amount of weight that it looked like they were each growing a mini basketball. They both had midwives and were both planning, as usual, to have natural births, Shaindy at home, Devorah in a hospital.

Shaindy tried to convince me to consider it. "It's the best kind of pain and the greatest high. You can't imagine what your body is capable of. Plus, you get to be part of a great tradition now, of women who've used midwives since the time of the Torah."

I knew homebirth was not for me. I wanted to be in a crisp, clean hospital bed with people whose job was to take care of me and my baby. I wanted every drug available to make everything hurt less. I felt angry and betrayed by my body until just before I gave birth to her.

The angel appeared beside me as promised, while Naftali stretched out in a chair, asleep. He reached for my hand, and his skin felt softer than before.

"Tears of joy loosen my skin," he said and smiled at me.

When I didn't respond, he said, "My dear, I understand why you are so afraid. Never does a life have a warmer and safer experience than in the womb. But did you know, that while they're there, babies are taught the entire Torah? And when they're born, someone like me taps their mouth and causes them to forget. It'll be up to you to reteach her."

"But I don't know anything," I tried to tell him.

"*Rachamana Liba Bahee*," he said. "The Compassionate One only wants what's in our hearts."

Then he disappeared.

When my daughter was born, she had huge brown eyes, just like mine, and golden blonde hair like Naftali's. I couldn't believe someone so big and beautiful had been living inside me. She stared at me and reached for my finger, and I knew I loved her in a way that I had never loved anyone before.

We'd been looking up names and talking about options for weeks, but when I saw her, I knew.

It was a name Naftali had suggested, a biblical name, Batya, and it meant daughter of God. It reminded me of a quote I'd read in rehab, about being a child of God and not being afraid of our light and not playing small. We'd agreed that we'd give her a middle name after Jillian. In Sephardic culture, people name after the living, and it was our way of saying we believed that she'd beat this. We offered to name her Miriam, but Jillian shook her head. "Call her Jillian," she said, so we named her Batya Jillian.

CHAPTER THIRTY-ONE

AT FIRST, I didn't feel like a mom. I was tired and bleary eyed all the time, but I could stay in my sun filled bed, the blinds and windows open all day, the high thread count sheets and duvets soft, with all the ice packs and adult diapers, Advils, and stool softeners that the hospital had given me. I felt like a celebrity convalescing at an expensive rehab because, as Jillian had predicted, the Goldwaters hired us a day nanny, a night nanny, and a part time housekeeper to clean the apartment, prep and cook food for us. I'd be asleep, and someone would nudge me awake and hand me the baby, I'd nurse her, half asleep, and hand her back. I'd fall asleep knowing she was probably in safer hands with them than she was with me. Someone would bring me food in bed, and when I woke up next, the plate would have disappeared, the floors mopped, my side table shiny with a new glass of ice-cold water waiting for me to drink it.

We had moved to a three-bedroom condo near where all the Goldwaters lived. I'd loved living downtown, but in my last trimester, his parents had excitedly announced that they bought us a home for our growing family. The one good thing was that, before all of this, Jillian had moved out of our old place and into a bigger one about a fifteen-minute walk south of our condo.

It made it so much easier to check on her. We texted or talked every day. She didn't want to FaceTime, she said, because she was insecure about how she looked now because of the treatments.

Naftali's siblings stopped by all the time. Shaindy brought organic coconut oil and shea butter. "These two will make your stretch marks disappear," she said.

Devorah dropped off Slim Fast drinks and meal replacement bars.

"Aren't you into doing things naturally?" I asked her. I'd watched her video about being kind to the body postpartum, about just letting it recover after the miracle of birth.

I'd actually liked it.

She sat down on the bed beside me. "Hannah," she said, "there's what you tell people you're doing and what you actually have to do. I do spin classes and Pilates until the very end of my pregnancies. I would love to take it easier, but my brand depends on the way I look. That and Max likes me a certain way. We've been sharing one plate of food for our meals since we first started dating."

She looked at me, then at the plate of leftover spaghetti beside my bed and shook her head.

"In the first few weeks, I always do a combo of slim fast and juices."

"And that works? You have enough supply to nurse and energy to function?"

She smiled. "My body is a well-oiled machine. I've done this a few times, remember? I know what I'm doing.

If you have to start eating again, go keto. It really works. I have no idea what my brother's into, but it couldn't hurt to try to look your best."

When she left, I got up and took a shower. I washed my hair and, instead of pajamas, I tried to get dressed. My maternity clothes were too big, but I couldn't fit into my regular clothes.

I put on a black dress from early in my pregnancy. I put on lipstick and mascara and blush.

Naftali's eyes popped when he saw me. "Wow, babe, you look incredible."

"Thanks. Your sister was here."

"Fuck, what did she say?"

"Nothing, it was basically just a bunch of weight loss advice. I tried to ignore her."

"Good."

"But it got me thinking, maybe I need to be more present in our lives."

"Babe, you only had Batya two months ago."

"Yeah, but when you have as much help as we have, it's embarrassing to just sit around. I've been thinking about Jillian. She should have someone there, taking care of her."

"Where's her family in all of this? Didn't you say they were very involved?"

"They are, but I think it's wearing them down. They agree that whatever can be done here doesn't seem to be helping. I can't imagine what they're going through, to watch your kid almost die once, and then to think it could happen again, but this time ...

"There's a doctor in the US that they know, that does treatments and surgery that are experimental, but he has a very high success rate. He's Israeli. I think she said his name is Dr. Nevo."

"Is it safe?"

"I don't know. She thinks the benefits outweigh the possible dangers. The problem is he's incredibly expensive. Her parents have done whatever they can. They even sold the unit we used to live in to pay for two visits with him, which is why she moved, but it's not enough for the surgery. In total, she said, the cost is $250,000. Her parents could only contribute $75,000."

"Which leaves $175,000," he said.

"Right. She said with the cost of medication and extra treatments she might need; it could be more. I wanted to talk to her parents about it, but she begged me not to. She said it's too embarrassing for them, knowing that there's nothing they can do."

I was crying now. "There's just, there's got to be something …"

Naftali put his arms around me.

"Of course there is. We can raise money. We can start a GoFundMe, we can do community things, you know, learning in her honour, having bake sales. Do you want me to talk to my family? Do you want me to see if they'll contribute?"

"I don't know if we should directly ask them for money. I don't think she'd be comfortable with that."

"You know, my mom and Devorah love to put on charity events. They know Jillian, and they know how important she is to you. I'm sure they'd help. Seriously, writing menus, creating a theme, picking décor, and furniture. They could organize a black-tie event, through

The Goldwater Foundation, where every seat costs five hundred dollars, and invite their friends, who have the money to donate on top of that. She's a girl in the community, and my wife's best friend. I'm sure they won't say no. Iris is great at stuff like this too, not just at making things look pretty, but at budgeting and making sure we make exactly as much as we need to. We'll talk to her, we'll have to do the exact math, but she's amazing at keeping everyone on task. We'll make it happen."

"Wow, that sounds incredible. You really think they'd do this for her?"

"For her, I don't know. For us, yes. They love doing stuff like this, and they'll love that you had this idea, and that you want to join them in something they find satisfying."

"Okay, so what do we do?"

"I think we should start by talking to them. I can give my mom a call, and we can see if she and Devorah can get started right away. The sooner the better, right? In the meantime, we can look into smaller, local things."

I nodded. "We should talk to Jillian and ask her what she wants. I have a feeling she won't want us to use her real name."

Naftali looked thoughtful.

"Okay," he said, "why don't we use her Hebrew name? Miriam Bat ..."

"Esther," I said.

"Pretty common names, so it'll be harder for people to identify her, unless they know her already. Let's see if she's feeling okay later. Maybe we can visit her and run all of this past her."

I texted Jillian, and she told us not to wait.

*COME OVER RIGHT NOW XO*

We waited though until Naftali had gotten in touch with his family and discussed the basics of the plan. Avrumi, of all people, and Devorah both seemed excited to help.

I was startled when I saw her. She had no hair, and her cheekbones looked like sharp blades. She was wearing gold eyeshadow, long, obviously fake eyelashes, and thick, dark penciled in eyebrows.

"You look like Natalie Portman in *V for Vendetta*," I said, and she actually looked happy.

She came close and touched my wig. "Maybe I should get one like this," she said and laughed, but it sounded wheezy. "All these years of me being against hair covering, and ironically now, I'm sitting here, envying your long, dark wig with its beautiful gold low lights."

I took it off and handed it to her. My hair was tied into a tight bun underneath it, and it felt good to let it out.

She shook it out and tried it on in front of her mirror. "Whoa, not bad."

"It looks amazing on you, better than on me."

The rich brown matched her skin tone perfectly. It made her cheekbones look softer, her eyes more liquid and Bambi like.

"Take it," I said. "I have another one, and if it makes you feel more like yourself..."

She looked emotional. "Wow, that's incredibly generous. I know how expensive *sheitels* are ..."

I shrugged. "It's nothing."

Naftali leaned in towards Jillian.

"Hannah and I both love you. I've been talking to my family, and with your permission, we'd really love to help you."

Jillian looked startled. "What do you mean?"

"Hannah told me about the cost of your treatments. My brother Avrumi teaches part time at Ohr HaTorah. So first things first, starting next week, they're having a marathon learning session, where they study a whole tractate of the Talmud over forty-eight hours in your merit. And people in that community, of course will donate. Devorah is busy setting up a five-school wide challah and bake sale that she thinks could raise up to five thousand dollars. Hannah and I want to set up a GoFundMe, where people can donate anytime. We think it should have a blog updating everyone on your progress, including photos, if you feel up to it, and if it's too much work, or energy, we can post too."

"I know it's kind of weird, #CancerWarrior, #InspiringWoman."

She interrupted me. "# blessed."

We all started laughing.

Jillian reached over and hugged us both at the same time.

"There's something about cancer," she said. "It really does bring out the best in humanity."

She was most impressed by the charity ball.

"My family can put something like this together fairly quickly," Naftali said. "My mom loved the idea. I just have to talk to my dad about the details."

"If I feel well enough," she said, "I'd love to be able to

sing at it. I wonder if it'll be the last time I'll ever get to sing like that in public."

I reached for her hand. "Jillian, don't say that. You're going to get better. If anyone could make a miracle happen, it's you."

"If you're not feeling the best, you could always just record a song and we could play it for everyone," Naftali said, and she looked touched.

"Thanks, both of you," she said. "You have no idea what this means to me."

CHAPTER THIRTY-TWO

A FEW DAYS later, we had our meeting with Jack to discuss the charity ball. Naftali was running late, so I got there alone, slightly panicked about exactly what I was supposed to say. He texted to say he'd be there in a few minutes, and I should go right up to his dad's home office, which was on the third floor.

I checked my watch. It was 3:45. I was wearing a silk grey and black striped dress, and heels so I decided to take the elevator. Jack's office had a slate grey door, and walls full of built in shelves that were outlined in gold. Jack was sitting with his back to me in his brown leather armchair. He was facing the window. A silver framed photo of his and Malka's wedding day peeked out from beside some books. His shelves were full of Jewish books: the *Shulchan Aruch*, the code of Jewish Law, along with books by Rabbi Soleveichik and Rabbi Jonathan Sacks. There were business and self-help books, like *The Innovator's Handbook* and *How to Win Friends and Influence People*. There were photos of his children: Avrumi graduating from yeshiva, Devorah covered in jewels and floor length white on her wedding day, the three of them as little kids, walking side by side in Jerusalem.

"Jack?"

There was a bump, and a small high-pitched groan. I saw some draping red fabric on the floor on the side of his chair.

"Shit, I bit myself."

Jack laughed, and I stared as Iris got up off her knees in front of him.

She held onto Jack's arm to steady herself. She smoothed a crease in her impossibly elegant dress. There was a faint flush in her cheeks, but she looked more amused than guilty.

"It's just Hannah."

I stared as Jack zipped up his pants. I forced herself to look away.

"I didn't know," I said. I looked at Iris and felt a flush of panic creeping through me. "Maybe I should go."

Jack got up and closed the door behind me. "We should probably talk about this."

Iris looked at me. "I thought you already knew. I mean, you know about Malka and Naomi, so I thought that someone would have told you. Or that you'd figured it out."

I drew in a breath.

Iris looked at me almost pityingly and laughed. "Stop looking so scandalized. It's the worst kept secret ever."

I stole another glance at Jack. He was smiling faintly. "We don't talk about it," he said, "but yes, everyone has always been"—he paused and coughed—"aware."

"Everyone," I managed to get out, "even Naftali?"

"Naftali, out of all my kids seemed to take it the worst." Jack bristled.

"You know how Nafs gets on his high horse about everything," Iris said.

"I ... I didn't know that," I stuttered. "So everyone else is okay with this?"

"Well," Jack said, "when you think about it, why shouldn't they be? 'My wife' has been involved with Naomi since before we met, and obviously she continues to be. This was always our arrangement. Malka seems to like you very much, by the way, which is quite the compliment."

I took a breath. "I like her too."

"Devorah was very unhappy about it at first, but she seems to be a little more accepting now. She's not the easiest person either, as you probably know. It hasn't affected my relationship with her too badly, although unfortunately Iris can't say the same."

Iris shrugged. "We were never very close, but when I was with Avrumi, she was more neutral." She looked up at Jack.

"It's hard for her to be mad at her dad, which I can understand, so she takes it out on me. It's okay, I can handle her."

I smiled in spite of myself.

"And I guess Avrumi's moved on?" I tried to ask gently.

"Of course. This wasn't a thought until Iris and Avrumi got their Jewish divorce. Although legally, it's obviously a more complicated issue. When everything happened, in our business, some of which I assume Naftali has told you, our family, our finances, and our reputations were saved entirely by Iris. Avrumi, as I'm sure you can guess, has a fragile ego and couldn't take that it was her, and not him, that did all the important work. On the other hand,"—he smiled and reached for Iris's hand —"my admiration grew tremendously for Iris. We literally owe her everything. Here was this formidable woman, this beautiful and brilliant person, being criminally unappreciated for everything she's done for this family. I couldn't take it. When they separated, then got their Get, she and Victoria needed a place to live. I discussed it with Malka, of course, but there was no question in either of our minds."

I wondered what in the world they'd told Victoria. I stared at a flower pattern in the lush green and cream Persian carpet on the floor. "Does that mean Victoria ..." I trailed off.

Jack's temples reddened. "My granddaughter is not my daughter if that's what you're asking, Hannah."

"I'm sorry," I said. "It's none of my business. I appreciate you both being so open with me. Iris has been like the sister I've never had since I first met Naftali."

Iris jumped in. "Or, you mean, like the stepmom you've never had?"

We both started laughing. The situation was so surreal and strange it was too much to think about.

"Naftali and I were supposed to talk to you at 4 about a fundraising event we want to hold for Miriam Azoulay."

Jack gave me his most focused look, which looked exactly like Naftali's.

"Yes, he mentioned it to me." He looked down at his watch.

I felt like a contestant on one of those business shows where they have thirty seconds to give their best pitch. "As you know, she has stage three cancer, and Naftali and I have been reaching out to the community to help raise the funds to get her treatment in the US. Part of the money will go to Jewish cancer charities in Toronto, but half will go to fund Miriam's treatments, and—" The words caught in my throat, I still couldn't get them out. "Part will go to helping her family with the costs if she doesn't survive. This was what she asked for."

Iris's expression turned somber. "I'd heard she was sick. I'm sorry, Hannah. She looked so beautiful at your wedding; I didn't realize that it was that bad."

"It's a charity ball, you wanted to have, correct? Something that would involve Malka and Devorah?"

I nodded. "Yeah, I just don't know where to start with all the details. Naftali's mentioned different hotels with kosher catering to fit the number of seats we need, and we only have two months to do everything ... it's a bit overwhelming. We'd need a place that has capacity for three hundred and fifty to four hundred seats, that has room for entertainment. We'd need to organize food, and a theme, flowers, possibly things people can bid on in an auction ..."

"Hannah," Jack said, "take a deep breath. For functions that size, our foundation normally uses the Four Seasons. They have capacity for six hundred. We have a good relationship with a kosher caterer who works directly with them. Don't worry about flowers and themes, even entertainment. Devorah and Malka are experts at this stuff. Just give them an idea of Miriam's taste, and they can get it done within days. They're basically professional party planners."

I heard footsteps and was relieved to feel Naftali's hand on my shoulder.

"As for the deposit on the ballroom, we'll take care of it. Iris will market the event to everyone, and whatever tickets remain, our charity has the budget to cover, so we'll have a full room. Don't worry, you and Naftali will help us, and together we'll take care of everything."

"Sorry I'm late," Naftali said quickly, "but it sounds like everything is under control."

"Your wife," Jack said, looking me in the eye, "is a very special woman.

"Tzedakah is important, especially for a member of our community, for a close friend of yours. Just send me an email with the details. We'll write the cheques this week."

He walked us to the door.

"Iris and I, earlier on," he told Naftali quietly, "told her about our relationship, and she handled it with a great deal of grace and understanding."

Naftali's cheeks reddened. "I walked in on them," I whispered and held his arm.

"Thank you both for your help. There's no way we'd be able do any of this without you."

Jack smiled. "We'll be in touch soon," he said, and walked behind us.

When the door closed, and we were halfway down the stairs, Naftali turned to me.

"What exactly did you see?"

I grimaced. "You don't want to know. But let's just say I didn't know Iris was so flexible."

He groaned. "Oh my God. You know my mom's not even out of town right now? Ugh."

I put my arms around him. "Why didn't you tell me?"

"I tried to hint at it so many times. You guys are close, I figured she alluded to it or maybe told you."

"Maybe she did, and I'm an idiot so I just missed it."

"You know why they wanted us out of the apartment? They both work down there; they probably want to go there together."

"Oh God, you think?"

"I don't know. However cool my dad acted about you finding out, I could tell he was freaked out. Thanks for acting like you're okay with it, however against common sense and Jewish law and everything else this is."

"I keep looking up at all his holy books, all these guidelines to living a pure and meaningful life."

"I know. And every time I've tried to point it out to either of them, they act like I'm being ridiculous. But I'm not. Even if my mom divorced him, they still couldn't get married. Legally, she's still married to my brother. Jewishly, she's his ex-daughter-in-law and no rabbi on earth would marry them. They could never be a legitimate couple, out in public and still live the lives they live right now. It's so messed up."

We walked out the front door and into the driveway.

"I was just trying to focus on Jillian, on getting what we needed for her. Should we just tell him we changed our mind?"

Naftali shook his head. "No, she needs us."

He turned to face me. "Do me a favour? I'm sure he told you that we're all okay with him and Iris, but we're not. None of us ever talk about it. Unless something else big happens, like today, are you okay with us just not talking about it?"

I nodded. "Yeah, I guess so."

I thought about all the conversations I'd had with Iris, all the time I'd spent with her.

"I can't believe I've been so close to her, but I had no idea."

He shook his head. "I've never seen her be as close to anyone the way she is with you. I'm sure she never meant to hurt you."

He squeezed my hand. "Thanks," I said.

He bent down and kissed my forehead.

"Let's go home," he said, and I wished we were going downtown, miles away from all of them.

CHAPTER THIRTY-THREE

E VERY DAY I logged into Jillian's GoFundMe page. I knew I didn't need to do it more than once a week, but I was addicted. I wanted to know how much people donated, if I knew them, or if they did it anonymously, if our goals were being met, and if Jillian, in between travelling to the States and all her treatments, updated the blog.

Her entries were short but always full of her personality and spirit.

GUYS, she posted one day, *today I had the hottest nurse. She had short blonde hair, all neat and pushed back, and these intense blue eyes. I could totally picture her, all dapper in a suit, listening to jazz while I sit beside her in a red dress with a flower in my hair, drinking a martini. Thank you for all of your donations. Thank you for giving me faith in humanity, so I can sit here and fantasize about a future that might actually happen, thanks to you.*

Lots of people donated in increments of eighteen and thirty-six. The number eighteen, or *chai,* symbolized life and was lucky in Judaism. On a good day it was encouraging to see, on a bad one it was depressing in how naïve it seemed, as if donating the right amount or doing the right thing automatically guaranteed anything.

People were donating in record time this month. Jillian's total costs were $3,890 a month, and we were already up to $4100.

So far, Jillian had been to the US for four treatments, and they'd worked better than anyone expected.

She'd gained back ten pounds, and her eyebrows were starting to grow back. She moved around more easily and made more jokes. The doctors were working her up to surgery, she explained, but if she continued to make progress like this, it was possible that she might not even need it.

"When that happens," she told me giddily, because she now believed in manifesting, "I want to donate all the money to cancer research."

For the first time in months, Jillian didn't want to spend all day in bed. She asked if she could run errands with me once and we went to Apollo Bakery together. Even though it took us twice as long, Jillian made small talk with the cashier and even ate a few bites of a mint chocolate cupcake. She started playing with Batya, who was now six months old and laughed every time she heard Jillian's voice.

I started sleeping more easily.

As she regained her strength, she started taking Batya out for walks in her stroller to a park that was two streets away. She told me that Batya sometimes looked up at her with the same soft, quizzical look as Naftali. My heart melted a little. She bought Batya dolls and stuffed animals, and she laughed when Batya threw them out of the stroller.

She started writing music again, calling me at night, playing songs for me.

I think I've discovered / what it means to recover / I've discovered how to be myself went the chorus of one of them. Her voice sounded good, almost as powerful as before, and it was such a relief.

One day, she told me she felt bad about the stress her health had taken on us. We had a nanny during the day, but Jillian offered to stay overnight so that Naftali and I could have some time alone together. Naftali had booked us a spa day in Niagara on the Lake, and the plan was to stay overnight and for Batya to stay at the Goldwaters'. Of all the siblings, I still trusted Iris the most.

Jillian had always been great with changing diapers and outfits, and sitting around holding her when we watched TV, reading her baby books and singing to her. Naftali seemed nervous when I mentioned it to him but knowing that his parents and Iris and Devorah and Avrumi were all minutes away seemed to help.

"We're only going for one night," I reminded him.

Jillian seemed thrilled. "You guys need this, so badly," she said. "Hannah's been looking like she's about to have a nervous breakdown for the past month."

"We'll only be gone for one night," he said quickly. "But thanks for doing this, it will be nice for us to get some time together."

I gave her a hug. "Send me pictures. Call me and tell me how she's doing and call me or Iris or even Malka if you need anything."

She shooed me away. "Just trust me. You're going to have a great time."

I made sure that everything was organized for her. I

set up all her outfits, the diapers, and diaper cream. I pumped milk and took some extra milk I'd pumped out of the freezer and defrosted it.

It took us almost three hours to get to the Prince of Wales Hotel. It was beautiful and luxurious, and I was overwhelmed with the relief of being unencumbered, no kid or responsibilities, less worries about Jillian.

We went to the swim on the hotel's gold mosaic pool, and as we got in, my phone pinged.

Jillian had sent me photos of Batya in her crib. I noticed she was frowning, her eyebrows knotted with worry, but she seemed safe, holding her favourite stuffed squirrel by the tail. Two hours later, when we were getting massages, she sent me a meme she'd made of Batya screaming on the swings in the park. Underneath it, it said Mood Swings.

I stopped my massage and called her. "Is she okay now?"

"Oh yeah, she's totally fine. Sorry, I didn't mean to scare you. She's having a nap right now, sleeping like a little angel."

She FaceTimed with me so I could see it for myself. Batya was passed out in her crib, lying on her back with her arms stretched out.

I noticed that Jillian was wearing a full face of makeup, including bronzer, purple eyeliner, and red lipstick. She was wearing the wig I gave her.

"Are you going somewhere?" I asked her. "Because if you want, I can get Iris or even Devorah or Shaindy to come and take her. I can call them right now; it's no big deal."

"No, I just have an interview with a music manager from New York and we're going to do it over FaceTime. I figure if Batie's sleeping, now is a good time."

"Okay," I said. "Just keep an eye on her. Call me if you need me to come back."

"Relax," she said. "I'm standing right outside her door, watching her from the webcam the whole time while she's sleeping."

I texted Josephine, the nanny, to see if she could check in on them since she lived down the street. She called me a few minutes later.

"When Jillian first arrived, an hour early, she was sick. She vomited in the guest bathroom, and I cleaned it up. Then I told her to rest. When she woke up, she seemed okay. I stayed with them an extra hour. Batya was sleeping when I checked on her."

Jillian texted us one more time before bed, but I tossed and turned.

I asked Naftali if we could check out early, and we drove home early in the morning.

They were both still sleeping. Jillian groggily told us that Batya been sleeping for hours, since maybe 7 p.m. or so the night before. I touched her chubby cheek gently.

She moaned but wouldn't open her eyes. I picked her up. I sang the "Itsy Bitsy Spider," which was her favourite. I said her name.

"Batya," I shouted, choking on the last syllable.

Naftali picked her up and lightly shook her. She stirred slowly and started crying softly.

"I don't like this, I don't like this at all," he said, the panic growing in his voice.

Jillian reached for his arm. He shook her off.

"We're taking her to the hospital," he yelled, and her eyes lit up. We called 911 and an ambulance took us to Sick Kids. It was small and cramped inside the ambulance, and Batya sat on my lap, alternating between crying and falling back asleep. I unbuttoned my shirt and tried to see if she'd nurse, for once not caring how exposed I was. She nursed for a minute and then fell back asleep. Naftali and I looked at each other helplessly.

When they got there, Naftali used his contacts to get the emergency doctor on call to see Batya sooner. Dr. Silverberg asked questions and Jillian attempted to answer them.

I leaned in close to the doctor. "She's recovering from cancer. This might all have been too much for her."

Dr. Silverberg gestured for Jillian to sit down and asked her a few questions about her condition. She grew more energetic with every answer. After a few minutes, he explained that they were going to take Batya to do some blood tests.

"We need you both to come with. Your friend can stay here and rest."

Jillian nodded. "I'm just going to text my sister."

We came back forty-five minutes later. Naftali looked ashen.

"The doctors said they found traces of codeine in her system. It damaged her stomach lining. She has to have emergency surgery."

Jillian paced manically. She spoke really fast. "What kind of surgery? Does she have to have it right now? Can I go with? Do they think she's going to be okay?"

Dr. Silverberg, who was standing behind him grabbed

Naftali by the shoulder and lead us into his office. Jillian followed us and stood outside the door.

"How the hell did the baby get codeine into her system?"

Naftali looked angry and confused. "I honestly don't know. It's not like we have any in the apartment."

He looked us both in the eye.

"Hannah, I know this must be difficult, but I have to ask you a few questions."

"Does your friend Jillian have a history of erratic behaviour or a diagnosed mental illness?"

"I mean, I think she suffered from depression when she was younger. I think she did have some issues, but she's never been very specific."

"She didn't have a diagnosis that you knew of?"

I shook my head.

"Do you think it's possible that Jillian intentionally gave your daughter Oxycontin?"

I shook my head. "Of course not. She loves Batya."

Dr. Silverberg rubbed the back of his neck. "I talked to her. The details she told me just don't make sense. I've never heard of the treatment she says she's doing. I know one of the doctors in the practice she's talking about in New York. Nevo exists but he's semi-retired. I've never heard of the nurse or the receptionist she mentioned."

He gestured outside the door to where Jillian was standing. "Can you come in here, please, Jillian? I want to ask you a few more questions."

I saw panic register on Jillian's face. "I just have to go to the bathroom," she said, and ran down the hall.

Dr. Silverberg reached over and grabbed me by the shoulder.

"If it were me, I'd look into it. You could even take her to psych ward at Toronto General, see what they make of it. CAMH has some great programs."

I shook my head and stared at Naftali.

We walked back out into the waiting room. Naftali started pacing, and I sat beside Jillian.

"Batya is going to be fine, Hannah," she said, her eyes glassy. "I just have a feeling."

I pulled away.

Two hours later Dr. Silverberg and another older doctor came to tell us that Batya was out of surgery. He led us into his office. "She's going to be okay," Dr. Silverberg said slowly. "We're going to keep her for another day for monitoring, but we expect her to make a full recovery."

"I'm going to bring in another colleague." A taller man, with dark, curly hair and bright blue scrubs stood behind him. "Jillian, this is Dr. Jones. He works across the street. Come with us for a second, we'll bring you right back here. You can leave your stuff."

We looked in her purse the minute Jillian disappeared. Naftali found a bottle full of Oxys, and I slammed my hand down on my chair's armrest so hard I yelped in pain.

He pulled out a small brown jar of Ipecac Syrup. His hands shook. "Do you know what this is?" I shook my head. "It's designed to make you throw up. It's quite dangerous. Devorah used it back when she was bulimic."

We also found a small bottle of Nair and a used razor. There were some thick, black hairs in it.

I picked up my phone and called Esther. I didn't

know what she was going to say, but I knew I had to do it. I put the call on speaker so Naftali could hear.

"Hi, Mrs. Azoulay," I said. "It's Hannah Goldwater. We've been worried about Jillian lately, and I thought we'd check in with you. I can only imagine how hard this has been for all of you, for Miriam to have cancer again."

"Cancer?" Esther's voice was so shrill, it was piercing. "There must be some kind of mistake, is this a joke?"

"What, no. She told us, Naftali and I, that the cancer had come back. She was taking care of our daughter, and our nanny told us she was sick, even though she told us she was getting better ..."

"I don't know what you're talking about, Hannah," Esther yelled, cutting me off. "You know my daughter, you know she struggles, she's sick."

"With cancer?"

"No, with her mind. She's not right in her head, you know it."

Esther started to cry.

"But she definitely doesn't have cancer?" I asked one last time.

"No, what is wrong with you. God forbid, no."

I hung up the phone. I heard footsteps coming up behind me, and Naftali put out his arm and blocked Jillian before I could take a swing at her.

CHAPTER THIRTY-FOUR

DESPITE EVERYTHING, LESS a week later, the charity ball for cancer was still happening. It had been Jillian's last wish to visit Paris, so the ceiling was full of pastel coloured hot air balloons, white and lavender, white and lemon yellow, mint green and peach balloons, with brown wicker baskets full of white roses that would land in the centre of each table. A big wall-sized flat screen showed the Eiffel Tower on one side and the Champs-Élysées on the other. There was an actual, working carousel, full of horses with ribbons and a grand white canopy that wouldn't have been out of place at a wedding. There were trays of several kinds of kosher French champagne and tables full of cheeses like brie, camembert and chevre, grapes, crepe stations ,and multi-coloured heart shaped macaron towers. There were peach and gold velvet couches to lounge on, a bar with unique drinks and gold chairs with black and white striped tablecloths. Devorah and Malka had outdone themselves.

I asked Naftali to tell his family because I couldn't bring myself to do it. It turned out, that they still thought the cause was good, so everything went on as planned with a few changes to the schedule. I was supposed to talk about my friendship with Jillian and her illness. I was supposed to be there to give a human face and a real story to something that felt abstract for people unless they'd been through it. I had a slide show of photos, some of her own, some that Jillian had given me that I could project onto the big screen with the Eiffel Tower. There was one of Jillian sitting on the sidewalk near her house in Israel, in cut off jean shorts and a maroon halter top, smoking *nargileh* with their neighbour's sons while a stray black cat lay sprawled across her lap. She still had the same penetrating gaze, like she could size up the person viewing her. There were more recent photos of her singing, all red lips and thick eyelashes, and one of her playing piano in her parents' living room in Israel. There was one of the two of us with our arms around each other at my wedding. I felt like crying. Even now, Jillian brought all of my emotions to the surface.

I wouldn't be talking about her at all now.

I'd texted her two days before as they were setting up the room.

I sent her a couple of photos. It was the first time I'd been in touch since the hospital.

 *HOLY SHIT.*

It was supposed to be for you, I wrote. *we did all of this because we believed you. What kind of person lies about having cancer?*

I saw the three dots from her text come up, but then they disappeared.

You took advantage of everyone, you caused us all to panic and this whole time, you knew there was nothing wrong with you. People were giving you money. Don't you feel guilty?

Like you never took advantage of people.

You're the most ruthless person I know. You take from everyone. You took an apartment from me for over a year. You took free shows, free drinks, free drugs. You became friends with everyone I introduced you to. You became close to my mom, close enough to name yourself after her. You took even more from the Goldwaters, the apartment, the new condo, the nannies, the fancy jewellery and wigs, your wedding. And what do you give them? Nothing but judgement. And you're doing the same thing to me.

WHAT?

"You think I'm an idiot, that I don't know what's dangerous and what's safe? I would've told you. I saw you were struggling Hannah, even though most people would kill to have your privilege, your new rich person problems. I just wanted to help you."

HELP ME? Batya could have died. No matter what you say, I can never forgive you.

Don't you feel bad at all for taking money from all these people? I mean, besides the Goldwaters, look at all those kids who baked challah or people who prayed or learned in your honour?

You're so naïve, it's all performative, Hannah. It's virtue signalling. What they're really saying is thank God it's not me who's deathly ill, maybe if I donate some money or act like I care it'll stop it from happening to me.

Was it fun, at least? I hope it was worth it to you. I hope the money and the extra attention was worth losing people who loved you.

So histrionic. Everything is so black and white with you. Did I really think you were interesting once?

I couldn't take it anymore. She didn't feel anything, and I couldn't begin to process my anger. I blocked her number and blocked her on social media.

For the event I wore my best wig and a cream and lavender dress with long chiffon sleeves. I had my nails painted into a hard, pearly pink. Frida did my makeup, and Iris lent me a strand of charcoal grey pearls. I felt like a doll, which I knew was the only way to get through this. Pretend that I was pliable because I was made of plastic, let everyone dress me up and tell me exactly what to say, and at the end of the night, maybe they could pack me up in a satin comforter and put me eternally to rest in Barbie's dream house.

Jillian's friend Marla had called me yesterday, distressed because she couldn't get in touch with her. I wasn't sure how it happened, but the next thing I knew she was offering me coke, and I was accepting. She dropped it off that night, and I made sure I saved most of it for today. The guests started coming and everyone started drinking and commenting on how beautiful everything was, and I laughed like everything was normal. Devorah's pink lace dress rustled when she moved. She was wearing a different blonde wig, less yellow and more gold, with enormous pink sapphire studs and six-inch heels. We posed for photos together.

Shaindy and Iris were both wearing pastel dresses, Iris's was blue and Shaindy's was mint green. Avrumi was wearing a pinstriped grey suit and a light green tie. He had trimmed his blond beard, but he still looked like a puffier version of Jack and Naftali. Naftali came up behind me and linked his arm through mine. Behind him, Josephine was carrying Batya, and all I felt was shame when I looked at her. She could have died. I trusted the wrong person with her well-being.

I walked over to the bar. Someone handed me a glass of pink fizzy lemonade, with an adorable pink and white straw. I took a few sips. I could almost feel the slow, tantalizing burn from my nostrils into the back of her throat. I licked my lips. I had that bump stashed in the hidden pocket of my purse, and I gripped the straps tightly in my hands.

I made a beeline for the bathroom. I chose the furthest stall and made sure that the door was locked. I took it out carefully and held it for a minute, and with Naftali's credit card, made two neat little lines with the powder on the toilet paper dispenser. I put my head down and covered my nostril. The straw was surprisingly soft. I tried to breathe out daintily.

Like a lady, I thought giddily. Like a society lady enjoying all the decadence of fancy balls.

I sniffed hard and put the lid down on the toilet seat. I was starting to feel better.

I drew back when I heard the door opening and people coming in. I didn't want to leave yet. I still had a little left. I peeked through the crack in my door. I could see the back of Devorah's dress, and I could hear the clack of Iris's heels on the marble floor.

I heard Iris's voice.

"Great job tonight."

"Thanks. It was a lot of work."

"You're always so good with the details. I told Hannah you'd know what to do."

Devorah murmured something that I couldn't hear, then I heard her continue.

"Too bad Miriam turned out to be a scammer. I thought nothing about her would shock me, but I was wrong."

I heard a makeup bag being unzipped.

"Do you think Hannah was in on this?"

The question hung in the air for a minute.

"No," Iris said quietly. "I don't. She's sincere and open like a little kid. I don't think she's capable of this kind of deception."

"Yeah, that's what I thought too," Devorah said, sounding somewhat disappointed.

"But it would've made so much sense."

"What do you mean?"

"You know, here's this average girl who won the lottery when she married Naftali. He's rich and beautiful and a good guy and just look at her. I mean I know they say opposites attract, but this was a little extreme, don't you think?"

"Your point?"

"If she could fool a family like ours into letting her marry in, why not fool a community? Once you get some money, why not go for more? You know if she was a professional gold scammer, I'd respect her more."

Iris let out a small laugh. "Wow, tell us how you actually feel. You really are your mother's daughter, Devorah."

"Hey, no need to insult me." I told him. "Look at her and look at us. Do you really think she's compatible? I even told him about Miriam, how she was gay and how she hit on me in high school, and how if Hannah was close to her, they must be more than friends, or maybe they used to be?"

I stumbled out of my stall. "Devorah," I spluttered, and she stared at me. I grabbed her by the shoulders and pushed her away from the mirror. We were inches away from the hallway in clear earshot of all the well-dressed pillars of her community.

"You're a hypocrite and a liar. Whatever happened between you and Jillian was mutual. You just wanted to do anything to avoid having a life like your mother's. If you hate Jillian so much, and you hate me, why are you even here?" I asked, my voice growing louder with each word.

"Hannah, I ..." Devorah started to stutter but I cut her off.

"Just admit it, you want to be seen as a good person so badly that you'll take credit for anything."

I took a deep breath. "You make people think that if they just do what you tell them to do, that you'll like them and finally treat them with basic decency, but you won't no matter how hard anyone tries."

"Hannah," Devorah screamed, "your nose is bleeding."

I felt the blood gush hot, full of anger and spite, full of everything I'd felt from the moment Naftali had forced me to deal with his brother and his sister. I looked at her, vaguely aware that I was ruining my dress. "You're not fooling anyone, Devorah. No one thinks you're a good person or a smart person or an interesting person. No one believes you're honest or generous. You're a fraud, Devorah, just like Avrumi."

I noticed that Malka was standing in the entrance of the bathroom, staring at us. I felt Iris reach out a hand to catch me before I hit the floor.

CHAPTER THIRTY-FIVE

I WOKE UP the next morning feeling like I had a migraine. My throat was dry, and my nose was on fire. Naftali had left me a note that he'd taken Batya to his parents for the day.

"Try to sleep it off," he wrote. "We'll talk later."

I wondered if our marriage was over. Even if all this time, Naftali hadn't agreed with Devorah, I was sure he would now. I got up and washed my face. I got dressed in one of my regular outfits, a black three-quarter sleeve dress, my wig, black flat shoes. I dug in the back of my closet for an old pair of jeans and a tank top, and I put them in a backpack. The driver played Rihanna's "Love on the Brain," which felt about right.

I stopped at the first Starbucks I found and changed in the bathroom. It felt great to feel the wind whipping my hair around on the street. Instead of taking the streetcar, I walked all the way to the tattoo parlour Jill had taken me to once. I was surprised when Johnny remembered me.

He gave me a long hug. "You look hot," he said, and I blushed. It had been months since Naftali and I had

had sex. His hands lingered on my sides, near my breasts, which felt surprisingly tender.

"I was thinking," I said, using my elbows to squeeze my breasts together for maximum cleavage, "of a piercing maybe."

He grinned. "Take your shirt off," he said.

I liked how forceful he was, how easy the transaction could be. He reached behind me and pulled my bra off. The metal snaps dug into my back. My nipples were pink and felt tender. He grabbed my left one and pulled. "Do you want it right here?" he asked.

My blood felt hot, and it was rushing in one direction. I put a hand on his neck and pulled him closer. I kissed him and heard the metallic clack of a streetcar whiz by. We should lock the door he said, and I nodded. I led his hands to my jeans. I might want to pierce here, I said. He turned up the music. Red Hot Chili Peppers' "Under the Bridge" was playing. My mom's next-door neighbour played *Blood Sugar Sex Magik* all the time when I was a teenager. It took me back. "No underwear," he said. "My kinda girl."

"You're dripping," he said, and I sighed, wanting to be swallowed completely in the here and now. I undid his jeans. What felt like a second later, he was on his back, on his tattoo table. I was on top of him, it was happening, we were having sex, and it felt like the biggest relief I'd experienced in months, like falling into a pile of down pillows. I screamed and dug my nails into his back.

"Wow," he said, afterwards, sighing and collapsing onto the floor. "That was everything I hoped it would be and more."

I reached down. Semen was dripping between my legs. I did the porn star thing and wiped it from my thighs with my hand, then licked my fingers. He shuddered. "Fuck, you're so hot," he said. He put his arm around me.

We hadn't used a condom.

He ran his hands along my back. "I want to tattoo you right here," he said, "just above your sexy ass." He reached down and slapped me hard and I moaned.

"Okay," I said. "What do you want to do?"

"There's this great Kanji I have," he said, "a Japanese character."

"Is it a symbol for strength or independence or some crap like that?"

He shook his head. "Actually, it's the symbol for a goddess."

I rolled my eyes. "Like the one you gave my friend Jill?"

"How is she?" he asked. "I haven't seen her for a long time."

"We're not talking right now."

"I'm sure you two will make up," he said. I found my jeans and my bra and put them on.

Then I changed my mind, emptied my bag and put on my dress, tied up my hair and put on my wig. I breathed in the scent of blood and sweat and sex.

Johnny's eyes bugged out.

"I have to go," I said, "but thanks. It helped a little."

He unlocked the door without saying another word.

I found a garbage can and threw the jeans and tank top away.

I called an Uber and shut my eyes until we got to the condo.

Naftali was waiting for me when I got to the door.

"Babe," he said, and he was holding up his phone. "You have to see this."

The headline read:

MIRIAM AZOULAY, 26, LEAPS TO HER DEATH FROM A LUXURY HIGH RISE.

CHAPTER THIRTY-SIX

READ ALL the magazine articles until I could put together a visual, until I could see and hear everything, until I actually felt like I was there.

I could see Jillian, her grey eye shadow smeared and orange lipstick faded, her bangs still charmingly uneven, like a wired Amelie, talking manically to the people she was with, endlessly, about New York and music.

I could see her growing frustration, see her eyes darting all around, see her tugging at her sweater sleeves as she paced. I could see her cousin getting nervous, asking Jillian if they couldn't maybe call someone to pick her up. I could see Jillian recalibrating, wondering why she couldn't just be normal and have boring friendships.

I could see her walking over to the window, momentarily assessing the drop. I could see her putting her ratty headphones on. I could hear Kanye West's "Diamonds from Sierra Leone" remix come pouring through, loud enough for the room to hear Jay-Z rap about people lining up to see the Titanic sink. I could see Jillian's face change as she heard the line "instead we rose from the ashes like a phoenix." I could see her jaw unclench; her posture loosen itself. I could see her delicately tapping the double-glazed window, tugging at the bronze bar across the glass.

I could hear her cousin sounding alarmed, pulling Jillian back, offering her tea.

"I hear you read tea leaves," she could have said to distract her, and Jillian would have responded with a kind of deflated enthusiasm. "Oh, yeah, I'd love to read yours after."

I could see Jillian getting distracted by her friend's books, picking up a copy of Haruki Murakami's *1Q84*, wincing at how heavy it was. I could see her walking over to the chair by the window with the book, as if she planned to read it. I could see her throwing *1Q84*, aiming for the right corner. I could see the glass smashing instantly, and Jillian pushing her hand and then her side through it. I could see the glass cutting Jillian's shoulder, see the blood drip, and Jillian not even registering it, for the exhilaration of smashing through so easily. I could hear her cousin screaming, her boyfriend standing, paralyzed as Jillian pushed with all her weight and tore through. I could hear Jillian's laughter, more joy than fear as she saw the building and the neighbourhood, the apartments with lights on, felt the music and the cold air.

I didn't expect to find a suicide note, but there was one, addressed to me, in the blog section of her old GoFundMe page. She'd made it private, but she knew I still had the password.

> *Hannah,*
> *I've been thinking about you so much. I know I couldn't say it before, but I am sorry that I hurt you. After everything happened, I thought*

about getting help. The way I see it, you can choose to get better, but there's a lot that you give up if you do. It wasn't worth it to me. I knew I had to leave, and I had this fantasy of heading to Philadelphia, of finding Jill Scott and introducing myself, hearing her in concert or bumping into her on the street and telling her how much she changed my life and helped me find my true self. She has such a warm, maternal energy, don't you think? I wanted her to hug me. But I didn't know where she lived. I didn't have the energy to try to track her down.

I came back to New York. I found a few old musician friends. I slept on a couple of couches. I slept with two random women. I told people my name was Mary.

I dropped acid on a roof in Brooklyn, and I kept thinking how much the sky, which was the colour of the rain smeared Tel Aviv sidewalk in February, looked like your eyes.

It's not clear to me how deep this religious stuff runs with you. Have you ever thought about Olam Haba, the word to come, and what it really means?

Here is my vision for the afterlife. I will be freer in my body and freer to move between worlds, to move from one space to the next, from suburban Toronto to the beach in Herzliya in the blink of an eye. I will be free from worrying about things like how I look, or how people see me. I will have access to books, to art, to events

*all around the world as they happen, but nothing
will ever completely cure my boredom. In the
end, I will always be me. I will always feel
unsatisfied, I will always feel like I don't fit in,
but I will always know that I have people who
understand, and you are one of those people. I'll
try to find a way to talk to you once in a while,
to let you know that even though I'm in a
different dimension, I'll always be here for you.*

*In another life, you'll have security and
stability, I'll have notoriety and stimulation, we'll
both have love, and none of these things will
come at the price we paid for them this time.*

Until we meet again,
I'll love you always,
Jillian

That night, I went for a walk around my neighbourhood. I stared at the apartment buildings, the people walking the streets, coming in and out of stores and kosher restaurants.

I thought about a conversation Iris and I had earlier, when I told how unhappy I'd realized I'd been. I asked her what would happen if I left, and she told me about her Get, about hearing Avrumi talk, and when it was her turn, having nothing left to say. She told me about watching the rabbis tear up her *ketubah*, how she let out an animal scream which surprised her, and the kind eyes of the rabbi who promised her that she still had her whole life ahead of her.

"Will you still be my sister if I leave?" I asked quietly.

I knew her well enough to know what she was going to say, and when I heard the tears in her throat I hung up. I didn't want to hear the words.

I wondered if this was how my mom felt when she finally decided to leave. I wondered if she'd lost people she'd loved too.

If nothing else it occurred to me now, Jillian had a moment of lucidity, a moment when everything was clear enough to know what she wanted. A teenage girl walked past me blasting Bjork's "Sun in My Mouth" on her phone. I knew it because it was one of Jillian's favourites. I closed my eyes.

I was in third year, sitting next to Jillian on her bed, listening to the whole *Vespertine* album while she raved about the nineties. I was full, for a second, of Jillian's optimism. I knew that even if my marriage was over, even if I didn't know how to handle the Goldwaters, or how to be a parent, I would be okay.

I could hear Jillian's laughter, and her voice in my ears, promising me that we had a whole lifetime ahead of us.

Acknowledgements

WRITING A NOVEL does not come naturally to me. I dreamed of writing short stories (and often did) throughout the writing of this novel. Thank you so much to my amazing publisher and editor, Michael Mirolla, for his patience, encouragement, and careful editing. It's a privilege and joy to get to work with you again. Thanks so much for believing in me and in this project.

Thank you so much to Anna Van Valkenburg, for all her hard work and for being so lovely to work with, Crystal Fletcher, and the whole Guernica Editions team, for being so fantastic. Thank you to David Moratto for the beautiful cover.

Thank you to Heather Wood, for being an amazing publicist and an equally amazing friend.

I was so lucky to do a first draft of this novel as my thesis when I did my MFA at Guelph. Thank you with all my heart to Dionne Brand (who is as fantastic as one dreams and had amazing insights). Thank you to Catherine Bush for believing so much in this whole idea and in the Goldwater family. Thank you also, so so much to my amazing MFA cohort. Reading your books makes me so happy.

Thank you to Alissa York and David Bezmozgis at Humber School for Writers for being amazing bosses. Thank you to the writers I work with for so much inspiration.

Thank you to the writing community; to Elyse Friedman for the amazing early notes, to Leah Eichler for the amazing reading and encouragement and friendship, Jean Marc Ah-Sen for a much needed pep talk, Carleigh Baker, Hollay Ghadery, Samantha Bailey, Anita Kushwaha, Sidura Ludwig, Leesa Dean, JJ Dupuis, Olga Stein, Nora Gold, Rebecca Rosenblum, Ian Colford, Karen Green, Susan Sanford Blades, Martha Batiz, and all the writers I was lucky enough to share a stage with, read, or do a panel with, judge a contest with, or be nominated with. You inspire me more than I can say.

Thank you so much to my amazing family, my husband and best friend, Micah, who reads everything and supports me endlessly, our amazing three kids, Lev, Zohar, and Nissim, our doggos, C and N, my mom Nurit, who has always been my second reader, my dad, Martin, who talks me through all kinds of things, my brothers and sister-in-law, Ari, Brooke, Yoel and Fleur, and my whole family, everywhere, for being amazing. I love you all so much.

And thank you, most of all, for reading.

About the Author

Danila Botha is the author of three critically acclaimed short story collections, *Got No Secrets* and *For All the Men (And Some of the Women) I've Known* which was a finalist for the Trillium Book Award, The Vine Awards, and the ReLit Award. Her new collection, *Things that Cause Inappropriate Happiness*, was published in 2024 by Guernica Editions. The title story, "Things That Cause Inappropriate Happiness," was nominated for a Pushcart Prize. The book was also a finalist for the Canadian Book Club Awards in the Short Story category. She is the author of the award-winning novel *Too Much on the Inside,* which was optioned for film. She is currently working on a new short story collection and her first graphic novel. She is part of the faculty at Humber School for writers.

Printed by Imprimerie Gauvin
Gatineau, Québec